TEMPT

A PEACHWOOD FALLS NOVEL

ADRIANA LOCKE

UMBRELLA
PUBLISHING INC.

Published by Umbrella Publishing, Inc.

Paperback ISBN: 978-1-960355-36-2

Cover Design by Books and Moods
Photography by Regina Wamba

This book is for Ashley.
You're one of the strongest, smartest, most incredible women I know.
I'm lucky to call you a friend.

Tumble | Tangle | Trouble

Standalone Novels

Sacrifice | Wherever It Leads | Written in the Scars | End Game | Like You Love Me | The Sweet Spot | Nothing But It All | Between Now and Forever | Play Me

For a complete reading order and more information, visit www.adrianalocke.com.

SYNOPSIS

It was a simple job—keeping his teenage daughter out of trouble for thirty days. But I didn't realize how my grumpy, gorgeous, blue collar, single dad boss would tempt me in all the wrong ways.

Chase Marshall is the bane of my existence. He's moody, gruff, and impossible to read. Sure, he's an incredible father, but with me? He's colder than a February night in this small Indiana town.

And now, because of a favor, I'm stuck living under his roof for the next thirty days.

He claims I'm the most infuriating woman he's ever met. But then come the lingering glances, the accidental touches that don't feel so accidental, and a smirk that I want to kiss off his annoyingly handsome face.

The longer we're together, the hotter it gets—until the tension finally snaps.

Now, nothing is simple. The job. Our boundaries. *My feelings.*

Will Chase watch me walk away when my time is up? Or will he be tempted to ask me to stay?

CHAPTER 1

hase

"Why does this always happen to me?"

My middle brother, Luke, sighs through the phone. His question, overly dramatic per usual, is rhetorical—or should be. *We both know the answer.* But he'll wait for a response because he likes to wallow in self-pity and because I'm a fool for answering his call in the first place.

Damn him.

"Oh, I don't know," I say, returning his exasperation. "Ever think that maybe you're just an asshole?"

"No."

"Well, maybe start there and work backward."

My windshield wipers squeak, working overtime to clear the rain from my view. Unfortunately, the precipitation hasn't let up all day. I'm soaked to the core, my bones ache, and the intense pain in my shoulder exacerbates my frustration—the frustration my brother compounds.

I want to get home.

"That's pretty rich coming from you." Luke laughs.

"Hey, *you* called *me.*"

"And *you* answered."

I remove one hand from the steering wheel and stretch my arm to the side, desperate for relief. "Do you want anything? Or did you call to remind me not to have an odd number of children?"

"Huh?"

I sigh. "Never mind."

"So back to this thing with Alyssa," he says, not missing a beat. "I don't think she's coming back."

She won't if she's smart.

I instantly regret that thought because it's not fair. I'm cold and exhausted and have a fourteen-year-old girl waiting at home for our weekly pizza-and-movie night. Luke might be a pain in the ass—and more of a diva than my daughter—but he's a solid guy.

I still don't want to do this with him.

"Are you listening to me?" Luke asks. "I'm having a crisis over here, and you're acting like it's no big deal."

"Do you want to know what happened to me today?"

"Well, I—"

"I was fifty feet in the air fixing a power line when an old lady came around the corner. She doesn't see the cones, plows ahead, and clips the back of the truck. Jason jumped out of the way, or else he'd be dead. I fucked up my shoulder on the corner of the bucket." *Thank God that was all that happened.* My jaw pulses as the memory of thinking I would meet my maker passes through my brain. "So excuse me for not classifying your pussy problem as a crisis."

Gravel crunches beneath my tires as I turn onto the old country road that leads to my house.

Luke's silent. He's unsure whether to press forward or

retreat from the conversation. *Wise.* Although there are a few things that I'd rather be doing *less* than acting as my brother's sounding board, I have ten minutes to go until I get home.

I can suck it up that long.

"Why did Alyssa leave in the first place?" I ask with as much *give-a-shitness* as I can muster.

"She said she was sick, and I told her I had all the vitamin D she needs."

I roll my eyes. "You're twenty-seven years old. Grow up."

"*I was joking.* What do you know about women, anyway? When's the last time you had one around?"

"If I don't know anything about women, why in the hell are you calling me for advice?"

"Simple. You're the only sibling who will answer."

When will I ever learn?

"Gavin is avoiding me for reasons we won't discuss," he says. "I talked to Mallet last week, and he said his trainer was taking his phone. He's been having a hard time concentrating for his fight, so Oscar was removing all distractions. And I'm not about to call Kate."

I grin. "Aw, Kate's your baby sister. I'm sure she has great advice."

"She's your sister too. Have *you* ever called her for advice?"

We laugh at the same time. Kate's *a firecracker. You risk setting your problems on fire if you ask Kate for help.*

"Eh, maybe I'm better off without Alyssa, anyway," Luke says. "Fucking the same person is a dead-end sport."

My forehead wrinkles. "How do you go from one extreme to the other? Two seconds ago, you were fucked up because she was gone. Now you're happy about it?"

"I just got my feelings hurt. I want her to want me."

"You want *everyone* to want you."

"Yes. *I do.* Not all of us are content with jacking off for the rest of our life."

Here we go.

I frown and grip the steering wheel tighter.

My family's ongoing push for me to find—I don't even know what it would be called at this age—*a girlfriend? Significant other? God forbid, a wife?* I don't want one, whatever it's called when you're sniffing forty.

Am I against casual sex? It's great for Luke. *Do I have a problem with dating?* Gavin loves it. *Is marriage a social construct that works in the modern world?* Mallet's wedding was the happiest day of his life—if you ignore the fact that the union ended in divorce. And I'm certain Kate will have the biggest damn wedding the world has ever seen someday, and an enormous brood of kids too. *Everything for that girl is extra.*

Relationships, in all their forms, are great … *for some people.* I even understand the draw. But I also understand the *drawbacks,* and quite frankly, I'm not interested in failing another human being in my life.

"You know what?" I ask, redirecting the conversation away from me. "You need to let Alyssa go. Just forget she exists."

"Why?"

"Because you can."

The line goes quiet while he ponders my suggestion.

The rain eases as I approach the bridge over Peachwood Creek. Through the drizzle, I spot a car on the other side of the waterway. It's barely pulled off to the side of the road.

What's going on here?

"What do you mean *because you can?*" Luke asks.

"You were fine with her leaving at the start of this conversation," I say, leaning forward and squinting to get a better look at the car. "If you can let her leave, you need to let her leave. Make sense?"

"Not really."

I squeeze the back of my neck in frustration.

I don't have time for this—any of it.

Luke rattles on, weighing the pros and cons of monogamy. On the other hand, I peer down at the white car sitting askew with its lights off. This is not unusual; many locals know this area is ripe for hunting and fishing. But locals typically drive vehicles with four-wheel drive if they're going to hit the backroads.

I slow down, hoping to see some dipshit climbing out of the ditch with a fishing pole. If that's the case, I can go home and get these wet clothes off. But something tells me that won't be the case.

As I roll by, I can't help but notice the glow of a cell phone in the driver's seat.

Shit.

I ease my foot off the accelerator and assess my options.

Do I go on? No one is asking for my help, after all. Or do I stop? Because someone might be in trouble.

I want to keep going.

"Are you still here?" Luke asks.

Groaning, I hit the brake. *I have to stop, or else it'll bother me all night.*

"Yeah, I'm here," I say, ignoring the sudden weight on my shoulders.

I throw the truck in reverse and roll backward until my passenger's side window lines up with their driver's side door. "Luke, I gotta go. There's a car parked half-assed on the side of the road by Peachwood Creek."

"That's weird."

"I know."

"Well, enjoy," he says.

"Yeah. Bye."

"Later."

I shift the truck into park and rest my head against the seat. My eyes fall closed. *Please have stopped to make a call and don't need real help.*

Water splashes around my boots as they hit the ground. I tug the hood of my sweatshirt over my head and approach the front of the vehicle. A cool breeze—the same one I've battled all day—washes over me, reminding me that a hot shower, sausage, and mushroom pizza are just down the road.

The windows are foggy, but someone moves as I get closer. I don't know what I expect—*someone to roll down the window? Crack the door? Step outside the car?* Regardless, none of those things happen. *Nothing happens.*

What the fuck?

I rap against the glass with the back of my knuckle. "What's going on?"

My hands go into my pockets, and I wait.

Nothing.

Frustrated, I clench my jaw. "Do you need help?"

"I don't know." Her voice muffled. "I don't know what's wrong."

Okay? "Are you hurt?"

"No."

"Out of gas?" I ask.

"I don't think so."

Oh, for fuck's sake. "Are you confused?"

"*No, I'm not confused,*" she says as if offended by the question.

I roll my eyes. "Look, if you don't need help, I'm gonna go."

"My car was … *steaming,* and I pulled over," she says, her voice shaky. "I'm afraid to start it again."

"You mean steam was coming from under your hood?"

"Yeah. I pulled over and turned the car off. But I'm panicking because cornfields surround me… and now there's a man at my window. This is how every horror movie begins, you know."

I glance around. Tall cornstalks sway on both sides of the road—just like every rural road in southern Indiana this time of year.

"I take it that you're not from around here," I say.

"Not sure how that information is pertinent."

The fuck? "Excuse me?"

"It just feels like a very personal question coming from a man I don't know," she says.

"Well, *this man you don't know* is only trying to help."

"I didn't ask you to stop, *sir.*"

My eyes go wide, and I half laugh. *Fuck this.* "No. No, you didn't. Good luck to ya."

I turn to leave when a knock comes on the glass. "*Wait.*"

Looking over my shoulder, I'm surprised to see the door swing open. I'm even more surprised to see someone climb out of the car. But none of that matches my amazement at the woman who steps around the corner of the door.

Holy. Fucking. Shit.

CHAPTER 2

egan

HOLY. FUCKING. SHIT.

A set of extraordinary green eyes capture my gaze. They're so intense that I stutter.

"Um, I …" I start, but the words just won't come. *What was I saying?*

Squarish jaw. Dimpled chin. A day's worth of stubble dots his cheeks. Thick brows frame those ridiculous eyes, and a slightly crooked nose parts his sharp cheekbones.

The chill that has tormented me since I broke down has vanished, and in its place is a heat that gathers in my core.

My phone in one hand, my other hand curled tightly around a hairbrush—the only weapon I could find to use in my defense at a moment's notice. I stand in the middle of a mud puddle and try to regain my composure.

He's too handsome to be helpful. Men this attractive are usually worthless.

"Do you want my help or not?" he asks, shifting his weight from one foot to the other.

I clear my throat. "Yes. Please."

Please don't make me regret getting out of this car.

"So what was it doing? Steaming?" he asks. "Anything else?"

"It started … boiling. Then there was a pop before it started hissing." I shiver against the wind. "Hard to hear anything over the car's frame smashing a pothole every three feet."

He lifts a brow. "How long have you been sitting here?"

"A while. Twenty minutes, maybe."

"Do you have a coat?"

I shiver again. "In my bags in the trunk."

Mentally, I kick myself for being in this situation. I should've gotten the earlier flight from Dallas, and I never should've trusted the navigation in this rental car. Ten minutes wasn't worth a gravel road after a storm. *I knew better.* And now, here I am, paying the price for my foolishness.

My best friend, Calista, tried to get me a tow truck. I called her as soon as I pulled over in a semi-panic. Before she could get my location, her boss beckoned her, and I forced her to go.

Now I wish I would've let her call for help.

"Any chance you're out of coolant?" he asks.

Really? "I don't know. If I knew that, I'd grab the sports drink out of my trunk and pour it into the radiator."

"A sports drink?" His brows rise. "*Tell me you're kidding.*"

"What? I was once stranded on the 405 with a similar issue. The internet said it would work, and it did. But I didn't check the gauges before I shut it off this time, so I'm not sure it was overheating, and I'm too scared to start it again to see." I sigh. "This is a rental, anyway. I don't know this car's quirks."

"The 405?"

I sigh and shiver again. "Yes. A highway in LA."

"You're from LA?"

"Can we focus, please? I'm freezing."

Whether he scoffs or snorts, I'm not sure. But the motion causes a whiff of his peppery yet sweet cologne to roll through the air and envelop me. My core tightens as if the scent is an invitation to climb him like a tree.

It's not.

He slips his jacket off, clearly annoyed. "Just pop your hood."

It's a command punctuated by a *don't fuck with me* look—a look that's so hot I'm pretty sure the look I give him in return says *please fuck with me.*

His jeans are dirty as if he's been working all day. His hands are thick and strong—and ringless. *I can't help but notice that.* He maintains a respectable distance as we chat, and despite his evident irritation at stopping, *he didn't just drive by.*

That has to say something about his character ... I hope.

Still, my risk assessment isn't scientific, and his broad shoulders probably contaminate it.

This is why I'm not a scientist.

"How do I know you know what you're doing?" I ask, my gaze dropping to his lips. "You could get under my hood and do bad things to me."

Oops.

A faint smirk settles on his lips at my unfortunate choice of words. *Damn you, Freud.*

"I meant that you could permanently disable my car and leave me stranded," I say.

He doesn't buy my pathetic attempt at an excuse. "Sure."

"Look, maybe I should just call a tow truck," I say because that's easier than crawling in a mud puddle and dying.

"That's fine. But let me give you a little heads-up."

"What about?"

"It's almost seven o'clock on a Friday night. Tucker, your savior tow truck driver, currently occupies the last barstool at The Wet Whistle, knocking back cold ones left and right. He isn't coming to get you until tomorrow afternoon at best. So if you wanna wait it out because I might *do bad things to you*," he says, deliberately arching a brow, "then I'd find a blanket. It gets cold around here at night."

He knows he made his point. Yet a smugness in his features gives him away.

I wish I were ballsy enough to wait for Tucker or, at the very least, call this guy's bluff. But unfortunately, I listen to too many crime podcasts. I'm scared of the dark, and all I want is to get to the hotel tonight and have a hot bath.

"Suit yourself," he says, turning like he's going to leave.

"*Here.*" I reach into the car and pull the lever. *Pop!* "There you go."

"Are you sure you can trust me?"

I narrow my eyes. "No. But it doesn't sound like I have another option, does it?"

He tosses me his jacket, dragging his gaze away from mine so roughly that I shiver. "Put that on." He shoves his sleeves to his elbows, walks to the hood, and lifts it open.

A blast of air whizzes by like a handful of tiny razors. It probably doesn't help that my feet are soaked, and enough drizzle has landed on my head to practically saturate my hair. I hold out as long as I can, hoping I can muscle through and not put on this guy's coat. But when my legs start to shake, I give in.

I take the risk.

The warmth is immediate. So is the burst of pheromones through my veins.

The headiness of his cologne rushes across my senses. It electrifies every nerve ending in my body, and I'm almost dizzy. *Would it be wrong to hold the collar to my nose and sniff?*

"When's the last time you had your fluids checked?" he asks.

"If that's a pickup line, it sucks."

He bends over the front of my car as I approach, his hands planted on the frame. Veins pop in his forearms as he grips the metal, playing out every blue-collar fantasy I've ever had.

Am I sure this isn't a fever dream? I've been under a lot of stress lately.

He looks at me over his right shoulder and *almost* smiles. Then I realize he's waiting on an actual response to his question.

"I honestly have no idea when those fluids were last checked," I say, tugging his jacket tighter against me. "This is a rental car."

"So you *are* from California."

He says it with pride like he just solved a riddle.

"Actually," I say, moving to stand beside him, "I'm *not* from California. You'll have to keep working on your super sleuth abilities, buddy."

"Are you always this much of a pain in the ass?"

"Absolutely."

He tries to hide his grin as he walks back to his truck.

"I'm from Dallas," I say, pausing to unstick one of my shoes from a mud hole. "I grew up there." *And live there again, sadly.* "But I lived in LA for a long time."

He yanks open the back door of his giant diesel truck and digs around on the floorboard.

"You do know what you're doing, right?" I ask, trying to peek over his shoulder. "Maybe I should've asked for your experience before I—*ah!*"

I yelp, jumping back as he stands abruptly. Before returning to my car, he fires me a look I can't quite read.

"Your coolant is empty," he says, pouring a gallon of water into my radiator. "The oil is muddy. I checked the wiper fluid for the hell of it, and it's empty too."

"Are you serious?"

He blows out an exasperated breath. "You need to call the rental company about this thing. It's not safe to drive too far."

The fabric of his black hoodie stretches as he holds the jug in place. The hemline pulls up just enough for me to catch a glimpse of his skin above his jeans. It's innocent, a quick flash of flesh, but it's enough to make my brain tizzy.

"So how far is *too far?*" I ask, wondering if I can make it to the hotel. "Can I drive it out of here without blowing it up?"

He looks at me out of the corner of his eye. "Are you going to accuse me of getting too personal if I ask how far you have to go?"

I lean against the car and watch him.

He's kind—he's helping me. But he's taciturn all the same. It seems like he cares for my safety but also like he couldn't care less if I drove off a cliff.

There's an invisible wall between us. He nailed that into place as soon as I got out of the car. Still, he fills the space around him with a certain warmth that makes me wonder if he's as disconnected as he seems.

One thing is sure—I'm not scared of him. My creep radar is as quiet as a church mouse. And I'm relatively relaxed for the first time since I got to the airport this morning.

"If I tell you how far I have to go, you're not going to stalk me, are you?" I ask, hoping to get a grin out of him.

I don't.

"No," he says.

"That's a shame."

A streak of surprise flashes through his eyes, making me laugh.

"I'm kidding. Don't panic," I say half truthfully. "I'm going to Peachwood Falls. That's close to here, right?"

"How the hell did you get out here if you're going to Peachwood Falls?"

"Chris."

He snaps the cap back on the jug and heads back to his truck. "Who's Chris?"

The hint of irritation in his voice is fascinating. I could tell him who Chris is—the name I gave the navigation system after I chose the sexy Australian accent to give me directions. But admitting that feels slightly like defeat.

"Oh, Chris is a guy helping me get to Peachwood Falls," I say. "He told me to turn on this road to save ten minutes, which was obviously bad advice."

"Chris was setting you up for failure because this way isn't gonna save you ten minutes. It's probably gonna cost you fifteen —twenty if the road isn't washed out."

In his tone, there's that warmth again, a thread of what might be concern. It's curious and slightly adorable—in a moody kind of way.

I smile. "All men set me up for failure. That's why I'm thirty years old, alone, and childless."

He tosses the empty jug into the back of his truck and then leans against the tailgate. Surprisingly, he seems vaguely interested, so I keep talking.

"From what I've read, it's subconsciously intentional on my part," I say, wiping a strand of hair out of my face. "I choose to have relationships that I know won't work out because it's my comfort zone—which is odd because there's nothing comfortable about it."

I tug on the sides of my shorts—shorts that end at a spot my grandmother would've said is highly inappropriate for public consumption. Shorts that Grandma would've also said are inappropriate for this time of year. *Not the proper attire for Indiana in the fall.*

He keeps his gaze glued to my face as if he's oblivious to the length of my bottoms.

"Come to think of it," I say, "you stopping to help me is the most romantic thing anyone has done for me in a long time."

"Don't get the wrong impression." He shoves off the truck as if he can't possibly stand still a moment longer. "There's an easy solution to your problem, you know."

"My problem?"

He stops just out of reach. The green in his eyes hosts a spattering of gold flecks as he gazes down, deciding what to say.

Energy crackles between us. My heart pounds. I don't know this man, which is not lost on me. Still, I don't move or feel compelled to put distance between us.

"Stop giving your time to unworthy men," he says, his voice softer. "Don't entertain clowns, and you won't have to go to the circus."

I rock back on my heels.

What did he say?

Is a man being logical?

Did I just fall in love?

"Car repair, romance, and inspiration? You could charge big money for this," I say, smiling.

He dips his chin and turns away, heading back to my car. As soon as he's a step away, my entire body sags. *Oof.*

My palms sweat around my brush and phone. He runs his tongue around the inside of his cheek as I approach him at my car door.

"So you're headed into Peachwood Falls," he says, redirecting the conversation. "What for?"

"I'm staying at The Ridges tonight. I start a new job this weekend, and I'm making a pit stop before I go on tomorrow."

"I hope you get directions from someone besides Chris."

Laughter topples from my lips. I think he wants to laugh, too —but he doesn't.

"Peachwood has a bar that moonlights as a restaurant when the sun is up," he says. "It's across the street from The Ridges. So if you're hungry, make sure you get a sandwich before it closes because there aren't any other options until dawn."

Is he serious right now?

His grin grows a smidgen at what must be the shock on my face.

"Relax," he says. "There are big box stores on the highway a little ways out of town. They have everything." He pauses. "Grab some pepper spray while you're there."

"Pepper spray?"

"Someone will take that hairbrush from you before you even swing it," he says, nodding at my hand.

How did he know I was going to use this as a weapon?

My heart flutters at his consideration. "Be careful. That almost sounds like you care."

"I don't." He nods toward my car. "Now go ahead and give it a try. Let's see if it starts up."

I climb into the car and press the brake. My finger touches the ignition button, and my car comes to life. *No steam.*

"So you do know what you're doing," I tease.

He flashes me the tiniest of smiles.

"Get the hell out of here," he says, swatting a lightning bug as it flies in front of his face. "I'll wait and make sure you get turned around. Then call the rental company and force them to figure out your car. I can't believe they let you drive it off the lot like that."

I slip off his jacket. "Got it. But one more thing. I don't know how to get back to Peachwood Falls. I can ask Chris, but he'll tell me to go straight, and that's apparently not the way."

"Go back out the way you came," he says, taking his jacket and ensuring our fingers don't touch. "Take a right onto the highway and go about eight, ten miles. You'll see the exit."

"Then why did Chris have me come down here?"

He shrugs. "He's your friend. You tell me."

"Well—"

"I was kidding. I don't give a shit." He smirks again and taps the top of my car. "Buckle up and get out of here. Watch for deer. They jump like hell this time of year."

"Thank you. Honestly, I don't know what I would've done if you hadn't stopped."

He bats a hand through the air like it's no big deal. Also like *this conversation is over*.

The last dark cloud clears, displaying a remarkable sunset. The sun hovers above the tree line, and the sky glows a beautiful color of oranges and reds. Without any noise from nearby towns, everything looks so peaceful and calm ... until he revs his engine.

I roll my eyes and close the door. I try to rev my engine too, but I don't think he can hear it over the roar of his truck. I'm also not entirely sure I'm doing it right.

It takes me five moves to turn my car around the narrow stretch of road. On the third attempt, I nearly slip off the dirt and into a ditch. By the fourth one, he's yelling at me and waving his hands like he's landing an airplane.

It doesn't help. I yell back that I don't work well under pressure, but I'm pretty sure he doesn't hear that either.

Once I'm facing the right way, he honks his horn twice and then barrels in the opposite direction as if he can't get away fast enough.

I'm left sitting in the middle of two cornfields, wondering what in the hell just happened.

I broke down and got rescued by a hot stranger.

A grin settles on my face as I hit the gas.

Not a bad start to my stint in Indiana.

Not a bad start at all.

CHAPTER 3

egan

I splash my way across the street.

Hit-or-miss streetlights project a hazy glow between The Ridges and The Wet Whistle. A handful of cars, primarily trucks, are parked near the establishment's entrance, which has shifted into more of a bar than a restaurant now that it's dark.

My first thought after my bubble bath was to climb into bed and sleep. But I know me. If I don't eat before I lie down, I'll be ravenous at two in the morning. Patti, the sweet receptionist at the hotel, confirmed that there's nothing to eat in town once The Wet Whistle closes. *"Sometimes the gas station has chips."*

How do people survive here?

My phone buzzes as I step onto the cracked sidewalk. I slip it out of my pocket and stand beside a whiskey barrel full of yellow mums.

"Quick question," I say before my mother can say hello. "Do you realize you sent me to a town without a pizza place?"

Mom's laughter is loud.

"This isn't funny," I say, laughing too.

"It's only a month, Megan. I'm sure you'll survive."

"I mean, maybe. *Barely*. Patti, the receptionist at The Ridges who has friend potential, advised me I'd be bored out of my mind here."

"Maggie said there were lots of restaurants and things to do outside Peachwood Falls," Mom says. "She's always talking about grabbing lunch from a sushi shop with Lonnie. I'm sure you'll be fine."

A man with a long, gray beard putters up the road in a golf cart. He stares at me so long that his neck must be in pain.

What? Is it that obvious I'm a tourist? I look around and sigh. *I don't think tourist would be the right word.*

"I'm starting to think you broke your leg on purpose," I say.

"I was going to say that I wouldn't do such a thing, but it *is* awful cozy wrapped up on the couch watching old movies."

Mom's unfortunate step off a sidewalk three weeks ago made her unable to fulfill her promise to her best friend, Maggie Marshall. How could she keep up with Maggie's *spirited* teenage granddaughter with a cast on her leg?

Answer: she couldn't. *But I could.* So my mom volunteered me for the position before I knew what was happening.

That's what being unemployed and moving in with your mom will get you—even if you're thirty.

"I'm taking it you made it to town," Mom says.

"Yeah." I tell her about breaking down but stop short of the story. She'll panic. "It's all good. I'm going to the Marshalls' tomorrow to meet Maggie's son and his daughter. Just standing outside The Wet Whistle to get a sandwich right now." I glance up at the sign. "Cute name, huh?"

"Go eat. I know how you get when you're hungry. Just let me know when you're back in your hotel room."

I smile. "I will. Love you, Mom."

"Love you."

I slide my phone into my pocket and tug open the door to the bar.

It's bigger than I expected based on the outside and much cozier. A couple sits under a giant stuffed turkey flanked by two deer heads. The man and woman smile politely before going back to their drinks. A man at the far end of the bar nods before turning back to the television and giving me a clear view of his Tucker's Towing shirt.

At least the diesel guy didn't lie.

I reach the bar beneath a ceiling covered with dollar bills and eighties rock music playing through hidden speakers. A light flickers at the back of the building, and I spot a chalkboard wall. Everything from song lyrics to tic-tac-toe games to a plate lunch menu for the upcoming week is written in different colors.

"I haven't seen you around before."

The bartender walks my way as I slide onto a barstool. His full head of sandy-colored hair is mussed up like he gave in and let it do whatever it wanted. His eyes are light, too, and playful —just like his smile.

"Probably because I've never been here before," I say.

He stops in front of me and sets his towel down. His friendly face is instantly likable.

"Where is everyone? Patti said this was the most exciting venue in town," I say.

"Patti isn't wrong. But she just must've forgotten that the Peachwood County Fair is this week, and everyone who's anyone is there."

I smile at him. "I see. So if you're here, what does that make you?"

"Someone who doesn't like kids, and all the kids are at the fair."

I laugh. "Fair enough."

"So what can I get ya this evening?" He grins. "A drink? Food? *Therapy?*"

"While I could probably use a little therapy and a drink after the day I've had, I was just hoping for a sandwich."

"I can make that happen." He digs around under the bar, then presents me with a laminated menu. "Ignore the stuff on the front. We're on a skeleton crew in the kitchen after dark."

I quickly skim the offerings. It's a variation of hamburgers and grilled cheeses.

"I'll take a cheeseburger and a Sprite, please," I say, handing him the menu back.

"Run it through the garden?"

"Huh? I have no idea what that means."

"You know, do you want all the stuff on it? Lettuce, tomato, onion, pickles."

"Yup. Run it, baby."

He points at me, laughing, and disappears through a set of swinging doors.

I pull out my phone and find the camera app. My best friend, Calista, always gets a kick out of the things I discover on my adventures. She was adamant that the blueness of Chefchaouen in Morocco was a filter. And when I paddled through an underground river in the Philippines, she thought I was lying. So while the dollars on the ceiling in this small-town bar aren't that exciting, she'll like it nonetheless.

As I open the app, a deep voice from the other end of the bar captures my attention.

"You must be the girl who was stuck out by Cotton's," Tucker says.

Cotton's?

"Um, I don't know," I say, resting my elbows on the bar. "Is Cotton's a spot with cornfields on either side of the road?"

His laugh is loud and gruff. "This is Peachwood. Everywhere is a spot with cornfields on either side of the road."

How did he know that was me?

I turn in my chair, the torn leather biting through my jeans. "How did you know that? How did you know I was out there tonight?"

He grins before taking a long slug of his beer.

"I mean it." My brain spins, searching for an answer. "Did that guy in the black truck tell you?"

Tucker shrugs and goes back to the baseball game. I stare at the back of his round head, unsure whether to demand an answer. I don't know these people.

Car problems in a cornfield. Hot guy to bait you. A small town with all-knowing residents waiting for darkness to fall …

I glance out the window.

Darkness has fallen.

The bartender comes back and glances at me. He sets my drink down and then plants his hands on the bar. "What's wrong?"

Slowly, I slide my gaze from the window to Tucker's mullet and then back to the bartender.

"Tucker knows I broke down today out by Cotton's—whoever that is," I say carefully. "How did he know that? It must have been the guy in the truck because that's the only person I saw. Unless …" My stomach drops. "You know …"

He snorts. *"Don't."*

"Don't what?"

"Don't freak yourself out." He thinks before he speaks again, clearly amused. *"Guy in the truck.* What was his name? I'm Gavin, by the way."

"I'm Megan." Since leaving him earlier this evening, I have run through my conversation with Diesel Man a hundred times. This time, I try to remember his name and not just his physical details … and come up empty. "I don't know. Somehow, he didn't mention it."

"What did the truck look like?"

"Big. Black." I pause. "Loud."

"And the guy?" he asks, grinning.

"And the guy what?"

"What did he look like?"

I study Gavin.

I like him, and not for the same reason I liked Diesel Man. Gavin is attractive, for sure, but Diesel is different. Gavin is *cute*. He's the kind of guy who's a good friend. The one who makes you laugh. He's the person you call when you have an extra ticket to a concert and no one to go with you.

He's not the kind of guy you fantasize about throwing you against the hood of a car and burying his face between your legs.

"He was in his thirties, probably," I say. "Complicated. Not sweet, but not a total dick. *Super determined* that I didn't think he was being nice, though—like that would've ruined his whole life."

Gavin's eyes sparkle.

"Despite his grumpiness, he was freaking hot," I admit, feeling comfortable enough around my new acquaintance to admit such things. *I'm only going to be in town for a month. What do I care what he thinks about me?* "Green eyes. Broad shoulders. Forearms that just ... *ah*."

Gavin bursts out laughing.

"What?" I ask, shrugging. "Do you know who it was?"

I glance at Tucker. He's watching me over his shoulder and grinning too.

"*What?*" I ask them both, holding my hands at my shoulders. "What's going on?"

Tucker shakes his head, then focuses on the game again.

"It's rude to eavesdrop, *Tucker*," I say.

His heavy shoulders bounce as he laughs.

I sigh and turn back to Gavin. "Who was he? You guys know, don't you?"

"How would we know from *that* description? So vague. I mean, think about it. My eyes are kinda green. Look at these shoulders." He flexes. "And I'll have you know I get compliments on these forearms all the time."

I stare at him. "What's your point?"

"My point is that your description could be anybody."

"*Hmm.*"

"Don't *hmm* me. I bet you'll figure it out once you're here for a few days—if you're sticking around."

I swirl my straw around my drink.

Gavin is easy to talk to—but most bartenders are. He reminds me of Calista in a weird way. They're both funny and open and have never met a stranger.

The exact opposite of Diesel Man.

"Yeah, I'll be around for a while. I'm starting a … it's a job, I guess, since I'm getting paid to do it. But it's not a *job-job*—more like a favor for my mother. Or for her friend, really." I grimace. "Whatever. I'm here for about a month. Let's keep it at that."

"What's the favor? Seems pretty complicated."

I take a sip of my drink before answering him.

"My mom's best friend, Maggie, is going out of town for a month to see her daughter. Mom was supposed to watch Maggie's granddaughter," I say, using air quotes. "She's fourteen and testing lots of limits. They don't want her home alone while her dad is at work especially considering he might be working out of town for stretches at a time."

"*Oh.* Okay. I see."

"Yeah." I sigh. "I'm sure it will be fine, even though I'm staying in Maggie's son's house, and I've never met him before."

His smile stretches from ear to ear. "That could get interesting quick."

"I suppose it could, but Maggie said he's working all the time now, and I probably won't even see him. Besides, he's *her* son. I'm sure he's as nice as they come."

Gavin nods his head.

"You're odd," I say.

He laughs. "I'm just thinking about how having to be with kids all the time must be the worst job in the world. I buy condoms by the boatload to avoid that situation."

"I like kids. I thought I'd have a few of them by now."

"Not me. That's not in my future."

"It's not in mine either because I can't find a man with daddy potential."

"I'm not touching that," he says, making me laugh.

My glass creates a ring of moisture on the bar top. I grab a coaster and slide it under the drink.

"Gav!" a voice yells from the back.

He holds up a finger and disappears behind the swinging doors into the kitchen again. I start to text Calista the dollar pictures when a text pops up.

Calista: I did some digging.

Me: STOP.

Calista: You don't even know the
guy you're moving in with, Megs.
Someone has to look out for you.

Me: 😕

Calista: He doesn't have an
online presence AT ALL. Nothing.

Me: That's a good thing.

Calista: That's a weird thing.

Me: Will you relax?

Calista: What if he's a creep?
What if he has some kink, and you
wake up in the middle of the
night, and he's standing in the
corner with his dick in his hand?

Me: Then that'll be more dick
than I've seen in a while.

Calista: I AM BEING SERIOUS.

I consider telling her about Diesel Guy but stop short of spilling the goods. Instead, she'll call me for all the details I don't have.

I'll wait until we're face-to-face.

Gavin comes through the doorway with a bag.

Me: I'll call you tomorrow. My
food is here. 😬 Thanks for
having my best interest at heart.

Calista: Love you, fool.

I laugh and set the phone on the counter.

"The kitchen thought this was to go," Gavin says, frowning. "I'll grab a plate."

"No, that's fine—perfect, actually. I'd rather take it back to my room and get myself sorted for tomorrow anyway."

He sets the bag on the counter. A coy smile plays on his lips. "Are you nervous?"

"A little. It's growing as I sit here." *And think about Calista's warnings.* I reach for the cash in my pocket. "I should've drunk my dinner."

"Put your money away. Dinner is on me," Gavin says.

"What? *No.* You aren't buying my dinner. Why would you do that?"

He shoves the bag toward me. "You've had a hell of a day. Sounds like the guy who stopped to help you gave you a hard time, and who knows what will happen tomorrow?"

My jaw falls open. "Gee, thanks. Did you miss that whole part about me being nervous? Because that doesn't help."

"I'm not saying something *bad* will happen," he says, rolling his eyes. "I'm just ... *saying.*"

I put a five-dollar bill on the counter for a tip and grab the bag. "I *am* going to let you buy my dinner for making me worry about that all night."

He grins cheekily.

"You are officially my only friend here, Gavin. Congratulations. If tomorrow is a shit show, I'll be back for therapy."

"Tell you what," he says, tossing the towel he had earlier over his shoulder. "If tomorrow is shitty, I'll listen to you whine and buy your dinner again."

"*Oh,* you're now my best friend here, even if Patti pans out in the friend arena."

He snorts. "I'll beat Patti for that title even if she makes it into the friend arena."

I laugh. "Good night, Gavin."

"Night."

"*Night, Tucker.*"

He throws up a hand in a salute without looking at me. *I kind of love this guy.*

I head for the door and step out into the cool night air.

My spirits are surprisingly good, considering the ridiculousness of the day. Although, physically, I'm disjointed from the traveling, and emotionally, I'm stressed from the anticipation of tomorrow.

I need to eat and get to bed.

My phone buzzes as I start splashing back across the street. No cars are coming either way, so I tuck my take-out bag under my arm. Then I slip out my phone.

Calista: He won an award.

        Me: Calista …

Calista: He was Lineman of the
Year two years ago. That's
electrician speak, not football
speak, to clarify.

        Me: Noted. I just got a burger
        and made a friend. I'm going to
        try to relax and get some sleep,
        so enough with the private eye
        work, okay?

Calista: Did you tell them you
have a best friend already?

        Me: LOL. Is that all you took out
        of that?

Calista: I mean it. You already
have a best friend.

        Me: I know.

I step onto the sidewalk in front of The Ridges.

Calista: Love you. Call me if you
need me. CHARGE YOUR PHONE.

Me: ☺ Good night. Love you.

Calista: Night, love bug.

I laugh and make my way to the front of the hotel.
Burger. Brush teeth. Bed.
I grin.
I'll try not to imagine a hot, green-eyed grump in bed with me.

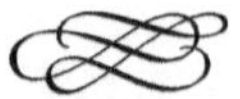

CHAPTER 4

egan

"I LEGITIMATELY HATE MY BOSS," CALISTA SAYS, NEARLY GROWLING into the phone.

"What happened now?" I squint through my windshield into the morning sunlight. "You sound extra passionate today, and it's Saturday. How can you be pissed at your boss on a Saturday?"

"Remember that guy I met at the airport? The hot guy in the suit and glasses?"

"Vaguely."

She sighs. "It's been a while. I can see why you might forget him."

"Or I might forget him because you've had—how many men have you been with since you met him?"

"*Not the point.*" She smacks her lips together. "We had a … I'm going to say a date because that sounds more politically correct. But it was really dinner and a hookup."

I grin and silence Chris's directions.

Calista and I have a lot in common—we love the beach, Brad Pitt movies, and everything that happened in the nineties. But in some ways, we're opposites. When it comes to men and dating, we're on different spectrums.

My friend dates fast and hard. There's an objective to it all. *Find a husband.* She's convinced there's one man out there created just for her, and she'll know it when she meets him. So why bother pretending to be serious about someone she knows isn't *the one*? It only prolongs or prevents her from fulfilling her happy ending.

Me? I date cautiously. The goal isn't … well, there isn't one besides a good time. The concept of *forever and ever, amen* makes me itch. My eye twitches, and I feel like I'm going to throw up. A clock starts ticking as soon as I get attached, and I've never found the pain of the loss to be worth the experience. I bow out before things get too serious.

"Anyway, there's no dinner and no hookup because I have to travel to Albuquerque tonight," she says, growling the words. "I've been traveling for our department for the past three months, and that bastard promised me he would give me a break so I could try to have a normal life."

"I'm sorry."

"Yeah, me too. LAX is going to be a nightmare. *But,*" she says, her voice brightening, "because I was running on fury and adrenaline last night after I got my travel notification, I spent a couple of hours online."

I know where this is going. "*Calista. No.*"

Gravel crunches beneath my car tires as I turn onto a country road. Strands of corn sway in the breeze on either side. *What is it with cornfields?* I hit the gas a little harder.

"Chase Marshall won an award last year for Lineman of the Year," she says. "I told you that last night. Anyway, there was a picture in the paper. The resolution online was surprisingly terrible, considering we aren't in the Stone Age anymore, but I liked what I saw."

I sigh. *Oh, friend. Don't start shipping us already.*

"I'm trying to arm you with information," she says.

"You aren't arming me with information by saying you think he might be good-looking."

"That was a side benefit. I didn't pull it up to see if he was hot. I was searching for red flags. But, again, I have a vested interest in you not dying."

"*Again,* I'm not going to die. *And* if I wanted to know what he looked like, I could've asked my mom. Or Maggie. Or I could've looked at Maggie's social account because she posts pictures of her kids. She's a very grandma-y type, you know?"

The cornstalks give way to a farmhouse in the middle of an extensive lawn. The siding is white, and a porch wraps around the corner by the driveway. Plants hang from hooks in the rafters, and the landscaping is tidy. *Very pretty.*

A bubble of excitement mixed with equal amounts of nerves fills my stomach. Although I brush Calista's fears off—and despite knowing that the Marshalls are great people—a thread of uncertainty about working for a man I haven't met in person exists.

"Calista, I gotta go," I say, my heart beating faster as I pull into the driveway. "I'm here."

"Okay. Be safe. If there are bad vibes, leave. You can break a promise once in your life."

"It's not my promise—it's my mom's. My guilt would be much less because of that."

"See?"

I laugh. "Love you. Bye."

"Call me—"

I hang up. *She'd go on about this forever.*

I park my car next to a small burgundy SUV and turn off the

engine. Sun filters through the trees that pepper the property, making it look like a postcard.

As I climb out of the car, Maggie comes rushing down the front steps with a giant smile on her sweet, familiar face. There are a few more lines around her eyes, and her hair has a bit more silver than the last time I saw her—which, come to think of it, was probably ten years ago. Otherwise, she's the same Maggie.

That's such a relief.

"There you are," she says, arms extended. "I'm so glad you made it."

I let her pull me into a hug and enjoy the warmth of a motherly embrace. "It's good to see you."

"You have no idea how good it is to see you, honey." She releases me. "You look as fit as a fiddle. *Look at you.* You are as pretty as a peach, Megan Dawn."

I giggle. "Keep talking like that, and I might not leave."

She hugs me quickly once more. "Oh, it's so good to see you. Thank you for coming. We're relieved that Kennedy will be in your competent hands."

I couldn't wipe the smile off my face if I tried. "Well, I'm happy to be here. I'm not sure how capable these hands are, but I'll give it my best shot."

"Just keep her from sneaking out and borrowing her daddy's truck"—Maggie makes a face—"and we'll call it a success."

"*Ooh.* Okay. I understand where the whole *spirited* thing comes from."

Maggie rolls her eyes. "She hit fourteen, and her sensibilities have gone out the window. Don't get me wrong. Kennedy's a good kid. She's just going through something, I guess." She grins, shaking a finger at me. "And she better get through it before her daddy drags her through it with her grandma behind her with a broom."

I laugh.

"This place is gorgeous," I say, spinning in a circle and taking it all in. "It's like a postcard from a quaint little bed-and-breakfast."

She beams. "Let's go in. I'll show you around."

We take a brick pathway to the steps. Solar lights line each side, leading us to the porch. A welcome wreath hangs beside the door.

"I've been cleaning all day," Maggie says, waiting for me to go through the doorway first. "It's not usually this organized."

"You didn't have to clean for me."

"Honey, it's the least I can do."

I'm greeted by the scent of freshly baked bread and the undeniable easiness that only *a home* can deliver. The sensation caresses my frayed nerves.

Hardwood floors extend from the small foyer in every direction. A small, cozy living room with a rock fireplace is beyond an arched doorway on my left. A stack of books sits in the center of a long table through the archway on my right. Stairs rise in front of me, and a hallway stretches beside them, leading to what appears to be a kitchen at the back of the house.

"This is it," Maggie says, closing the door behind her. "Lonnie and I live just down the road. So if you need something and don't want to drive to town, feel free to see if we have it. I'll leave a key with you. Kennedy and Chase each have one too, of course."

"I'm sure we'll be fine. Don't worry about us."

She motions for me to follow her down the hallway. "Oh, I'll worry. That's my job. Just wait until you're a mother. You'll understand then."

"If my life doesn't get on track soon, my eggs might be dried before I find viable sperm."

Maggie laughs. "You're your mother's daughter, that's for sure."

"Don't tell her that. She's convinced she's never going to be a grandma. I keep telling her that she should've had more kids to up her chances."

"Oh, she doesn't think that. She wants you to be happy."

We enter the kitchen. The bright and airy room has white cabinets and buttery-colored walls. The appliances are stainless steel, and a farmhouse sink sits under a wide window with gauzy curtains.

"Mom should relax because I want to be happy too," I say, peeking out the window at the expansive yard.

"How are things going with you? Your mom said you were pretty bummed to be back in Dallas."

I press my hip into the island and watch her piddle around the kitchen, putting up a few cups that sit by the sink.

"Moving home at my age isn't exactly a reason to celebrate," I say. "But my company felt the pinch after the pandemic and downsized. I can't blame them."

Maggie frowns. "Well, I know Denise loves having you back home. She missed you and worried about you in Los Angeles alone."

"I know. She keeps asking me if I'll move back to California, and I keep telling her I'm not. As much as I loved my job and the beaches and the weather, I'm not a West Coast girl." I laugh. "I don't think she believes me, though."

"Where *do* you see yourself?"

I can't answer that question.

My dream job was a dream job that I didn't know I had. It fell into my lap like a gift from above.

Who thought you could get a job designing nail polishes? And who would've guessed it would be so fun and inspiring? Not me. I worked with the most incredible creative team and public relations division to select each season's themes based on current events, movies, or travel destinations. Visiting sets of music videos, traveling to exotic destinations, and meeting some of the most interesting people in all facets of the business were more than I imagined was possible.

Sales rose during the pandemic. Our older lines sold out. We devised an at-home kit that went bonkers … and then the world reopened. Sales slowed. Budgets were cut, and so was I.

"I don't know, Maggie. I have a few feelers out there and am hoping something pans out before this month is up."

"I'll keep my fingers crossed for you."

"Thanks." I move around the island toward a china cabinet in the corner. "When do I get to meet Kennedy? Is she here?"

"She's with her grandpa. They have a standing Saturday morning breakfast date, and Lonnie wasn't about to miss it because it'll be the last one they get for a long time."

My heart warms. "I love that."

"They do too." She dries her hands off on a kitchen towel decorated with fall leaves. "They'll be back soon. Chase should be back anytime too. He helped his brother with a fence this morning." She shakes her head and tosses the towel onto the counter. "That man works so much that you'd think he'd want to sleep in on the weekends. But he's just like his father. He didn't get that waking up early nonsense from me."

I laugh but bristle when a door slams on the other side of the wall.

"That's the mudroom," Maggie says, nodding toward a door I didn't notice to my left. "Chase uses that when he comes in filthy. He put a whole bathroom in there last summer. It keeps the floors much cleaner in the rest of the house."

The energy in the room shifts. It's heavier, more electrified—chock-full of anticipation.

"Did you have an easy trip yesterday?" Maggie asks. Despite her attempt at nonchalance, her eyes sparkle. "I wish you would've called last night."

"Actually, it was a bit of a shit show."

Maggie lifts a brow, amused. "Oh?"

"Yeah. I tried a shortcut and ended up somewhere by Cotton's—whoever that is. I sat there for a while before a guy stopped to help me."

"*Oh?*"

"I was expecting a Michael Myers situation with the cornfields," I say, laughing. "But I was pleasantly surprised to discover it was a total hottie."

"Really? A hottie, huh?"

"Let's just say I wasn't mad about watching him work on my rental car."

Maggie laughs, clearly smitten with my story.

"I don't know what it is about grumpy men, but I think his broodiness made him even hotter," I say.

"You're right. Grumpy men can be very attractive."

I smile, imagining my mom and Maggie prowling for guys back in the day.

"He wasn't mean, was he?" she asks, her features sobering.

"Not at all. I think he *wanted* to be nice, maybe even sweet. He was all …" I pause to think of an analogy that is PG-rated enough to share with Maggie and one that she'll understand. "He was a grumpy cat. Scowly and moody, but deep down, he just wanted to be petted."

Her face lights up as she walks toward me. "*Ha!*"

"I just enjoyed the arm porn and overlooked the irritation."

A coy smile plays on her lips as she stops in front of the mudroom door. "Smart move. I would've done the same."

My heart begins to pound again as I anticipate … *something.* I'm not sure what's about to happen, but a definite undercurrent ripples through the room.

"Maggie?"

"Come here," she says, motioning for me to join her beside the mudroom door.

Once I'm standing beside her, she smiles. *And throws the door open.*

My.

Jaw.

Drops.

A man with incredible green eyes and broad shoulders stands in front of me in nothing but a pair of black boxer briefs.

His gaze snaps to mine and locks into place. The aforementioned scowl covers his lips.

What in the hell is happening here?

I suck in a haggard breath as my eyes nearly pop out of my head. I grip the doorframe to steady myself.

Holy freaking hell.

My brain screams at me not to ogle him—*not in front of his mother. Oh my gosh, Maggie is his mother? Diesel Man is Maggie's son?*—and try to process this situation. But my body overrides the logic.

His body is a freaking playground.

Strong arms. A thick chest. Narrow waist.

He's muscled and proportioned perfectly as if his strength comes from physical labor and not just hours at a gym.

Don't drool, Megan.

His underwear hugs the lines of his thighs and gives a not-so-vague idea of what he's packing between his legs.

I gulp. *Lord, have mercy.*

"Chase, meet your new nanny," Maggie chirps.

Her words sling me back to reality.

No. No, no. no. This can't be happening.

Chase doesn't look at his mother. He doesn't acknowledge that he hears a word she's saying. Instead, he stares at me as if I've somehow overstepped my bounds.

"Megan, this is my son, Chase," Maggie says as if she's all too happy to make the introduction. "Kennedy's dad."

I gulp again. At the same time, my brain explodes with the weight of this information.

How is this possible?

How is Diesel Man the single dad?

Did he hear me say I thought he was hot?

I force a swallow down my very constricted throat.

Is Maggie going to put two and two together?

A silent wail echoes through my brain.

Kill me now. Someone, please put me out of my misery.

Chase lifts his chin, exposing the long lines of his throat. It's entirely hotter than it should be, and I wonder somewhere in the back of my mind if he knows it and is doing it intentionally.

"A grumpy cat?" he asks, his brows lifting to the ceiling in displeasure mixed with surprise.

He heard me.

My cheeks flush as my conversation with Maggie replays in my head. Just as I'm about to excuse myself and flee, the corner of his lips twitch into a hint of a grin. It's as if a button is pressed, and my shoulders fall.

"Yes, Chase," I say, lifting a brow. "*A grumpy cat.*"

I grin, watching him try his best not to react to me. It's a decent attempt. Too bad for him that I see right through it.

"Megan also said you were a total hottie," Maggie says, nodding emphatically.

My cheeks burn from embarrassment. *Guess she put it all together.*

"Really, Maggie?" I ask.

"What?" she asks, her arms stretched out to her sides in a show of innocence. "You did say that, didn't you?"

Chase crosses his arms across his chest. "*Mother,*" he says, his voice cool and calm. "Would you mind giving me a minute to get dressed?"

"Why are you standing in your skivvies anyway?" she asks.

He looks at her like he can't believe they're having this conversation. "Does it matter?"

"I guess not. We'll be in the kitchen. Take your time, dear."

I turn to leave the room when my gaze slams into Chase's

again. His eyes nearly burn holes into mine. They're so intense —*yet so absolutely unreadable*—that I freeze.

The gold I saw in his icy greens last night reappear one fleck at a time. It brings a light to his face, a slight approachability, that I know how to work.

I smile sweetly. "Yes, Chase. Take your time, *dear.*"

His eyes narrow.

I wink. And then, with a fire in my stomach that I can barely contain, I walk out and shut the door behind me.

CHAPTER 5

hase

I run a hand down my face. The scruff I didn't bother to shave last night is rough against my palm. I open my mouth and work my jaw around once, then twice to dispel some of the *surprise ... frustration ... tension* of the last few minutes.

How is she *at my house?*

Bits and pieces from my conversation with Megan—a name that I went to great lengths last night not to learn—come barreling back at me.

Her new job. Being in Peachwood Falls. Not being familiar with the area.

She probably had my address in her GPS instead of The Ridges.

I growl into the air.

Megan is so damn hot that it's almost unreal. Blond hair. Bright blue eyes. A beauty mark off-center below her left eye. Her body is ridiculous, with curves that my fingers itch to skim.

Her laughter mixes with my mother's voice outside the door, and I can't help it. I smile—because *that's* the shit that kept me up all night. That's the shit I can't shake.

Every time I think of her little smirk and playfulness when she's teasing me, I can't help but grin. She brushed off my scowl like she wasn't concerned with my obvious irritation at stopping to help. Instead, she pestered me, joked around, and her boundless energy and never-ending mouth were somehow ... cute.

She's everything I don't need to fuck around with. Period.

I toss my soiled clothes into the laundry hamper by the sink and then pull on the clean jeans and flannel I set out before I left for Gavin's this morning.

She's the nanny? She's staying here for a month?

How did this go from one of Mom's friends to a sexpot?

I button my shirt.

This isn't what I signed up for. I didn't agree with this. I have my hands overflowing with Kennedy's teenage bullshit and work. There's no bandwidth left to deal with—Megan's and Mom's voices grow louder—*that every day for thirty damn days.*

"This is never going to work," I grumble. "There's no reason to start it. I didn't want a fucking nanny anyway. I'll call in favors from Luke and Gavin. God knows they owe me anyway."

Mom's laughter rings through the closed door again.

"Maggie Mae Marshall, we're going to talk about this," I mutter.

I yank open the door with more force than necessary. I'm unsure if it's to affirm that I'm taking a stand or to broadcast my irritation before entering the room. Both heads turn toward me as I step into the kitchen.

Megan leans back in her chair, an arm draped over the seat next to her. *Casually confident.* Her lips are pressed together like she's waiting patiently for me to explode.

I want to explode all right. So that's why you gotta go.

"Can someone clue me in as to what's going on?" I ask, ripping my eyes away from her mouth.

"Megan is Kennedy's new nanny," Mom says, chirping like a damn songbird. "I had her come by this morning so we could have brunch and show her around before she meets Kennedy and moves in."

Move in? Oh, hell no.

I hold out a hand. "Let's …let's back this whole thing up a minute, Mom."

"What? Why?"

I sigh.

My explanation should come quickly and easily. *I'm too attracted to have Megan in my house twenty-four hours a day for a month. She'll hinder me a hell of a lot more than she'll help.*

But I can't exactly say that.

"I didn't realize you'd hired someone," I lie. "I thought you were bringing people by so we could interview them."

"Chase Ryan, you know that's not true."

"So, what? You just chose someone for me?" I ask as if this shocks me. "You chose a random woman I've never met to live in my house and care for my baby girl?"

"*She's fourteen,*" Mom says, her no-nonsense tone hard to argue with.

But I do.

"I wouldn't give a shit if she were five," I fire back. "Actually, it might be easier if she were a toddler and not a teenager hell-bent on coming up pregnant or dead."

Mom sighs. "You're exaggerating."

"*Barely.*"

Megan drops her hand from the chair and leans forward. "Excuse me. The teenager part of this I can handle. The rest of it? This is not what I expected."

"That makes two of us," I say, lifting a brow.

"What are you saying?" she asks.

I look at her. *I want to fuck you senseless is what I'm saying.*

"Can we just take a breath?" Mom asks, rolling her eyes. "I know this situation isn't what any of us expected, but Denise breaking her leg changed things, and I thought we were all in agreement that this was the best solution."

"I don't even know her," I say, gesturing to Megan.

Megan stands, her eyes narrowed. "Are you implying that I'm untrustworthy?"

It's not you that I don't trust, sweetheart.

My chest rises and falls with more force than necessary as I watch her hand clench the bend of her hip. Her anger should make me feel embarrassed for my behavior, maybe. Or guilt-ridden for making this whole thing a big deal. I should probably feel like a dick for being one.

The only way her confidence makes me feel is … *damn.*

"*I trusted you*—on a backroad at dusk, no less," she says. "And now *you* have trust issues? That's rich."

I narrow my eyes at her, hoping she'll back down. She doesn't. She doesn't even flinch.

"You trusted me because you needed me," I say, irritated that she's making this more complicated than it needs to be. "I can be more discerning. I don't need you."

"Yes, you do, Chase," Mom says with exasperation.

I slide my gaze to hers. "Please let me handle this."

"I'll do no such thing." Mom gets to her feet, the pink sequins on her shirt catching the sunlight and almost blinding me. "Megan is the daughter of one of my very best friends, and I trust her implicitly. I—"

"Well, that's great," I say. My blood pressure rises at Mom's assumption that my opinion doesn't matter—and the fact that I'm grasping for control. Probably mostly the latter. "But *I* don't know her. I don't know anything about her. Maybe I don't want—"

"Okay, *hold on a second*," Megan says. The fire in her eyes burns a straight line to my cock. "First, I'm standing here, so please don't talk about me like I'm not. Second, I don't *need you* either. And after listening to your rant, I'm not sure I want to work for someone with such a ..."

"*A what?* Go on. Finish it."

She narrows her eyes. "*A bad attitude.*"

"I don't have a bad attitude," I fire back.

Mom sighs. "Yes, you do."

"Mom, *please ...*"

Megan bites her bottom lip. Sometimes people do that when they're thinking. Megan's thinking all right—she thinks she'll get me to crack. To give in. To backtrack and apologize.

Not happening.

"Okay, let's look at it like this," I say, approaching the problem from another angle. "How am I supposed to trust a woman with my child who thought *a hairbrush* was an acceptable weapon?"

"It was all I had."

"You were unprepared."

She huffs. "Hardly. I was *resourceful.*"

I roll my eyes.

"Fine. *Let's look at it like this,*" she says, her voice growing cocky as she throws my language back at me. "Why should *I* trust a man who threatened to leave me sitting in the middle of a darkened cornfield?"

Mom gasps. "*You better not have.*"

Megan's lips purse together. "Maybe *I* need to rethink this commitment."

"I didn't threaten to leave you. I told you I'd leave you to your own devices because you thought I would *do something bad to you.* There are two reasons for that—one of them being trust issues," I say, smirking. "You didn't automatically trust me either, sweetheart. Hell, you barely trusted yourself."

Megan narrows her eyes. I give her a smug grin that only

irritates her more. And that only makes her hotter, which is a problem I can't remedy—a problem I'm not willing to extend over a month. *I'm not Luke. I'm not a glutton for punishment with no responsibilities and lots of time on my hands.*

"I could barely trust myself? Are you projecting, Chase, *dear*?" Megan asks. The pulse of her jaw negates the sweetness in her voice.

"I—"

"I think you two are getting off topic," Mom says.

"This is Megan's comfort zone," I say, my eyes not leaving *the nanny's*. "She lets *Chris* lead her astray all the time."

She grins. "*Oh*, are you jealous of Chris? Is that what this is?"

"*Chris doesn't know jack shit.*"

"Chris is practically a superhero, thank you very much."

I scoff.

"Will you two *please* stop it?" Mom says with a giant sigh. "You're fighting like an old married couple."

Megan gives me a final glare before turning to my mom. "I'm sorry, Maggie."

"No apologies needed," Mom says, patting Megan's shoulder as she walks by. "I know this situation is stressful for all of us. *Right, Chase?*"

I look at the ceiling and sigh.

Mom has made her point, and she knows it. None of us wants to be here, in the position of needing someone to stay with Kennedy. Not me, not Kennedy, not Mom, and apparently not Megan. Yet *here we are*.

If I ask Gavin and Luke to help with my daughter, Mom will stay home. She loves my brothers, but she also knows her sons would let Kennedy get away with much more than she deserves. Mom would cancel her vacation with my sister, and she needs to see Kate. And Kate needs her. It's been too long.

Mom hasn't had a real getaway since Child Protective Services called ten years ago to tell me I was a single dad.

Shit.

I look at Megan, my resolve waning. "Did you call the rental company about your car this morning?"

She blinks slowly.

"I told you it wasn't safe to drive around," I say, frustrated with her lack of concern for her safety.

"Well, I had an appointment this morning. You know, to have brunch with a family I would be staying with to help them out of a pinch."

The intensity flowing from one to the other makes my heart pound. I have no idea what I'll do with her or how to handle this situation, but I better get a grip on it and do it fast.

"I'll tell you what," Mom says, picking up her cell phone off the table. "I'm going to step outside and call Kate to book the massages we discussed last night. God knows I'm going to need one. And, while I do that, the two of you will work this out. Understood?"

Megan and I stare at each other, the energy between us crackling.

"You have ten minutes," Mom says, heading for the door.

Ten minutes to work this out.

Like that will be possible.

CHAPTER 6

egan

THE DOOR SHUTS WITH A BOOM.

Point taken, Maggie.

Chase works his jaw back and forth, watching me like I'm the enemy. I roll my eyes at his ridiculousness, hoping it irritates him as much as his behavior irritates me.

His gaze narrows.

I smile. *Fucker.*

"Let's get one thing straight," I say, jumping into the thick of the matter. "I'm not begging to be here. As a matter of fact, *I don't even want to be here.* So don't act like you're doing me a huge favor by letting me watch your daughter."

He takes a breath and grabs the back of a chair in front of him. The severity of his features eases. A wariness, a cautious curiosity settles in its place.

"Tucker does basic mechanic work," Chase says. "Have him look at your car today."

I lift a brow. "That's what you want to spend the next ten minutes talking about?"

He releases the chair and then paces the kitchen.

Frustration drips through my veins as I watch him blatantly *not talk*. Not look at me. Refrain from giving any indication that he wants to have this conversation.

If that's the way he wants it, fine. I'll go back to Dallas and get on with my life.

"Your point is taken," I say. "When your mom comes back, I'll let her know this isn't going to work for me."

He stops pacing and sighs. "Megan ..."

"What did you say to me last night? *Good luck to ya?* Well, good luck to ya, Chase."

He rolls his eyes. "Will you shut up?"

I gasp. "No, I will not."

"Of course not. What was I thinking?"

"At least I'm not acting like a child. Are you sure your mom didn't need a babysitter for *you?*"

He throws his hands in the air.

I move around the room—careful to stay on the opposite side of the island from Chase. My heart pounds as the words I just spoke echo back at me.

What are you doing, Megan? Don't act like this.

"I'm sorry for saying that," I say, stopping beside the sink. "I'm just ... worked up."

He pulls his hands down his face. "That makes two of us."

The tension between us thickens. It's heavier and more cumbersome. Even if we're firing back and forth, the levity we've shared seems to have evaporated.

"I'm sorry too," he says, blowing out a breath. "You just surprised me."

I see my opening—the sliver of an opportunity to bring some light into this conversation—and take it.

"When I walked in on you practically naked?" I ask.

Chase stops in his tracks and smirks. The longer I say nothing, the deeper his smirk grows. The deeper his smirk grows, the more his shoulders relax and the lines in his handsome face ease.

"What?" I ask, playing it cool. "Do you want me to be embarrassed that I saw you in your boxers?"

He shrugs.

"I'm not," I say, hoping my voice is void of the tremble in my stomach. "I think your romantic, inspirational car repair side was my favorite. It turns out that I prefer you naked and not talking."

"Maybe that's our problem."

"Excuse me?"

He shifts his weight from one foot to the other, his grin slipping. "Nothing. Never mind."

I don't know where to go with this. We aren't getting anywhere, and I don't foresee progress. We might have partially defused the situation, but the problem remains.

The thought of disappointing Maggie—and my mother—hurts my heart, but what can I do? This is out of my hands—even if I wanted to stay. And, at the moment, I don't.

Finally, he sighs and folds his arms over his chest. "You called me a grumpy cat. What kind of a description is that? *A grumpy cat?*"

"It's a meme you would know if you had social media."

Shit. This is why I didn't want information, Calista!

A shadow falls across his face for a split second.

"But I didn't say you *were* a grumpy cat," I say hurriedly, hoping he doesn't catch my slipup. "I said you have the personality of one, and, you know, my observation wasn't wrong."

He narrows his eyes. "Chris led you into the middle of cornfields, and you called him a damn superhero. And I get a grumpy fucking cat?"

"What does Chris have to do with this?"

He rubs his forehead.

"*Again*," I say, emphasizing the word, "I'll tell Maggie you'll need to find another *nanny*. I can't imagine staying here and arguing with you for a month. We'd kill each other."

And probably without hate fucking and then makeup sex, to boot. Because that's my luck.

"Megan ..."

For the first time, buried just beneath his steely exterior, there's a flash of vulnerability. It's just a flash—a quick blur of emotion—but it's there.

He covers it as quickly as it appears.

"What?" I ask.

A truck rumbles into the driveway. We turn toward the window to see Maggie making her way to a silver truck.

Chase watches as an older man, whom I recognize as Lonnie, and a young girl with long, dark hair hop out. *That must be Kennedy.*

"Thank you for helping me last night," I say, turning my attention back to him. "I appreciate it. To be safe, I'll get someone to look at the car before I head to the airport."

"Well, look who we have here," Lonnie says as he walks through the mudroom door. "Megan Kramer, if you aren't a sight for sore eyes."

I smile at the teenager beside Lonnie as he hugs me. The buckles of his overalls are cold against my skin—almost as cool as Kennedy's reception.

"How are you, Lonnie?" I ask.

"Good. Ready to see my girlie Kate, that's for damn sure," he says. "I haven't hugged my daughter in far too long."

"I'm sure she'll be just as happy to see you." I pivot to Kennedy and smile. I don't know what to say to her, but I can't not say anything at all. "You must be Kennedy."

She eyes me with a heavy dose of typical teenager suspicion. "Are you *my babysitter*?"

That's how we're playing this, huh? "I—"

"Hey, Ken," Chase says, inserting himself into our little circle. He pulls her against his side. "You're back early. How was brunch?"

I breathe, relieved to have a moment to get my bearings.

How do I answer that? I'm not her babysitter—but Maggie doesn't know that yet. Neither does Lonnie.

I gulp. *This might get awkward.*

"It was brunch," Kennedy says, keeping an eye on me. "They had baklava this week. I brought you some but left it in Pap's truck."

Chase kisses her on the side of the head. "Thanks, kiddo."

"Is that your car out there?" Kennedy asks me, pulling away from her dad.

I nod.

"You have an Iyala Nails bag in the back," she says. "The turquoise tote from the spring collection."

"The turquoise was much prettier than the pink, despite popular demand. I have the pink one, but I never use it."

Her eyes widen. *She has her dad's green eyes.* "You have the pink one? That was *impossible* to get. The turquoise one was too, but *no one* could get the pink one because it came with the summer manicure set and the Relatively Rare red polish."

My smile is wide. "You know a lot about Iyala polishes."

"Yeah. Well, not just the Iyala ones. I love all nail stuff. But the Iyala special collections are always the best."

"I've always been partial to the winter collections. They're always a bit more magical. Don't get me wrong, the summer ones are great. But the winter ones ..."

"The winter ones are always different. Not just red or pink or orange. They come up with some cool colors for the winter collections. They're kind of funky."

I nod, delighted that she picked up on the things I strove to achieve in my years with Iyala Polishes. "Yes. Exactly."

Kennedy grins, satisfied. *I've passed her inspection.*

I'm reveling in my success when I realize I don't need to pass her inspection because I'm not staying.

I clear my throat and avoid Chase's gaze. "I need to get back to the hotel, Maggie. I have a few calls to make this afternoon." *Namely, to buy a ticket home.* "Can I give you a call later today?"

Maggie quickly glares at her son before settling her smile on me. "Absolutely, sweetheart."

A lump settles in my throat, and I turn toward Lonnie.

"Good to see you again, Lonnie," I say. "It was nice to meet you too, Kennedy."

Her brows wrinkle. "Yeah. You, too."

"I'll walk you out," Chase says, his voice rough.

Now he's being nice? It takes everything I have not to roll my eyes and tell him not to bother.

"I'll see you all later," I say, waving as I make my way across the room.

"I hope so," Maggie says.

Chase holds the door for me as I step outside.

The air is blustery, filled with the promise of winter in the distance. I slip my hands into my pockets and hurry down the sidewalk. If I walk fast enough, maybe Chase won't follow.

I'm reaching for the door handle when he speaks.

"*Megan.*"

"What?"

I pop open the door before looking at him.

His eyes are foggy as if a storm is rolling through them. He lets his arms hang at his sides, and his jaw slips.

Why do you have to be such a dick?

At first, this situation was entertaining. Riling him up was fun and watching him squirm made my day. But now? Now that I've seen Maggie again, hugged Lonnie, and met Kennedy—it's not such a joking matter. And neither is the bullshit he was saying about not trusting me.

Because it is bullshit. I don't know why he doesn't want me here, but that's not it.

And it's not my problem.

I wait for him to explain why he stopped me, but he doesn't.

"It was nice to meet you," I say, climbing into my car.

"*Wait.*"

I sigh, resting my head on the headrest. I squeeze my eyes closed for a second. "What do you want, Chase?"

"I think things got away from us today."

"You think?"

"Yeah."

But it doesn't change anything.

"Look, I'm going back to my hotel," I say. "I'll tell your mom tonight that I can't do this. I'll take the blame."

"Oh, she'll put the blame where it's due regardless of what you tell her."

I can't do anything about that.

I smile at the handsome man despite my irritation with his behavior. "Good luck to ya."

Then I close the door, turn my car on, and back out of the driveway.

As my tires hit the gravel, my stomach twists into a tight knot.

I need to walk away from this whole thing.

I know that. Hell, *I want that.*

So why does it feel like a loss?

I shrug and press harder on the gas pedal.

Good luck to me, too.

CHAPTER 7

hase

Mom stands as I walk in and shoots me a dirty look.

"What are you looking at me like that for?" I ask, the words coming out snippy.

"She better come back."

I glance around the room as I barrel my way to the refrigerator.

Mom trails me across the kitchen. "Want to know why I'm looking at you like this? It's because I'm excited to hear about your plan. You just ran off your help for the next four weeks, so I'd love to know how you plan on finding someone to cover for me. I leave on Monday morning, you know."

Yeah, I know.

I wish it didn't have to be this way—that I didn't need to rely on people to make things work. And if Kennedy wasn't freshly fourteen and had a greater sense of her own mortality, I might chance it. But she's making emotional decisions, seems to think she's immortal, and I'm waiting on the call that I'm back on the traveling crew again. *I would never leave her overnight or for days at a time. No fucking way. She's never been alone one night, as a matter of fact.*

I take the orange juice out of the refrigerator and pour myself a glass. I need something to do and drinking a glass of juice is the only thing I can do that I won't regret later.

"I'll figure something out," I mumble.

"You better figure something out."

"Where's Kennedy?" I ask, not wanting to have this discussion in front of her.

"She went with your father down to the lake."

The drink is sweet and smooth as it slides down my throat. But, unfortunately, it does nothing to help dissipate the heat and frustration inside me—frustration at myself more than anything.

My heart pumps so hard that the pulse is evident in my neck.

"You know," Mom says, straightening the toaster, "I would understand if she was a stranger. And I know you don't know her. I get that. But do you think I would allow someone who might hurt or neglect Kennedy in any way into this house?"

I hang my head.

"I love that little girl just as much as you do, Chase."

Dammit.

"Mom, I know," I say, sighing before my gaze rises to hers. "I know you do. I didn't mean to insinuate that you didn't."

She shoves a hip into a cabinet and crosses her arms over her chest. Then she does the one thing I hate more than anything else—the *Mom guilt* look.

Three seconds of that stare has me backtracking. *I hope I have that kind of power with Kennedy someday.*

"I'm sure ..." I clear my throat. "I'm sure Megan is great."

In so many ways.

"She's wonderful, Chase. So smart and kind—and she won't be bowled over by Kennedy."

I believe that.

Mom sighs. "I don't know what all that was about with Megan, Chase, but you need to get your head on straight. Megan is exactly what your daughter needs right now. Someone young, someone fun—someone to model herself after." She shoves off the cabinet. "That polish brand that Kennedy was talking about? Megan was the head color designer there for several years."

Was she? I set my glass on the counter.

"She's been around the world," Mom says. "She's met people and seen things. And she's willing to come into *your* house and help *your* child for a month." She snorts. "She doesn't need this shit, Chase. But she's doing it for her mom. For me. *For you.*"

"Why? Why would someone like that want to come here and deal with a teenager?"

Mom shrugs. "I know she got laid off. Iyala is a smaller business, from what I understand, and they had to restructure to stay afloat. Megan moved from Los Angeles to Dallas while she figured out her next move. Nail polish designers aren't in high demand."

The fact that this all makes sense is even more frustrating. Why couldn't she have some massive flaw that makes it easy to justify not wanting her here? Why does she have to be perfect on paper?

And probably fucking everywhere else …

I have enough problems on my hands. There's zero doubt that Megan would be another. It's not hard to imagine the thirty days ending, and Kennedy has fallen in love with her and then acting out even more because Megan leaves.

Nor is it difficult to imagine that I would struggle to keep my hands off her if we shared the same living space …

But I have to do something.

I have to stop being selfish and do what's right for my family. And, right now, that's the little minx that has me tied up.

I grin. *Things that I wish were true.*

"Chase, honey," Mom says, placing a hand on my shoulder. "You're a good daddy—"

"Hey, everybody …" Luke stops on the threshold and looks at Mom, then at me. He grimaces. "I'll come back later."

I motion toward the table. "*No.* Sit. *Stay.*"

"Yeah, see … this looks like one of those conversations where Mom is about to let you have it," Luke says. "I'm familiar with the lead-up. While it would bring me joy to watch someone else get reamed for once, I'm afraid that sticking around might change the focus to me, and I don't need that kind of negativity in my life today."

Mom snorts and kisses my brother on the cheek. "You act like I'm always … what did you say? Reaming you?"

"Um, *you are,*" Luke says, ducking to avoid her swat. "I came to your house on Monday, and what happened? Oh, that's right —*you yelled at me.*"

"You brought your dirty laundry to my house and shoved half of a load in the washer."

"Isn't that where it goes?"

"Not when there's already washed laundry in there that needs to go in the dryer."

Luke cringes.

"Really, Luke?" I ask.

"I didn't see it."

"How could you not?" Mom asks, her voice rising. "Lucas, I love you. I've loved you since the day you were born. But you'll have to grow up at some point." She looks at me. "Where did I go wrong with him?"

Luke gasps. "Excuse me, Mrs. Marshall?"

"You call me Mrs. Marshall again, little boy, and see what happens—"

"Hey, Uncle Luke!" Kennedy comes in from the mudroom and taps my brother on the back as she walks by. "Pap and I are going fishing." She lowers her voice. "It's not what I want to do today, but he's acting like he's never going to see me again after tomorrow, and I feel bad."

We all laugh.

"Wanna come?" Kennedy asks, taking three water bottles from the refrigerator.

"Yeah, I'll come down there. Gavin tried getting me to go dirt biking with him this afternoon. Maybe I can talk him into fishing instead."

Kennedy grabs another water bottle. "Cool." She looks at me with a little grin as she walks toward the door. "I can't wait to tell you about my new babysitter."

My stomach drops. I fire her a look to be careful, but she ignores the warning in typical Kennedy fashion.

"Oh, that's right," Luke says, suddenly interested in my parenting decisions. "She was starting today. Is she here?"

"Nope," Kennedy says. "She just left. You should ask my dad about her. She's hot."

"*Ken ...*"

She ducks out of the room, laughing. "See you at the lake, Uncle Luke! I'll tell you all about it. Love you, Gram!"

"That kid," Mom says, chuckling.

That kid, all right. I heave a breath.

Discussing this with Luke was not on my agenda today—or ever. But now that he's been clued in on a *hot nanny*, there's no way to avoid the conversation.

"*Okay,*" Luke says, smirking like the bastard he is. "Let's talk about this nanny."

"Yes, let's," Mom chimes in.

"Let's not."

"She's hot?" he asks, taunting me. "She must be smokin' hot to elicit this kind of a response."

"You're wrong, Luke. She's not hot—*she's beautiful.*" Mom's mocking tone is as irritating as my brother's. "You should see her. Blond hair. Blue eyes. Built like a … what do they say? A shit house? A brick house?"

Luke snickers.

"*Mom,*" I say, exasperated. "Please don't do this."

She turns to me. "Don't do what? Tell your brother how delightful the woman is? The same woman you ran off from here, for some reason unbeknownst to me?"

"You ran her off?" Luke asks, his eyes bugging out. "*I can't wait to hear this.*"

"He did," Mom says, egging him on. "She's staying in town. Maybe you should get her, Luke, and see if she needs someone to take her to dinner."

I fire a glare at my brother. This only makes him laugh.

Mom launches into a second-by-second replay of our meeting with Megan. I gaze out the window and mentally chastise myself.

I'm being ridiculous. I've let this whole thing get out of control, and even I am embarrassed at this point.

I block out my family's conversation and close my eyes.

The two most important things are that Mom gets a break and that Kennedy doesn't steal a car and head to Mexico with a motorcycle club while I'm gone. My feelings are completely irrelevant.

I hold my forehead.

"I mean, I can watch her on Tuesdays and Thursdays," Luke says, chiding me. "But I'm gonna need money for dinner."

Mom smacks his arm.

"There's no need for that. Chase is going to march his ass over to The Ridges and talk to Megan," Mom says.

I look at her.

"It does seem like the perfect solution," Luke says, smug. "What's the problem?"

My brother knows the problem. I can tell by the glimmer in his eye. He manages not to notice obvious things that don't benefit him, like clean laundry in the washer. But give him the slightest detail that allows him to ride my ass, and he's all over it like some genius.

Mom's phone rings. She pulls it out of her bra, her face brightening.

"It's Kate. I'm going to take it outside." She starts toward the door. "Talk some sense into your brother, Luke." She tugs the door open. "I can't believe I just said that. What's this world coming to?"

"I heard you," Luke calls after Mom. Then he flops into a chair and makes himself at home.

"Whatcha gonna do?" he asks, settling in for the long haul. "If it were me, I'd go get the girl and enjoy my thirty days. She sounds like a stunner."

I sit across from him.

"What's the problem?" he asks. "Or is that the problem?"

The levity slowly melts from his features, and in its place is a seriousness that Luke doesn't often possess.

I start to admit that the idea of having Megan in my house feels like a terrible idea. It makes something deep inside me uncomfortable in the most comfortable of ways. It's as though she absolutely should be here, which is why she shouldn't be.

I've spent an hour with the woman—if that. I have no reason to suggest I don't trust her. *Lame excuse, Marshall.* But I have made it an absolute hard limit not to have women around.

That rule exists for a reason.

Kennedy was in first grade when I ended a relationship with a woman I'd seen for a couple of years. Watching my child lose yet another woman she'd come to love was ugly and heart-breaking. *Devastating.* I vowed never to do it to her again.

And I haven't.

I sigh. *But Megan won't be here for you. She'll be here for her.* I imagine Megan getting all over my daughter's ass for acting up. *Kennedy will hate her before it's over anyway.*

It's thirty days. I can deal with jacking off in the shower for thirty days.

"I'm being a jackass," I say, resting my forearms on the table.

"Yeah, well, you're a jackass every day."

"You know what I mean."

He leans forward, mirroring my posture. "I do. And as much as I'd like to rib you about it, you don't have much time to spare. Mom leaves Monday. Who knows when your nanny will skip town?"

Yeah. I know.

I need to find Megan and ask her to stay.

My body tightens, struggling against the chaos erupting inside me.

"I'm going to take a shower and find something to eat," I say, my jaw tensing. "Then I'm going to figure this out."

"And?"

"And go into town," I say.

"And?"

"Fuck off, Luke."

"Are you gonna grovel?" He laughs, his eyes sparkling with mischief. "You are, aren't you? She has you groveling, and you haven't even touched her yet. This is amazing."

"Please leave."

Luke snickers and gets to his feet. "Fine. I'll be over on Monday to meet the new nanny."

I hold my head in my hands.

How can one thing simultaneously feel like the right and wrong answer?

CHAPTER 8

egan

It's too early for the leaves to fall.

I tug my sweatshirt closer to my body as a barrier to the breeze. The temperature must've dropped ten degrees since I set out on a walk of Peachwood Falls a couple of hours ago, and I wasn't prepared. I was too preoccupied with my thoughts to grab a jacket.

The quaint town is reminiscent of a backdrop in a cheesy cable drama. I looked for a coffee shop, Peachwood Falls's version of Luke's Diner, but came up empty.

There is only The Wet Whistle.

I stroll down a residential street and take in the small homes on either side of the road. They're modest with cozy porches complete with swings. Many chairs, coffee tables, bicycles, and topiaries are wound with twinkling white lights. I imagine the townspeople congregating on their porch swings after dinner and waving to one another while the children play.

It makes me smile.

My phone buzzes as I turn onto the street that leads back to the hotel. A glance shows Calista's name.

"Hey," I say.

"Hey, you. Sorry I missed your call earlier. I was … *busy*."

I roll my eyes. I know what that means in Calista's language.

"How did it go?" she asks. "Tell me all the things."

I sigh and step over a puddle.

I left my room two hours ago to sort out *all the things*, as Calista put it. But, to my surprise, there's more rolling around my head than I realized.

The more I walked, the more my brain felt like an over-stuffed coat closet. Finally, today I opened the door, and it all fell into a cumbersome heap on the floor—or sidewalk, as it were. Things I thought I had put to bed resurfaced and demanded attention.

I've accomplished much in my life—more than I ever dreamed. I never imagined I would live in Los Angeles or have a worldwide magazine interview me about what inspires my creative direction.

I didn't even know I had *creative direction*.

The past ten years have been a whirlwind, and not a day went by that I didn't feel like an impostor. So how did I, Megan Kramer, from a single-parent household in Dallas with average grades, get a corner office at the trendiest at-home salon experience company?

When I started to believe it, it was yanked from me.

An uncertainty I've tried to ignore—an unsettledness about my life's direction, goals, and possibilities—roared to the forefront this morning. I realized that as much as I didn't want to be anyone's nanny, I was excited to stay with the Marshalls. I was excited about the break from life.

For the chance to gather my thoughts. To regroup. To

breathe and focus on something besides my problems for a change.

But, thanks to Chase Marshall, it's just me and the gaping holes in my life once again.

"It didn't go well," I tell Calista.

"What? *Why not?*"

I bite my lip. "You know, I don't know. He said he couldn't trust me because he doesn't know me, but I don't buy that."

My stomach swirls as if hit with a shot of adrenaline.

The way he wouldn't look at me. How he asked me to wait. His preoccupation with my car. *It doesn't make sense.*

"I can't figure him out, Calista. But I'm also not going to expend the energy to try. He's another guy in another city who wants to be a pain in my ass."

"Good for you."

I laugh.

"What are you doing now?" she asks.

"What do you mean? What am I doing this minute? Tomorrow? In life?"

"I don't know. Any of it."

I snort. "Well, the answer is the same. I don't know."

"Want to stay with me for a while?"

My shoe slips on the damp pavement. I catch myself before I topple to the ground.

"No," I say, getting my footing once again. "Thanks, though. I'm going to grab a sandwich from The Wet Whistle and then call Maggie and tell her I'm not coming back. Then I'll book a ticket back to Dallas."

"So you haven't told Maggie?"

"No." I make my way across the street toward the restaurant. "I didn't want to have that conversation with her family there. It was awkward enough the way it was."

But, also, it wasn't awkward. It was comfortable. Being with them made sense—it felt natural. Mom and Maggie have been friends for so long that I've always considered her and Lonnie distant family. I felt so welcomed by them. But how did I not know their oldest son was such a … jerk?

Ugh.

"You know I'm a phone call away if you need help figuring things out. I'm here for you—whatever you need, friend," Calista says.

I grin. "I know. Thank you. I love you."

"Love you too."

"I gotta go. I haven't eaten today, and I'm starving."

"You're always starving," she says, chuckling. "Call me later."

"I will. Bye."

The phone goes back into my pocket as I grab the restaurant door handle. I tug it open and can't believe my eyes. It's a different place than it was last night.

Last night, the lights were dim, and the televisions—all three of them—were lit up with sports games. Rock music played. Gavin was tending the bar in a plain black T-shirt and a smile that I'm sure got him a lot of tips … and phone numbers.

But today, there's none of that. Instead, the bright room shows the country aesthetic chosen as decoration. There's a giant pie counter that I missed before, and a small vase with what appears to be wildflowers decorates the center of the tables. *Absolutely precious.*

"Grab a seat, sweetie," a woman with a white apron and beehive hairdo from the fifties says with a giant smile. Her name tag reads Tabitha. "I'll be over there in a second."

"Sure thing. No rush."

I grab a table for two by the wall—the one *not* under a giant deer head. I reach for my phone when the table shakes as if something has run into it.

My head whips to the side to see a grinning Gavin sliding into the seat across from me.

"Sorry," he says. "Did I spook ya?"

"No. Yeah, kind of." I settle back in my seat, relieved to see a friendly face. "You're working today, too?"

"Nope. I saw you walk in, so I thought I'd check on ya."

I motion for him to lean across the table. He does, with a heavy dose of skepticism, and I rub my thumb over his cheek.

"Check your face before you go in public if you're going to kiss someone with red lipstick." I grab a tissue and wipe my hand. "Unless you don't mind. But free tip—women won't be open to flirting if they think you just got out of bed with someone else."

Gavin places a hand on his cheek and laughs. "You just might be the best friend I've ever had."

I laugh too.

"So how'd the job go?" he asks. "Are you employed?"

I snort.

His brows pull together. "What's that about?"

"It turns out that the best friend you've ever had is leaving Peachwood Falls tomorrow morning."

Gavin frowns. I find myself frowning too.

"I don't understand," he says, confused.

"It didn't go well today. The guy I would be working for—coincidentally the same guy from last night, mind you—I don't think he hates me, necessarily," I say, scrunching up my face while I think. "But I think he wants to."

He crosses his arms over his chest and studies me.

"But you know what?" I ask with growing irritation. "That's on him. I mean, did I poke at him a little? Yeah, probably, but only because he made it easy. And I don't think he cared, either. But that doesn't justify his stance that I'm somehow not trustworthy."

Gavin cocks his head to the side, amused.

"It's not about that," I say, the filter to my mouth nowhere to be found. "*What is it about?* I don't know. Maybe he has a girl-friend and thinks she'd be uncomfortable with a single woman living with him. That could be it. Maybe it's a control issue with his mom, and he's rebelling because she had me show up without his consent."

Gavin chuckles, his eyes sparkling. "Maybe he's just a dick."

"He is *a dick*."

I fall back in my seat with a huff.

"So all bets are off?" he asks. "You've told them you're done?"

My shoulders rise and fall.

"What's that mean?" he asks.

"It means I have, but I haven't. I mean, I pretty much told Chase, but I haven't told Maggie yet. I have to call her, but I'm procrastinating."

Tabitha comes to take my order. Gavin declines anything but takes the opportunity to flirt with the older lady. She blushes but razzes him right back. Their interaction is so wholesome and adorable that it dilutes my irritation—just a little bit.

Once she's gone, Gavin settles his sights on me again.

"What did you do today?" I ask, needing a reprieve from talking about the Chase issue. "Anything fun?"

"If you call building a fence with my brother fun, then yeah. Also did a little fishing that ended with a hook in my palm because my brother is an asshole." He holds his hand in the air. A Band-Aid stretches just below his thumb. "That hurt like the dickens."

"Did you have it looked at? Did it need stitches?"

"Dad closed it with some skin glue stuff. I don't know. He was in the Army, so he can piece you back together as long as you don't lose too much blood."

I wrinkle my nose, making him laugh.

Tabitha sets my drink in front of us and pauses to talk with Gavin again. I watch their interaction. It's clear why I like him so much. His effortless way about him makes everyone feel comfortable in his presence.

Unlike Chase freaking Marshall.

I swirl my straw around my lemonade and think about my options.

I can go back to Dallas and find a place to rent. *God knows I love my mom, but I can't live with her for long.* But where will I work? What will I do for a living? I have no idea. Despite Dallas being my hometown and my mom living there, it no longer feels like home. Being away for over a decade will do that to you. It's not that I've outgrown it or think I need the glitz and glamour of LA or New York. I just don't fit in Texas. I don't think I ever really did.

My other option is to keep looking for work in LA or New York, but the idea of moving back to the city doesn't excite me. Of course, if I must do it to work, I will, but I genuinely feel like that part of my life has passed. The trouble is, I don't know what part of my life I'm in now.

"What's that all about?" Gavin asks.

I pull my attention away from my thoughts and to my friend. "What's what all about?"

"That shrug."

Did I shrug? "Nothing. I was thinking about what I want out of life."

"And that is …?"

I don't even know for sure. "I'd take a cabin in the woods and a million dollars."

"Come to think of it, I'd take that too."

Tabitha delivers my grilled cheese with a friendly smile. I decline anything else, and she scurries back toward the kitchen.

"What are you going to do?" Gavin asks, folding his hands in front of him. "Are you gonna call Maggie?"

"I don't have another choice. What will I do—move in tomorrow when Chase doesn't want my help?" I fiddle with the edge of my sandwich. "Besides, I have no interest in staying in Peachwood Falls anymore. I was only helping my mom. I mean, Maggie would pay me well, which helped my current state of unemployment, but I don't *need* this job. And I sure as hell don't need this headache."

He sits up and rests his elbows on the table. "Maybe you should give this guy another shot."

"*What?*"

"You know, maybe he was having a bad day."

"Two bad days, you mean."

"Okay, maybe he's just an asshole every day, and that's something you'll have to get used to, but you can't let Maggie down, right?"

I gasp. "Whose side are you on, Gavin?"

"Yeah. Whose side are you on, *Gavin?*"

My head whips to the side—to the grumpy voice I've become all too familiar with. His green eyes peer into mine.

What's he doing here?

CHAPTER 9

 egan

GAVIN SCOOTS HIS CHAIR BACKWARD. "I THINK I'LL GO—"

"*Sit down,*" Chase says, his tone unwavering.

"Yup. Sitting," Gavin says, scooting back up to the spot he just held. He looks at me and grimaces before looking away.

I laugh in confusion. "What the hell is going on here?"

Gavin settles in as if resigned to what's to come. On the other hand, Chase gives me a look like I'm a fool.

Words are on the tip of my tongue, and my lips part to launch them into the air. I turn to Chase … and then stop.

My head swivels back to Gavin, and I gasp.

Broad shoulders.

Green eyes.

Overconfidence.

My jaw drops. "Gavin, you little shit."

He holds his hands out to the sides. "What?"

"How do you know her?" Chase asks, focusing his gaze on Gavin.

"*Her?*" Gavin nods toward me, his face paling. "I don't *really* know her. She's … a customer."

"A customer?" I ask, making Gavin flinch. I point at Chase. "And how do *you* know *him?*"

"*Him?*" Gavin sneaks a look at Chase and then quickly looks at me again. "I don't really know him—"

"*Really?*" Chase barks. "You don't know me?"

Gavin cringes. Again.

The twinkle in his eye. His growing amusement …

"You're related, aren't you?" I ask, my blood pressure rising. "What are you—brothers?"

Chase drags a chair from a neighboring table to ours. It screeches as the legs dig into the laminate floor. Even in my state of shock, I can't help but notice how his ass fills out his jeans.

Now is not the time, Megan.

"Will someone explain this to me?" I ask, ripping my eyes away from Chase.

Gavin sighs. "Well, Meg—"

"Meg?" Chase asks, screwing his face up like something is foul. "*Meg?*"

"What? We're friends," Gavin says.

"*Were,*" I say, pointing at him. "We *were* friends. Our friendship is on shaky ground right now."

"Why? Because I didn't tell you that Chase was my brother? In the spirit of transparency, I have two other brothers, Mallet and Luke. And a sister named Kate."

I glare at him. "Cute."

"*What?*"

I lean forward, resting my chest against the table. "You knew, didn't you?"

Gavin looks offended. "I knew what?"

"Last night, you knew I was talking about Chase."

"You were talking about me?" Chase asks.

Annoyed at the situation, I whip my head to him. "Can you please stay out of this conversation?"

"Hell no, I can't."

"Why are you even here?" I ask, desperately trying to hold tight to my annoyance. "Aren't you afraid I'll rob you or something?"

"Have you been drinking?"

"No, but you make me want to." I roll my eyes and turn to his brother. "Yes or no? Did you know I was talking about Chase last night?"

Gavin bites his lip and watches me.

"Gavin ..." I warn.

He sighs. "Maybe. *Kind of.* I put two and two together when you started talking about Mom."

I throw my hands in the air.

"So that means you knew all about Megan when we were building the fence this morning," Chase says.

"Oh, *so you were talking about me?*" I ask, throwing his question back at him.

Chase glares at me before leveling it at Gavin.

Gavin looks back and forth between the two of us. With each turn of his head, the smirk on his face grows wider.

"Careful ..." Chase warns.

Finally, as if he can't restrain himself a moment longer, Gavin bursts into laughter.

I lean back in my seat and shake my head. *The men in this family are killing me.*

Gavin stands and pushes his chair toward the table. "You two need to talk. This whole thing you're doing is the most bizarre but entertaining thing I've seen in a long time—*and Luke is our brother.*" He walks backward away from the table. "I'll see you both later. Enjoy."

I try to stare a hole into him, but he practically skips out the door.

My chin tilts toward the ceiling in what feels strangely like defeat.

Chase moves at my side, his knee brushing against mine. A lick of fire races through my body. *Nooooo, Megan. We don't like this rude Neanderthal.*

"Why are you here?" I ask without looking at him. My voice is dull, free of emotion of any kind.

"We need to talk."

"That's funny. I distinctly remember *you* refusing to talk a few hours ago."

He groans. "Will you look at me, please?"

I don't want to look at him because, if I do, I'll lose the upper hand. *If I even have the upper hand.* But I can't sit staring at the dollars on the ceiling all afternoon. If nothing else, my neck will ache.

Stay in control.

Grinning because I know it'll annoy him, I lower my chin. "Only because you said please."

He's not entertained. But I am.

Holy fuck, he's something to look at.

Chase is handsome in the traditional ways—excellent bone structure, great lips, and thick lashes. But it's the more subtle things—the way he flexes his fingers, the calluses on his hands, an implacable look that makes me wonder what he's thinking— that make it hard to breathe.

"There," I say, looking as far into his eyes as I can. "I'm looking at you."

His tongue sweeps around his lips. "Look, Megan ..." He takes a long, deep breath. "We got off on the wrong foot."

"I think we already established that."

He flashes me a look. "Let's ... restart."

I don't want to begin again with Chase, mostly because I'm

not sure why he wants to. I'm leaving town in the morning. There's no need to be friendly or to end our acquaintance any differently. We'll never see each other again … unless he wants to walk back his position on me helping him with Kennedy. In that case, I'm better off just keeping things as they are.

The man gets under my skin like no other.

I'll get under his before he can get under mine any more than he already has.

"Are we starting over before or after I saw you naked?" I ask, resting my chin on my hand.

His gaze shifts to the ceiling this time.

"Let's go with *after* that particular moment," I say as his cheeks turn slightly pink. "It's the only interaction we've had so far that I've thoroughly enjoyed."

Slowly, he lowers his gaze back to mine. When it connects, it's so intense that I shiver.

"I'm trying to be serious here," he says.

"Me too."

He runs a hand down his face and then down his thigh. There are stress lines around his eyes; surprisingly, I feel bad for teasing him.

"Okay, fine, I'm sorry," I say, frowning. I shove a hand toward him. "Hi. Fancy meeting you here. I'm Megan Kramer. What's your name?"

He takes my hand warily and shakes it. A zip of energy shoots through me.

"I'm Chase."

"It's nice to meet you, Chase," I say.

He drops my hand. "Are we doing all of this?"

"Hey, this was your idea. You said you wanted to start over."

He stares at me.

I rest my chin in my hand again and stare back at him.

"You know this isn't necessary, right?" I ask. "We can leave things as they are. As they were. I'm leaving town tomorrow, and you'll never have to see me again."

He starts to speak but stops.

Something in the way he watches me—a heated promise, maybe—has me holding my breath. *Why are you here, Chase?*

"I acted a little out of pocket today," he says carefully.

My brows shoot to the ceiling. *That's not what I expected.*

"I was surprised to see you, and I didn't handle myself very well." He slides his hands down his legs again. "I think we both got fiery and should've approached the situation more calmly."

Okay … "Well, you make me fiery when you accuse me of being a bad person."

"I didn't do that."

"You *did*."

He sits back in his chair. The legs squeak with the movement.

I study him, picking up on his frustration, which seems higher than mine. His right leg bounces to a beat I can't hear. He folds his hands on his lap, his thumbs flicking each other back and forth.

There's a slight, *so freaking slight*, softness about Chase that I feel the fight dissipating from my body.

"Let's not argue," I say, sitting back too. "You're right. You didn't handle yourself very well. And, honestly, in retrospect, I didn't handle myself the best either."

He stills, and the corners of his lips turn slightly to the ceiling. "Was that an apology?"

"Was yours?"

He shrugs.

I shrug too.

Then, at the same time, we both chuckle.

The relief I feel from this small, simple action is massive. My shoulders relax, and the muscle across the back of my neck eases. The heaviness of a few minutes ago lifts—even if only a bit.

Chase bends forward. His body angles toward mine, giving me an unobstructed view of his face. I wonder if it's intentional—if he wants to permit me to see him openly.

To see the clarity. The caution. The … *hope?*

"If I made you feel any way, I didn't mean to," he says.

I lift a brow and smirk.

The dimple in his chin deepens as he fights a smile.

"Well, if I made you feel any sort of way … *I meant to,*" I say, grinning.

The air between us shifts. It almost feels natural.

Chase chuckles. "You're a piece of work. Do you know that?"

"It's been said." I take a napkin out of the dispenser and fiddle with it. "So what brought you all the way over to The Wet Whistle?"

He rolls his head around his neck. His eyes never leave mine.

"The grilled cheese is good if you want some lunch," I say to keep the conversation going. I don't want to lose whatever rapport we've established.

"I'm not here for a sandwich."

"Oh. Why are you here?"

His Adam's apple bobs. "I need you to reconsider."

"Reconsider what?"

"I need you to reconsider working for me."

What?

My eyes widen, and I drop the napkin. I wait for him to recant. Or laugh. Or … something. But the longer we sit at the table surrounded by patrons enjoying their cheeseburgers and persimmon pudding, the clearer it becomes that his words were a complete sentence.

Chase sighs. "I *want* you to come and work for me."

"What happened to all that *you can't trust me* bullshit?"

"It was bullshit."

I wait for him to expound, but unsurprisingly, he doesn't.

"Why did you do all of that, then? Why did you make such a big deal if you're going to circle back this fast? It doesn't make any sense."

"I was concerned."

"And you're not now?"

His jaw sets into a hard line. "Can't you just say yes?"

"Come on, Chase. Do you think I'll say yes and skip off to your house with stars in my eyes?"

He rolls his eyes.

"I think—for your daughter's well-being more than anything else—that if we were to come to an agreement, we need to clear the air," I say. "I'll be in your house for a few weeks. We can't devolve into bickering every time we turn around. I, for one, don't have the energy for it. Two, it's not good for Kennedy."

He smiles. The bastard finally gives me a genuine smile. *It was so worth the wait.*

The movement brightens his face, making him look five years younger. There's a playfulness that I didn't expect, a warmth that seeps into my soul by proxy. From his smile alone, I can imagine him sitting with a beer and telling stories from days gone by.

It feels so good to be on the receiving end of his smile that I have to look away.

"I just want to make sure that we can get along," I say, studying the plaque on the wall commemorating the local coal mine like it's the most interesting thing in the world. "I don't want to feel weird."

"What do you want from me then?"

I look at him again. *I'll answer you.* "I want two things."

"Spit them out."

Ignore that. "First, since you've apologized for being a dick already, I want your assurance that you won't be a jerk again. I'm not going to do this if you're going to have a bad attitude. I don't need it."

He starts to speak, then reconsiders. "I won't be a jerk."

That was easier than I anticipated.

"What's the second thing?" he asks, his brows pulled together.

"I want to know why you were so adamant that I wasn't the right person for the job."

His smile fades as quickly as it appears. "What does it matter?"

"It matters to me. I won't look at you daily and wonder what you're thinking. Whatever your reasoning was, it must have been important for you to jeopardize your mom's vacation over it."

His leg stops bouncing.

"Tell me, and I'll reconsider," I say, drawing a line in the sand.

Chase sits up again in one swift motion. His hands rest on the table; they nearly touch mine.

Everything about the man just got serious. Stone-cold sober. The severity stills me, making me wonder if I want to do this.

But I do. The flame in my stomach begs me to hear what he has to say.

My heart thunders, pushing blood through my veins so fast that I'm dizzy. A million thoughts shuffle through my brain at max speed—postulating what might come out of his mouth.

"Are you sure you want to know?" he asks, his voice rough.

"Yes. And don't lie to me. We must be able to tell each other the truth, or else I'm not even entertaining going through this."

I think.

That sounds like a professional answer. It feels like poking a bear all the same.

Fire dances in his irises, the gold flecks nearly taking over the iciness—but not entirely. Just enough to keep me frozen in place while also melting into a puddle.

My mouth goes dry as my attention is drawn to his lips. He licks them slowly. Deliberately.

What are you doing, Chase?

"Okay," he says. "You want the truth? I'll give it to you."

"Okay ..."

"I didn't want you to work for me because you would make my life much harder than you'd help it."

My brows pull together. "How?"

A smile flirts against his lips. "Because I'm not sure how I could go thirty days with you in my house and not fuck you."

egan

"You're going to need to move your hands a little farther away from mine," I say, gulping.

His fingers flex before he draws them back onto his lap.

Holy.

Frigging.

Shit.

"Because I'm not sure how I could go thirty days with you in my house and not fuck you."

I'm acutely aware that he's waiting for a reaction—besides my suggestion that he put some space between us. I'm also cognizant of the fact that he can't gather too much of a response out of that sentence.

That's too bad. He'll have to wait.

My face heats as I stare at the spot his hand just vacated. Every nerve ending in my body tingles; every erogenous zone flickers to life, swelling so much that I nearly burst into a puddle of need.

I shift in my seat to relieve the pressure between my legs. Naturally, it doesn't help. It just makes me more conscious of the fire in my belly.

"Well," I say, clearing my throat. "That was unexpected."

I pick up my phone and ignore the pull to look at him. I scroll through my contacts list until I find the name I'm looking for. Then I press the screen.

"Are you really making a phone call right now?" he asks, borderline pissed. "For fuck's sake, Megan."

I suppress a grin as the voice on the other end of the phone says hello.

"Hi, Maggie. It's Megan," I say sweetly.

Chase moves at my side. I still don't look at him.

"Megan, hi, sweetheart. I didn't expect to hear from you so soon."

"Well, I didn't expect to call so soon either. But I left with things up in the air, and I hate doing that to you."

"I understand. Trust me. I'm so sorry for the way my son acted. I don't know what's going on with him."

I do. I bite my bottom lip to keep from smiling.

"What are you doing?" Chase grumbles.

"Oh, don't worry about Chase, Maggie," I say, turning slowly to him.

His eyes are wide as he watches me. Each breath is measured. It's as if he's deliberately working to keep it under control.

"I think your son was just dealing with a lot of pressure that he didn't know how to release," I say, looking at him and smirking.

He rolls his tongue around his mouth. His chest rises and falls like he's having difficulty keeping himself in his seat.

Good.

"As a matter of fact," I say, my eyes glued to his, "I called to tell you that I will take the job after all. I'm pretty sure Chase and I can figure things out."

I have no idea what Maggie says. Vaguely, I register that she seems happy with the revelation. But as far as the specifics go, I don't have a clue.

Chase scoots to the edge of his seat, his knees spread apart. My heart beats so hard that it overtakes every other sensation.

He folds his hands on the edge of the table and grins. It's not a smile or a smirk—it's the most sinful, delicious look I've ever seen on a man.

Fuck. Me.

Literally.

I blow out a steadying breath.

"That's great, Maggie," I say, hoping that's the right answer to fill the gap in the conversation. "I'll talk to Chase next and see what he wants to do and how he wants to do it."

He chuckles.

"That's wonderful," Maggie says. "I'll come by tomorrow and check in before we leave town. All right?"

"That's great. See you then. Goodbye."

"Goodbye, Megan."

I hang up before the end of my name is entirely spoken.

There. I place my phone next to the napkin on the table. *Decision made.*

I take a massive breath hoping to clear the endorphins from my brain.

"I take it you reconsidered," he says with a teasing lilt.

"Well, you were honest with me. I'm a woman of my word."

He chuckles. "Yeah. You gave in because I was honest."

"Do you think I did it for another reason?"

He shakes his head and ends his laugh with a sigh. "We need to talk about some things."

I like doggy style. "What are you thinking?"

It's as if he can read my mind. He lifts his brows and places his hands safely in his lap—the place farthest from me.

"The reason I didn't want you to work for me was that I want to fuck you," he says.

"Yes. I heard. That was quite the admission, but I'm not mad about it."

"I'm glad."

We watch one another, finding our way through a dance that neither of us is familiar with. He seems to want to be careful with his steps. I want to be smart about mine.

Does he believe I feel the same way he feels? Is he waiting for me to admit that I feel the same attraction?

Finally, after a long couple of moments, Chase breaks the silence.

"As long as you're in my house, I can't touch you, Megan."

The words are strained as if saying them is as hard for him as hearing them is for me.

But I get it.

Tabitha returns to check on me. She says something about my grilled cheese, and I smile and nod in return. My head continues to process Chase talking about fucking me. *Or not fucking me.*

My breath wavers.

As soon as she leaves, Chase switches gears. He's all business.

"Maybe I shouldn't have admitted that to you," he says, "but you asked for the truth."

"I did, and I'm glad you told me. It's an ego boost if nothing else."

He tries not to smile.

"But in light of your admission, do you think this is a good idea?" I ask. "Your attraction is reciprocated."

He lifts his chin.

"When you consider that along with how we seem to communicate …" I shrug. "It might be a recipe for disaster."

He shrugs. "It might be. I can't swear it won't."

I fall back into my chair. *What do I do?*

"We're adults," he says, his voice holding steady. "We can control ourselves. Right?"

"Yeah."

He looks around the room before dropping his gaze onto me again. "Kennedy is going through a phase right now that's making me want to drink. I'm trying to give her boundaries and a routine, and expectations. I'm trying to save her from herself. The last thing I want to do—*that I will do*—is confuse the kid more than she already is."

"What's going on with her?"

"Hell if I know," he says, running a hand over his head. "She's fine one minute, then skipping school the next. I found cigarettes in her room. She's snuck out more than once and has a group of friends that need some discipline—shit that I don't understand. She tried to forge my signature and get a fucking tattoo." He groans as if he's at his wit's end. "Why would she act like this? What am I not doing? What am I not giving her to make her act like a vigilante?"

I giggle even though it's not funny. What *is* funny, or endearing, is how sweet he is when it comes to Kennedy … and his complete lack of understanding of a teenage girl.

"It might not have anything to do with you," I say. "I don't know why she's acting like that because I don't know her. But this is normal teenage behavior."

He blinks. Twice.

"Well, rest assured that none of that has stamped her ticket to juvie," I say.

He sighs. "Do you see the problem? It doesn't matter how badly I want you. I'm not willing to risk either of us getting distracted and losing Kennedy in the process. So my focus is on her. That's why I need help—to keep Kennedy on the straight and narrow."

The worry etched on his face pulls at my heart. Suddenly, some of his reaction to me makes sense.

I bet Chase *was* irritated with me last night. Helping a random woman at the end of a long day while trying to get home to his worrisome daughter must've been a hassle. *And finding me in his house the next day?* He had to have been as surprised as I was.

Although I understand where he's coming from and his reasons for not wanting to act on his attraction, that doesn't mean we can ignore it. Ignoring it would only make it worse. We'll have to find a way to ignore it while acknowledging it.

"She's my priority," he says. "If I'm open to messing around with you, that leaves room for mistakes."

"I understand your point. For the record, I respect that. It seems like you are a good dad, and I wouldn't want to do anything besides help you with Kennedy."

He sinks back into his chair. Relief washes across his handsome features. "Mom swears you're the right person to help with Ken and, honestly ..." A grin twitches against his lips. "I might not disagree."

"You might not, huh?"

"Well, I mean, in your favor, you seem like you'll be hard for Kennedy to steamroll."

I laugh. "That, I assure you."

"So we have a plan then?"

I study the small cut on his bottom lip and the calluses on his hands as he folds them on the tabletop. I want to do this. But I don't want to have it turn into a soberfest.

"Okay," I say, smiling. "We have a plan. No action on the attraction. Besides, not knowing what your cock feels like in my mouth will make it easier to focus on your daughter."

He adjusts himself. "Seriously, Megan?"

"Kennedy isn't here, and I don't officially work for you yet."

"Fine. Then for the record," he says cockily, leaning toward me and lowering his voice, "not knowing what your pussy tastes like will make it easier when you're asleep a few doors down the hallway from me every night."

I tug at the hemline of my shirt to get some air around me. *Did it just get hot in here?*

"That's what we're doing, then?" I ask, fanning my face. "I'm staying in your house, and we're going to move around each other like we're two people who didn't just confess we want to perform oral sex on the other?"

"Yes."

I lift a brow. "You think that's possible? This is your life, your kid. You better be sure."

"It'll work as well as pouring a sports drink in your radiator."

"Hey, that *did* work."

"Speaking of, did you make an appointment for your car? Or call the rental company?"

I laugh in disbelief. "No. When I walked in here an hour ago, I thought I'd be leaving town in the morning, so I wasn't worried too much."

"Suit yourself," he mumbles, shifting in his seat. "I'll make an appointment for you."

"No. I need to turn it in tomorrow. Your mom said I could use her car while they're gone."

He stretches his arms over his head. The corner of his shirt slips up, displaying the expertly crafted muscles lining his sides.

How will I do this for thirty days?

I pause.

I'll do this because it's what's best for me. This time away from life is what I need.

Besides, I can already see why a relationship—sexual or otherwise —with Chase would never work. He's gorgeous and probably amazing in bed with those rough hands and scruff, but he's a package deal. He and Kennedy ... but there's also Maggie and Lonnie to consider. They're long-term people. And I'm ... not.

I'm thirty-day people.

"We're going to need some ground rules," I say, looking at his face again.

"For what?"

"To make this arrangement work."

"Okay. Like what?"

I lean forward, pressing my chest together to create cleavage in the V-neck of my shirt. As expected, his gaze falls on my breasts.

"Like that," I say, sitting back again.

His eyes lift to mine. "Point taken."

"No undressing me with your eyes," I say.

"No flaunting that little body around in my face."

I snort. "Oh, okay. Well, how about this? No walking around the house in your underwear."

"I wasn't walking around the house."

"Fine. No getting naked in a room without the door locked because now that I know your cock got hard when I walked out, I'd rather not walk in on you like that again."

His eyes burn.

"Also, I'd appreciate it if you didn't bring girlfriends home," I say, feeling out his dating situation.

"I don't bring anyone home. The only people who will come over are my brothers." He narrows his eyes. "By the way, I'm talking with Gavin."

"Me too."

Chase flinches, looking uncomfortable.

"What?" I ask. "What's wrong?"

"Is there something I should know about you and my brother?"

"Not really. Gavin is my only friend in Peachwood Falls, and I'm pissed at him for playing me like he did."

He blows out a breath. "I'm not sure I like you being friends with him."

"Well, I'm not sure I give a shit if you like it or not."

He lifts his chin. I do the same.

He straightens his shoulders. I do, too.

He gives me a look like I'm pushing his limits, and I raise him an *I'll walk out of here if you don't like it.*

Finally, he shakes his head and growls.

"Glad we took care of that," I say smugly. "When do you want me to start?"

"Tomorrow."

"What time?"

"Eleven thirty."

"*So specific.*"

"You asked."

I roll my eyes. "Fine. What do you need me to do while I'm there? Your mom told me you would let me know what you expected."

A couple with a wheelchair comes down the aisle toward us. Chase jumps up and apologizes before putting his chair back where it belongs. He stands out of the way as they push through. Then he takes the seat across from me.

His leg brushes mine as he gets situated. I pretend I don't feel it, like a rip of heat didn't just blow through me like a hot knife.

"I'm not ... I don't know," he says. "I've never had someone do this before. What are you supposed to do?"

"I don't know. I've never done this before either."

"Oh." He pauses and looks around the room. "You can do whatever, I guess."

That doesn't help.

"Look," I say, resting my forearms on the table. "Your mom is paying me well. I'll be at the house anyway, and Kennedy will be at school during the week. I don't want to overstep my bounds or get into something you don't want me to do, but I don't mind going to the grocery store or doing laundry. Dishes. I can cook a little, too, if you want."

He lifts a brow. "You cook?"

"It's not the greatest stuff you'll ever eat, but I can put together a simple meal."

"All right."

"All right."

We grin, both relieved, I think.

Tabitha swings by the table. "Do you need anything else?"

I glance down at my untouched grilled cheese. *I bet that was delicious when it was hot.*

"Put that on my tab, Tabitha, please," Chase says.

"*No.*"

Tabitha smiles. "No problem, Chase."

"Hey," I protest as she walks away. "That was unnecessary."

"If I hadn't shown up, you would've eaten your sandwich. Do you want a to-go box?"

I stand. "No. Cold grilled cheeses aren't great. However, my mom told me you have many options in the next town over. I might head that way this evening and check it out."

"Sounds good. I'll follow you out," he says, motioning for me to take the lead to the door.

The afternoon is warmer than it was during my walk. The bright sun filters through the colored leaves and makes them look magical. It lifts my spirits as Chase stands beside me on the sidewalk.

I inhale, hoping to get a cleansing lungful of air. But I get a straight shot of Chase's cologne—my kryptonite.

My stomach pulls. *I wish he didn't smell so divine.*

"Tomorrow," I say.

He nods. "Tomorrow."

"See you then."

"See you," he repeats and heads to his truck.

I walk across the street, aware he's watching me. I might shake my ass a little for his benefit. After all, this is the last time he can check me out per our agreement.

My lips twitch.

This might be fun. Chase is off-limits, so there's no hope that anything will blossom between us. I'm too smart to get attached to him because I'm leaving in thirty days—on to bigger and brighter things than a small town in the middle of nowhere.

If it all works out, it's exactly what I need. It's time, money, and a chance to make plans. Maybe I can even have a bit of fun while I get my life sorted. What harm can come of this? I don't want anything Chase has.

Well, maybe I do want some of it.

I laugh.

Let's hope I have more self-restraint than I think I do.

CHAPTER 11

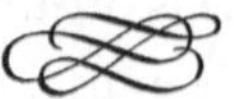

hase

I rinse the breakfast skillet and set it in the strainer beside the sink. Water gurgles down the drain, sucking the remaining suds with it. A part of me wishes I could slip down the pipes in one of the bubbles and get as far away from this place as possible.

I reasoned at three this morning that a large part of my frustration with this whole Megan situation is my lack of control. Frankly, *I don't have any.* What's worse is that I can't demand control or make moves to get more of it without being a complete and utter dick.

Not that I give a shit about that, except I won't be a dick to my mother.

"Can I go to Neve's?" Kennedy's voice echoes through the kitchen, taking me by surprise. "Her mom can pick me up."

My head hangs for a split second before I turn to face her.

"No, Ken. You know Megan is coming."

My daughter stands on the other side of the room. Her hands are pulled into the sleeves of a sweatshirt that's three sizes too big for her, and she gives me a look like I'm the dopiest person on the planet.

This is going to be fun. I grip the counter behind me and steady myself for battle.

"From what I understand, she'll be here for twenty-nine more days, right?" she asks, her dark hair swishing across her shoulders as she speaks. "Pretty sure we can get to know each other tomorrow."

"Can we not do this?"

"I just want to go to Neve's."

"You were there last night."

"And you made me come home."

Because I don't trust that Neve's mom will make sure she stays home all night. I scratch the top of my head and give another thought to jumping down the drain.

"This is going to ruin my life, isn't it?" she asks, crossing her arms over her stomach. "This whole Gram being gone and Megan thing will ruin everything."

"No—"

"*I* don't need a babysitter, you know. *You* need me to have one because you don't trust me."

I drop my hand and stand tall.

Usually, Kennedy has the sense to back up when I don't relent. She might sneak out later or skip school, but she doesn't typically go toe-to-toe with me.

Perfect time to level up your teenage drama, child. I'm irritated anyway.

"Yeah, you're right," I say, holding her gaze. "I don't trust you."

Her jaw falls to the floor.

"I've told you a million times. Give me a reason to trust you, and I will."

"What do you mean?" she asks, her voice shrill. "I always give you reasons, but you won't see them. You don't *want* to see them. You want to lock me up in this house like a little kid and never let me out."

I steal a glance at the clock. "You have to earn trust, Kennedy."

"I just want to go to Neve's."

"And I just wanted you not to call me from a cornfield last month—"

She rolls her eyes. "Here we go again."

"—because you were in the car with some boy you weren't allowed to be with in the first place, and he *hydroplaned off the road and almost killed you.*"

My stomach bottoms in response to the memory of Kennedy's voice on the phone. *"Daddy? I need you."*

In the period it took her to utter those three little words, my life stopped. Everything paused. Nothing mattered but getting to my kid and making sure she was safe.

And then grounding her for three weeks for lying to me and flouting the rules.

"*Fine.*" She narrows her eyes. "I won't call you next time."

My jaw clenches as I attempt to avoid losing my cool with my child.

I remind myself she's not always like this. She can be a sweet kid. She *is* a sweet kid.

Breathe, Chase.

"That's not what I mean, and you know it," I say.

"Pretty sure you just said you didn't want me to call you."

I growl in frustration. "Kennedy, *stop it.*"

"Is that a no on Neve's?"

Her shoulders stiffen as if she's trying to appear bigger and older than she is, but it has the opposite effect with her tiny frame draped in that sweatshirt. Vulnerability shines in her jade-colored eyes despite her fierce attempt to hide it.

She's a child standing in front of me. *My child*. A little girl trying to grow up without a mother.

"Come here," I say, crossing the room.

She pulls away from me.

"I love you," I say.

She leans farther back but doesn't move her feet.

I smile at her as I reach for her. She scoffs as if it pains her to give in, but she relents anyway. My arm stretches around her shoulders, and I pull her into my side. Then I kiss the top of her head.

"I know it's going to be hard for you while your grandparents are away," I say.

"It's not that. It's that *I'm fourteen*. I don't need a babysitter, Dad."

I smile against her hair. "Maybe you don't. Maybe you'd be fine on your own."

She turns to me with a set of hopeful eyes.

"But I can't go to work every day and chance it. Besides, I'll probably have to go out of town once or twice while Gram is gone. There's no way in hell I'm leaving you home alone all night. Sorry, kiddo."

She groans and shakes my arm off her.

"Kennedy, you're barely fourteen—"

"I know. You remind me all the time."

"—and I can't let you screw up your life." I hold her shoulders gently, turning her in a half circle to look at me. "I love you, little girl. The thought of anything happening to you is my absolute worst nightmare."

"But I'm not dumb. I know you think I am, but I'm not."

I smile softly. "I don't think you're dumb. But the world is evil and mean, and it will swallow you up and spit you out before you know what happened. The only thing between you and all of that is me. That's *my* responsibility. You might not understand it, like it, or appreciate it and, hell—maybe, I'm screwing this all up." I lower my chin. "But if I can keep you from ending up like your uncle Luke …."

It takes a few seconds, but a smile slips across her face.

Before we can say anything, a car pulling into the driveway catches our attention.

Any progress we've made disappears.

Kennedy rolls her eyes and sighs. "The babysitter is here."

A door slams in the distance.

"Look," I say, turning to her. "You get to decide how the next month goes. Megan and I both want you to be happy and have fun. But if you want to be a twerp about this, then it can suck. It's up to you."

"Oh, you and Megan, huh? It's already the two of you against me?"

Fuck. "Kennedy …"

Megan knocks on the mudroom door.

"She uses the mudroom already?" Kennedy asks. "Only our family uses that. We have a front door for visitors."

Wow. I make my way across the room. "It's a door. Let's not overthink it."

She hums.

I stop before leaving the room and face my daughter. She's watching me with a hesitancy that relieves me a little.

"Hey," I say.

"What?"

I grin. "It will never be me and anyone against you. We're always on the same side, all right? So even if you're mad at me, this is still a Dad and Kennedy Show."

She sags against the corner of the table. "All right."

"Now, be nice."

Her arms cross over her stomach, and that's good enough for me. At least her fangs are gone.

My heart pounds harder with every step through the mudroom. The knob slips under my hand as I pull the door open. A tightness forms across my chest as my gaze lands on Megan.

Motherfucker.

She's piled her hair on top of her head in a messy knot. It probably took her all of three minutes to arrange it. I don't see a speck of makeup on her face. A navy shirt with a collar across her clavicle—nice and high, covering her cleavage—and a pair of denim shorts that would be acceptable in any social situation adorn her body. Nothing suggests she gave a single thought to her appearance this morning.

And it's somehow the hottest thing I think I've ever seen.

"Eleven thirty," she says, smiling. "On the dot."

I glance over her shoulder. Gavin sticks his middle finger out the window as he speeds down the road. "Where did your car go?"

"I needed to return the rental, so Gavin followed me to the rental office this morning. Then he dropped me off here."

She lifts a brow, a coy grin dancing across her lips. Instead of pressing, which I want to do, I take her bags. Then I step to the side to make room for her to walk in.

"That's it?" she asks, a trail of jasmine floating behind her. I only know the scent because Kate broke down women's perfumes one Christmas. She was sure she could control men's reactions to her based on her chosen scent. Jasmine, I recall, increases libido.

Kate was right about that one. Damn.

I shut the door behind Megan, making an extra effort not to touch her.

"You seem extra grumpy today," she says, amused.

"Let's just say that Kennedy is ..." I search for the right explanation while setting her bags on the floor. "She's not thrilled with this situation."

"Oh."

"She'll be fine." *I think.* "Just, you know, be warned, I guess."

Her smile wobbles for the briefest moment. "Gavin said I was extra charming this morning, so I think I'll be all right."

"He did, did he?"

"He did." She smiles, sensing my irritation. "He also said I looked very pretty and smelled nice. Oh, and he's happy to be my Peachwood Falls best friend."

I lift a brow.

"I mean, what if you give me a night off?" she asks. "Who am I going to hang out with?"

The words ring with an innocence put on for my benefit. Even if I couldn't hear through the bullshit, I'd see it in her eyes.

Little minx.

I lean forward. Her confidence falters, her breath hitching as I inch closer.

"Guess what?" I ask.

She hums.

I lick my lips as I gaze down at her.

I want to say that I'll break Gavin's kneecaps if he thinks about fucking around with her. It would be too easy to tell her that I can occupy her if she wants to *hang out* with anyone while she's here. But both of those responses are a one-eighty from reality. From what's possible.

In the other room, my child is most likely plotting ways to test every inch of Megan's nerves. Megan will need to spend her time not getting swindled by a teenager.

Ugh.

"Gavin wouldn't know charm if it bit him in the ass," I say instead.

"Is that because he grew up around you?"

I stare at her.

She leans closer, splitting the distance between us in half.

Her tongue swipes across her bottom lip. It sends a bolt of energy straight to my cock.

"Why do I think that's not what you were going to say?" she asks.

"Because it wasn't."

"Now I'm curious."

Me too—about a million things I have no business being curious about.

I take a giant step back, blowing out a breath. "Don't be."

"Why? Didn't we agree not to have secrets between us?"

My brain scrambles, trying to block the jasmine-scented air from fucking with me while I attempt to remember our conversation from yesterday. It becomes apparent very quickly that it's a lost cause.

I take a deep breath, my gaze landing on the door leading to the kitchen before I flip it back to Megan. "That wasn't in the agreement."

Her forehead wrinkles as I approach her. I stop a couple of feet away.

"Do you know what we did agree to?" I ask.

"Yes. We're moving around this house like two people who didn't admit they want to fuck."

I growl. The sound of the word *fuck* coming out of her mouth catches me off guard. Lust surges through my veins, entertaining *the nanny.*

She smirks. "Was that what you were referring to? Or did I misread the room?"

"Are you going to be a pain in my ass for the next thirty days?"

"Probably." She laughs and walks toward the door. "But don't worry. It'll be fine."

Oh, I'm worrying.

She stops with her hand around the knob and looks at me. The playfulness slips away, and a mask slides into place. "As soon as I walk in here, it's game on. This is about Kennedy. Just like you said."

Yes, just like I said.

Ugh.

Her smile softens, going from suggestive to somber. "You said you need the focus to be on your daughter, and I heard that. I respect that. So that's what we'll do." She turns the handle. "Don't worry about me. I won't make this hard."

Oh, it's too late for that. I adjust myself as she opens the door.

"Ready?" she asks.

I clear my throat. "What? Yeah."

"Then let's go."

hase

HERE GOES NOTHING.

Kennedy sits at the table with her knees pulled up to her chest. No fire is coming out of her nostrils, and the daggers in her stare are relatively dull. *I'll take it.*

"Hey, Kennedy," Megan says.

She doesn't smile but doesn't frown, either. It's a shield of well-constructed apathy. "Hi."

"Your uncle Gavin is a lot to deal with in the morning," Megan says as she pulls out a chair and sits. "He gave me a ride from the rental car place a little while ago, and I swear he didn't take a breath. Talked all the way here."

"Dad is that way too." She tilts her head toward me. "But I guess you'll know that soon enough."

I watch her carefully, pausing before I respond. The more time passes in silence—with me looking straight at her—the stronger my point. Eventually, she sighs and turns her attention to the sleeve of her shirt.

"So you aren't a morning person?" Megan asks her.

"Me? No," Kennedy says. "Having to get out of bed in the morning ruins my day every day."

"Good," Megan says.

Kennedy eyes her curiously. "Good?"

"No, it's not good," I say. "I make Mom wear a shield to wake her up just in case she throws things."

It's a joke, mostly. Kennedy isn't easy to deal with before school. But as soon as I admit it, I worry that will throw Megan for a loop.

She surprises me.

"You better buy Kennedy a shield, too, because I don't function before the sun is up," Megan says. "And the only thing worse than actually getting up is dealing with someone happy about it."

Kennedy fights a smile. I do too.

"I don't want to be anywhere early," Megan says, reclining in her seat and speaking directly to Kennedy. "I don't need to discuss the weather. And please don't tell me you're a big breakfast person because, if you are, we'll need to figure out a grab-and-go thing. I can't eat before ten."

Kennedy sits up, dropping her sleeve to her side. "Okay, *same*. Gram gets upset that I hate breakfast. So she sends a cereal bar with me every morning, and I give it away in first period. If I eat that early, I want to puke."

"Breakfast is the most important meal of the day," I say.

"Actually, that's not true." Megan grins, her blue eyes sparkling. "Recent studies have shown that lunch might be the most important meal of the day."

"Oh, bullshit."

"No, Daddy, it's true," Kennedy says. "Think about it. It

makes sense. If you eat a little lunch, aren't you ready to eat anything you can get your hands on by the time you get home? But if you eat a bigger lunch, you're not dying. Right?"

What the hell is going on here?

I suppress my smile—because God knows that an indication that I'm happy with how this is going might set off my child—and settle back in my seat.

"You know," Kennedy says slyly. "Maybe I should warn Megan about what a grump you can be when you get home from work."

"Excuse me?" I say over their laughter. "I work hard for ten, twelve hours a day and then come home to you fighting with Neve or crying over algebra or—"

"Whoa, let me cut in here," Megan says, holding up a hand. "Crying over algebra is excused. *Come on, Chase.* Have a heart."

"Yeah, *Dad.* Come on. Have a heart."

I wonder if Megan hates algebra and mornings or if she's rolling with the punches to win over Kennedy. Because by the looks of things, they're forming a team. And for whatever reason—reasons that I won't give too much thought—it's cute.

"Algebra never killed anyone." I smile. "That's all I'm saying."

Megan winces. "Well, except Hippasus."

"Hippa-who?" I ask.

"Hippasus. He was an early follower of Pythagoras. Legend says that he was executed for demonstrating the existence of irrational numbers."

"I knew it." Kennedy throws her arms in the air. "I knew math was dangerous. I've felt it in my bones for years."

Megan smirks and shrugs.

"Can I use this as an excuse to get out of algebra?" Kennedy asks. "I think death by the mob over irrational numbers is a solid argument."

"Good try. *No,*" I say quickly before shifting in my seat

toward Megan. "How did you know that? That's the most random thing to know."

"It doesn't matter."

Kennedy laughs. "It didn't matter, but now it does. How *did* you know?"

Megan's cheeks flush. "Fine. When I was a teenager, my mom married this guy, Rick. They were married for almost ten years. Anyway, he had a son, Rodrick, and I despised that kid. He would come over on the weekends, or every other one, and was such a know-it-all. It didn't matter what you were talking about; Rodrick knew all about it. I got so mad at him once that I brought up menstruating, thinking he'd bail on that conversation. But nope. He tried to tell me all about how women's bodies worked, and I've never wanted to punch someone in the face so hard in my entire life."

"How old was he?" I ask, chuckling at the idea of a younger version of Megan trying to fight.

"Fourteen." She looks at Kennedy, who is watching her, amused. "Fourteen-year-old boys don't know shit. *Ah*," she says, making a face. "I'm sorry. I shouldn't have said that."

"Said what?" Kennedy asks.

"Shit."

I laugh. "You're fine."

"Yeah. You've met my dad and my uncle Gavin. I mean, everyone is allowed to curse but me," Kennedy says.

"Because you're still building your vocabulary, and you don't need to resort to cheap words to express yourself," I tell her. *Again.* "And if you," I say, turning to Megan, "know some random fact that goes against this theory, keep it to yourself this time."

Megan narrows her eyes, trying to decide whether I'm kidding. I toss her a wink and watch the air exhale from her lungs.

"I would like to reiterate that part about fourteen-year-old boys not knowing shit," I say, grinning. "That was the best fact of the day."

"You'll never think boys know anything, Dad."

"You're right—because they won't. I know because I was one."

"So when, exactly, does that change?" Kennedy smacks her lips together. "Otherwise, how do I know you know what you're talking about? You're a grown-up boy."

"Simple. When someone, not just boys, can make decisions based on character and not emotions, you can give things they say a little credit."

Megan nods emphatically. "Oh, I like that. I like that a lot."

"That's good, huh? It came to me one day while I was driving home from work."

She lifts a brow. "So you think about emotional maturity while driving home from work? What do you think about before going to sleep?"

Last night, your ass. "Depends on the day."

A slow smirk slips across her lips as if she just read my mind.

I shift in my seat again. *Change the subject, Chase. Fast.* "On a serious note, I'll update the school contacts list with Megan's name tonight. Ride the bus home, Kennedy, and do homework before you even think about asking to do anything."

"Dad. Seriously?"

"Yes, seriously."

She groans as if I just told her she was grounded. "I thought that since Gram isn't here, maybe we could modernize things a little bit. You know, ease up on the reins."

"Negative."

"*Dad.*"

"No."

Kennedy doesn't give up. Instead, she banters back and forth, countering every point and reason I give with a surprisingly strong argument. A part of me is exhausted from the constant bickering with her—the poking at boundaries and her challenging me on practically everything.

But another part of me is proud of that very thing.

I don't want her growing up too ready to agree with anything someone says. I want her to think. To stand up for herself. To not be afraid to push back for the things she wants. *Things that matter.*

Even if it is biting me in the ass at the moment.

Megan watches us with an amused grin, her chin cupped in her hand and elbow resting on the table.

Just as I'm about to ask if she has anything to add—for no reason other than to include her in the conversation—the door to the mudroom flings open.

"Hey, Mr. Marshall. Miss me?" Neve says, her curly red hair bouncing against her shoulders.

"Terribly."

She laughs as she prances around the room until she's standing behind Kennedy. "You must be the babysitter."

Megan laughs. "It's nice to meet you, Neve."

I groan. "Not you with the babysitter crap too."

"Well, I'm the best friend," Neve says, pleased with herself for irritating me. "I would say I'm Mr. Marshall's favorite non-relative, but"—she makes a point of looking at Megan before returning her gaze to me—"I think that's probably not true these days."

Kennedy pushes her head back against Neve's stomach.

"Neve," I say, ignoring Megan's stare, "pretend you have manners, okay?"

"Sure thing, boss. Moving on, I bet you're wondering why I'm here."

"You know—I'm not, really." *I just wish you'd leave.*

Neve sighs. "I'll cut to the chase. No pun intended." She giggles at her joke. "Can Kennedy please, please, please come over today?'

"Please, Dad?"

"Mom said she'll bring her home tonight—whenever you want," Neve promises. "And we'll be on time because I know you got a little upset when we were, like, five minutes late last time."

I snort. "Five minutes, Neve? Are we just lying outright now, or what?"

"Fine. Thirty-five or whatever it was."

"It was forty-five, and none of you, including your mother, answered your phones."

Megan grimaces.

"Do you have any fun facts about tardiness?" I ask her.

She shakes her head. "Don't pull me into this one. You're handling it fine on your own."

"Oh, come on," Kennedy says. "Where's the girl bond now?"

"Are you girl bonding with someone besides me?" Neve asks, gasping. "I'm shocked."

Megan laughs. "I just knew that math killed someone once. I'm not here to steal your best friend, Neve. Relax."

She stands tall. "I would hope not. We've been through it together."

"Been through it? Through what?" I ask. "You're fourteen."

"Can we not point out how old I am for the fourteen hundredth time this week?" Kennedy fake cries. "Will this stop when I'm fifteen, or will you just change the language?"

Megan lifts a finger. "Okay, I'm going to chime in here. She has a point, Chase."

"Whose side are you on?" I ask, dropping my jaw.

Her smile could defuse a bomb. "No sides. I'm on a balcony over here as an unbiased third party."

I intend on flipping my attention back on the girls. There's still a battle to be fought, after all. But the rosiness in Megan's cheeks, the sparkle in her eyes—the hint of debauchery hidden in her sweet grin—distracts me.

Focus, Chase. Don't go there.

I clear my throat.

Megan turns away. "What are you two wanting to do this afternoon? What do teenagers do for fun in Peachwood Falls?"

"Nothing," Neve says, wrinkling her nose. "There's nothing to do in Peachwood Falls."

"We'll probably just hang out. *We won't be making videos,*" Kennedy says, side-eyeing me. "We might … do our nails. Who knows?"

I fire Kennedy a warning glare to remind her I wasn't playing. If she makes any more half-clothed videos for social media, she'll not have a phone until she moves out of this house.

A horn beeps in the distance.

"Fine," I say, giving in. "Go. Be home before six."

"Thanks, Dad." Kennedy hops up and kisses me on the cheek. "You're the best."

"Six. Not six oh one."

"Got it." Kennedy follows Neve to the door, sticking tight to her heels. "See you later, Megan."

"It was nice to meet you, Megan," Neve calls out.

"Bye, girls."

The door closes swiftly as if they're afraid I'll change my mind.

As soon as we're alone, the air shifts. Shadows dance across the tabletop. Megan's jasmine perfume scents the air, and my body temperature rises.

I struggle to remember our conversation yesterday. I remind myself that my child—the same one that occupied the seat next to me a minute ago—is my priority. Over and over, I replay all the reasons I can't afford to get off track.

Why I can't touch Megan Kramer.

My muscles tighten in my stomach and across the back of my neck as I lift my gaze from the tabletop to her.

She grins. It's simple, but when coupled with the heat in her eyes, nothing about it is sweet. "That was fun."

I hold her gaze, unable to look away.

This is the first day, Chase. Twenty-nine more to go. Don't blow it already.

I smirk and push away from the table.

I need to put some distance between us before things get really fun.

CHAPTER 13

egan

"Coffee?"

Chase's chair screeches against the floor as he pushes away from the table. He doesn't wait for an answer. Instead, he heads to the coffee pot like a man on a mission.

His question throws me. *Do I want coffee?* It's almost noon.

"I guess ..." I shrug when he looks over his shoulder. "I mean, it's lunchtime, but I won't turn down coffee."

"Yeah." He exhales, leaning against the counter. "Hungry?"

I scoot my chair around so I can still see him.

He's crossed his long legs in front of him. His waist digs into the edge of the cabinet. With his contented annoyance—a look that's wildly amusing and hot beyond measure—he's the picture of single dad perfection.

Thank God Calista can't see this.

"I'm always hungry," I say.

For once in the three days I've known Chase Marshall, I

answer his question directly. No sarcasm. No prodding. No innuendo dripping from my words. But it doesn't matter.

Chase's gaze heats anyway, pinning me to my seat.

My heart pounds. The room spikes ten degrees. An array of goose bumps spill across my skin in anticipation of his touch … that never comes. That can't come. *That's not why I'm here.*

Yet I'm convinced that if I stood and walked across the kitchen, Chase would have a hard time turning away. My instincts say I could kiss him—that he wants me to.

And dammit if I don't want to.

But I can't.

"Want to make something?" His gravelly voice prickles against my skin. "Or we could go into town and grab a sandwich. I probably need to go to the grocery store anyway. I don't know if we have anything here."

He's talking about sandwiches, but I can only focus on the snack right in front of me.

His hair is tousled at the top—just needing a trim. The veins in his forearm rope around the muscle. His eyes tell me he wants to grab ahold of me and toss me against the wall.

I steady myself. *We need to break this moment.*

"Why don't you show me around instead?" I say, figuring movement is the best form of defense. "We can figure out food later—or I can go shopping tomorrow while Kennedy is at school."

His shoulders sag as if he, too, were holding his breath. "Are you sure? I can put together a ham and cheese sandwich at worst."

"Yeah, unless you're hungry."

He crosses the room. "Nah, we had bacon and waffles this morning." He disappears into the mudroom and comes back carrying my bags.

"Should I expect homemade breakfasts every weekend?"

He grins. "Ken goes with Dad for brunch on Saturdays, so I

usually grab cereal or a sandwich if I'm out fucking around. But we do usually cook together on Sunday mornings."

"You two seem close," I say, following him into the hallway and toward the foyer.

"Who? Me and Dad?"

"No, you and Kennedy."

He stops by the steps leading upstairs. "We are close. I think. *I hope.*" He looks up, giving me a front-row seat to his long eyelashes. "She wants to hang out and watch movies one day, and the next, she hates me for no apparent reason. She's emotionally erratic, and it's borderline abusive."

I giggle.

"It's not funny," he says, shaking his head and switching his gaze to mine. "I know I'm a grown man who shouldn't be scared of a little girl, but I'm terrified of her most days. I find myself approaching her door with a brownie as tribute."

My giggles turn into outright laughter. "Stop it."

"This is the living room."

He motions toward the left before dragging his eyes away from mine like he isn't done with that part of our conversation.

I peer into the cozy area in the front of the house. There's a mantel over the fireplace that I overlooked yesterday. It's dark lumber, resembling a railroad tie, and hosts a variety of picture frames in various colors.

"We live in there," he says.

"Fitting."

"And the dining room we never use is over there." He tilts his head toward the other side of the foyer. "I keep thinking I ought to do something different in there. But, hell, I'm not home long enough to get involved in a huge project, though Mom keeps insisting that a day will come when I'll need it."

I lean against the wall, absorbing the sun's warmth from where it filters through the transom window above the door.

The house is quiet, perfectly still, but I can imagine it filled with fun and laughter—the sound of big family dinners.

I only realize I'm smiling when Chase catches my attention. He watches me curiously.

"What are you thinking?" he asks.

I push away from the wall and sigh. "That I agree with your mom. It needs to be a dining room."

"Even if we never use it?"

"You will someday."

He rolls his eyes and heads upstairs. "I'm sorry for Kennedy's cool reception today, by the way."

"No, she was great. I imagine it was hard for her to have another woman in her house."

His lips twitch.

"She is the woman of the house, you know," I say. "You might see her as a kid, and she *is* a child by all definitions. But in her mind, she's a woman, and this is her house."

"Are you telling me I'm worrying too much?"

I think about it. "No, I think you're right to worry. I think it's great that you worry, actually."

He scoffs like he's embarrassed at being caught for being nice. It makes me laugh.

"I'm just saying maybe you don't totally understand her," I say. "So some of what she does looks like it's coming out of left field when maybe it's not."

"Yeah, well, left field would be better than outer space."

My smile grows.

I'm sure I was a handful for my mom when she was a single mother. Although we could get on the same page, she was still my mother, and I was still a bratty teenager. We butted heads. Even so, she could come at our issues from a place of understanding.

We get to the top of the stairs and stop. There is a door to the left, one in front of us, and a hallway to the right. Pictures adorn the walls—most of Kennedy at various stages of her life. A little table sits next to the hallway with an oddly shaped vase on it.

"Were you this way with your dad?" he asks. "Did you fight him all the time? Make everything hard?"

My smile slips. "No."

"Then what did he do differently because I'd like that kind of relationship with my hell-raiser."

"Well," I say, my thoughts going to a man I've not thought about in a while. "I guess the biggest reason we didn't fight was that he wasn't there."

Chase furrows a brow.

"It's hard to fight with someone who doesn't know you exist," I say.

He regrips the handles of my bags, studying me with a quiet intensity. I'm unsure if he wants me to elaborate—if he wants the messy details, or if he's trying to determine how to get out of this conversation.

Probably the latter.

"Think of it that way," I say, giving him an exit. "You might fight with her right now. But she'll grow up and appreciate that she had a dad who cared enough about her to stick around."

His lips twist into a semblance of a smile. "Right." He tips his head toward the lone door on the left. "That's my room. The one in front of you is a closet. Extra blankets, board games, candles because I swear every time Kennedy has an extra dollar to her name, she buys another damn candle."

"Yeah, well, I relate."

"Of course you do," he mumbles, heading down the hallway. "The door on the right is Ken's. The one at the end is the bathroom. You can get situated there. And this is your room."

He pauses by the door on the left and flicks the handle.

We step inside the small but gracious bedroom. It smells faintly of cinnamon and has a window that overlooks the driveway. A small bed is covered with a blue-and-white quilt that looks like it was plucked out of an Amish store.

A wooden rocking chair sits in the corner, and a large dressing table with an oval mirror rounds out the furniture. The only other item of interest is an accordion door in the corner segregating the tiniest closet known to man and the rest of the room.

Chase places my bags on the floor next to the chair.

"This is the cutest little guest room," I say, checking out a picture of a baby Kennedy on the table.

"No one ever uses it. Mom put fresh sheets and pillows on it this week, so you should be good to go."

"I'll be fine. I don't need much to make me happy."

He sits on the edge of the bed. The springs squeak with his weight. "Thank you for doing this."

I stand across from him with my back to the mirror. The room is so tight that only a few feet separates us.

He folds his hands together, elbows resting on his knees, and leans forward. His eyes are bright and clear, and unlike every other time we've been this close, he doesn't want to hide from me.

"Can I ask you a question?" I lace my fingers together in front of me. "If you don't want me to, just say so."

He shrugs. "Depends on what it is."

"Where is Kennedy's mom?"

He hangs his head for a long minute, and I'm not sure he will answer. I hold my breath, second-guessing my decision to prod into this area of his life, and start to change the subject. But before I can take back my question, he speaks.

"Monica, that was her name …" He looks up at me. "She's gone."

"Oh."

"She died when Kennedy was four," he says.

"*Oh.*"

His tone is void of feelings, but his eyes tell a different story. There's pain there—sadness. There's a pit of emotion that I'm unsure how to handle.

Suddenly, I want to wrap my arms around Chase Marshall and hug him. Only hug him, for once. I don't know his relationship with her—*were they married? Dating? How did she die?*—but I can tell her passing affected him deeply.

"Chase, I'm sorry. I didn't know."

"It's okay. How would you have known?"

I blow out a shaky breath. "I ..."

I stumble with words. They all feel wrong and heavy—inappropriate. I hate that I don't know what to say to him and even more that I put him in a position to discuss all of this.

"It's okay," he says. "You don't have to say anything."

"Good, because I don't know what to say. I feel like I just stuck my foot in my mouth."

He runs a hand down his face and groans. "Monica and I weren't a thing. We never were."

Oh. "You don't owe me an explanation."

"I know. I don't. But if I don't tell you, it'll hang between us and make things weird."

"Okay ..."

He takes a long, deep breath. "I was working in Michigan after a storm. We were there for about a month trying to get shit back together. Then one night, I met Monica at a little pizza restaurant, and we started talking."

"I'm a grown-up, you know."

He furrows a brow.

"I get you did more than talking. You have a kid," I say, teasing him in hopes it'll lighten him up.

He shakes his head ... and grins.

"So you're talking to her," I say, motioning for him to continue. "I've already gotten you this far. There's no turning back now."

He holds his hands out. "There's not a lot more to say. I came back home after the job. We talked a couple of times, but she never told me she was pregnant or wanted anything more with me. I had no idea, or else I would've been there."

"Why didn't she tell you?"

"I have no idea." He sighs, meandering through the room. "I was here living my best life, and she was ..." He laughs sadly. "I don't even know where the hell she was or what was happening to her. I'll never know."

None of this has anything to do with me, and a part of me thinks I should stay out of it and stop asking him questions. But when he stops moving and looks at me, there's an expectant look in his eye as if he wants me to ask. Like he wants to talk about it. Like no one has ever asked him this story and how he feels about being left out of his daughter's life—*for years.*

I sit on the edge of the bed. "How did you find Kennedy?"

"Child Protective Services called me one Tuesday afternoon. I hung up the first time, figuring it was Luke being a prick. But, no, I had a four-year-old child I'd never met sitting in an office in Ann Arbor."

"Wow. I'm ... speechless."

He snorts. "Well, I wasn't."

I smile at him.

"Monica was killed in a carjacking, and Kennedy was strapped in a car seat in the back." A flash of anger bolts through his features. "They found her crying in the parking lot of a gas station that night."

"Oh, Chase."

He nods, agreeing with the sentiment. "I'm just happy they found me, you know?"

"How did they find you? I mean, if she hadn't contacted you before, how did anyone know you existed or how to find you?"

"Monica had written down my name and where I worked

and gave it to her best friend. Just in case." He smiles sadly. *"Just in case."*

I have so many questions. *How does he feel about all of this? Did Monica take care of Kennedy? Was she okay?* But as I consider which to ask first, my stomach knots.

Instead, I stand. "She's really lucky to have you, you know."

He rolls his head around on his neck.

"Thank you for sharing all that with me," I say. "You didn't have to, but I think it'll help me understand Kennedy better."

He stands before me, taking me in like it's the first time he's ever seen me. *And I probably like this look the most out of all I've gotten so far.*

"Hey," I whisper.

"What?"

"I'm still hungry."

His cheeks split into a wide smile. "You're a pain in the ass."

My laughter follows us out of the room.

egan

I'VE NEVER SEEN THE SKY THIS DARK.

Water droplets fall to my shoulders, and I dab them quickly with my towel. Whiffs of roses, peonies, and other intense florals dance through the air every time I move. Kennedy showed me where she keeps her shampoos and soaps, kindly offering to let me use them. The flower bomb body wash was her favorite, so she thought I'd love it too. It felt like a peace treaty, an extended hand drowning in freesia. I couldn't say no.

But by my budding headache, I wish I had.

The house is quiet—strangely, it's too silent to be comfortable. The absence of sound gives my brain too much leeway to think. Unfortunately, thinking isn't always good.

I toss the towel onto the chair and grab my phone off the bed.

"Hey, Meg," Mom says after two rings. "Are you okay?"

"What are you doing up so late?"

"At the moment, I'm answering your call."

I snort. "Don't get an attitude with me, young lady. You're still indebted to me over this whole thing."

Mom stills. "Is everything going all right?"

"Yeah, it's going just fine." I mosey around the room, stopping again in front of the window. "It's so quiet here."

"The first time I visited Maggie, I could barely sleep. I kept waiting for a siren or a car alarm. How do people function if an emergency isn't happening in the distance?"

I grin. "Same."

"Besides being unable to sleep, how are you, sweetie?"

I turn away from the window and shuffle around, eventually sitting on the edge of the bed.

How are you, sweetie? It's such a loaded, complicated question from my mother.

My feet swing back and forth as I consider how to answer her.

On paper—and what she wants to hear—is that I'm fine. She wants to know that Chase and I are getting along and that I'm safe. She'd be thrilled to find out that Kennedy isn't the foregone conclusion she made her out to be. I think she and I can find a middle ground between a rebellious teenager and a pseudo-adult.

And while all that is true, it's not all that's true.

I'm also lost. I have no idea what I'm supposed to do with my life or what my goals even are. How can I be thirty years old and unsettled? Is it normal to look in the mirror in the morning and recognize the face but not identify with the person looking back at you?

I stand, blowing out a breath. "I'm great. Chase has been very kind, and Kennedy is probably a handful, but I think we'll figure it out."

"That's so great, Meg. I've been worrying about it all day, and you didn't answer my text."

"I know. I saw it come in, but …" My cheeks split into a wide smile. "Kennedy got home from her friend's and demanded that Chase show me the lake. There's this huge lake behind their house, and they have this paddle boat you can take out. It's propelled by your feet. So anyway, Kennedy wanted me to see it, so she and her dad took me down there."

"*Oh*. A lake? That sounds fun."

I laugh. "Well, it's rained on and off all day, so it was chilly. *And muddy*. Oh, my gosh, Mom—you've never seen this much mud in your life."

Mom laughs too.

"We mud-skated all the way home, which basically means we ice-skated on mud in boots," I say, giggling at the memory. "I had mud in my eyebrows."

"And here I was feeling lonely. But I'd take lonely all day over mud."

Her comment catches me off guard. Usually, *I'd take lonely over mud, too*.

I hate that Mom's relationships weren't healthy. She deserves love and happiness. Not that she received those things from any of the men she's entertained in the past, but every time she met another, I hoped he would be the one for her.

"It was fun," I say, still thinking about my revelation. "I don't know why because I just had to shower again to get the rest of the mud out of my scalp. But, yeah, it wasn't terrible."

"Sounds like it was more than *not terrible*."

I stand and head to the dresser. Rifling through it, I find a pair of socks. "Have you heard from Maggie? Did she make it to Kate's okay?"

"They'll be there tomorrow. Lonnie insisted on driving, and he stops a lot to look at every touristy thing, which drives Maggie nuts."

I chuckle.

"Well, honey, if all is good with you, I'll talk to you tomorrow," Mom says. "My sleeping meds are about to kick in, and I'll be on the line snoring in ten minutes if we don't hang up."

"That's fine. I was checking in with you."

"I'm glad you did. I love you. Talk to you tomorrow."

"Love you, Mom. Bye."

"Bye, sweetie."

I end the call and set the phone on the bed. As I put on my socks, my stomach starts to rumble.

"There are leftovers in the fridge if you're a leftover kind of person," Chase says. "Help yourself."

My mind whips to the image of Chase peeling off his muddy shirt this evening. It was a striptease—his abs were revealed like a slowly opened present … inch by delicious inch.

Or it would've been if Kennedy wasn't a few feet away taking her boots off, and I wasn't trying desperately to appear oblivious to the porn beside me.

I shiver at the reminder of the heat in Chase's eyes—a lascivious glimmer peeking through his otherwise unaffected demeanor. The slight licking of his lips. The way his fingers drifted along my lower back as he walked around me leaving a flurry of goose bumps in their wake.

And then the smirk over his shoulder as he walked away.

My stomach growls again. It wants food this time too, I think.

My socked feet hit the hardwood, and I grab my phone. With a few quick taps, Calista's name appears on the screen.

"What's up, buttercup?" she asks. "How are things in Mayberry?"

I laugh. "Peachwood Falls, but they're fine."

"Peachwood Falls is such a pretty name. I imagine antique shops and waterfalls. Old men sitting on benches, chatting about the good ole days."

"Well, that's a lovely little vision you've dreamed up, but that's not quite reality."

"Right. You always downplay your adventures. You describe things like they're average and then send me pictures of paradise. Every. Freaking. Time."

Grinning, I remember the dollars on the ceiling of The Wet Whistle. "I'll send you some pictures tonight. You'll see what I mean. This place is your typical Midwestern small town, but it is kinda quirky."

"I love me some quirk."

"Quirk can be fun."

"So," she says, sighing. "What's it like? Are you okay? I haven't checked in every hour like you probably expected, but my flight from Albuquerque got delayed, and I just got home."

I open my bedroom door and peer down the hallway. The night-light next to the bathroom glows a soft orange hue. Otherwise, there's no sign of life.

"Hang on," I whisper, tiptoeing to the stairs. I descend them as fast as I can in socks on wood and turn toward the kitchen. "Okay. I can talk now."

"Where are you?"

"I was coming downstairs for food."

"Imagine that."

I laugh, flipping on the kitchen light. The brightness makes me wince, and I cover my eyes until my pupils adjust.

"Why were you whispering?" she asks, chewing something with gusto. "Can't you talk in the house, or is that, like, a rule? You're there to be seen, not heard?"

"Hardly. I've talked and laughed a lot today, as a matter of fact."

My cheeks ache from the smile etched on my face.

Talking about Chase to Calista is a whole hell of a lot different than it was talking about him with my mother. First of all, my mom would be thrilled if I told her that Chase and I fell madly in love and were getting married and having seventy babies. Second, she's too invested because Chase is Maggie's son. But third—that's the part that keeps me from opening up too much.

Down deep, I know Mom blames herself for my singleness. Everything in her life reminds her of one of her various relationship disasters. *Even me.*

Whether she thinks I've learned to avoid similar situations by proxy or have been burned enough through her failed relationships, I don't know. But the disappointment and regret in her eyes when she looks at me are always there.

I can't share my dating life—or my life when it involves any man, for that matter—with her. It gets her hopes up that maybe she hasn't screwed me up. And when that relationship, friendship, or situation ends, she's devastated all over again.

"I like the sound of that," Calista says. "Continue with details. Lots of them."

"FaceTime me real quick. I'm going to heat chicken and rice from dinner."

The screen buzzes. I grab the food from the refrigerator and accept the video. Calista's freckled face smiles at me.

"Hey, gorgeous," she says, making a kissing face at the phone. "You look radiant. Did you exfoliate?"

I burst out laughing. "Stop it."

"Fine. I'll keep my compliments to myself. Talk."

"I'm going to set you here." I prop the phone up against the toaster. "Can you see me?"

"Yup. Talk."

I glance over my shoulder. "I need to keep my voice down because Chase and Kennedy are upstairs in bed. So don't shriek or yell at your cat or anything, okay?"

"Take the fun out of it, but okay."

I laugh, taking a plate out of the cabinet. "Things are going good. Chase and I have managed to find common ground. We haven't argued today, so that's a plus. And Kennedy sort of flew a white flag, so I think we'll figure it out."

"I don't envy you, my friend. Teenage girls can be wicked."

"Oh, I remember." I spoon some food on the plate and pop it in the microwave. "But she's not like that. She's not mean. Or petty. She's just …" *A lot like me.*

Calista rattles on about a story from high school that I've heard a thousand times. I nod and comment on the necessary parts, but my mind is elsewhere.

As the microwave goes around and around, my brain swirls with how much I fear Kennedy and I are the same. It's a feeling I've never shared with anyone, mostly because I don't think anyone will understand. And if anyone tries, I'm afraid they'll dismiss me as dramatic.

"She died when Kennedy was four."

My heart squeezes. *I'm sorry, Kennedy.*

The microwave beeps. I remove my plate and set it in front of the camera.

"I'm going to eat in front of you, okay?" I say, finding a fork.

"Won't be the first time."

I take my spot facing the phone and mix the food up to help cool it off.

"What are you wearing?" she asks, squinting at the screen. "Is that new?"

I step back and model my tank top. "No, it's not new. I found it in the back of my closet while packing my shit up in California before moving to Mom's. Cute, huh?"

"Adorable."

"I'm not showing you the shorts, but they're cute too," I say, then blow on my food. "They're red and silky. You know, like that expensive crap you wear to bed."

She huffs. "You look like a sweet little nanny. I, however, go to bed looking like I'm ready to fuck your brains out in case the opportunity arises."

"Shh," I say, laughing.

"Oops. Sorry."

"It's fine." I scoop up a bite and shove it in my mouth. "Let's just keep things PG-13 while I'm here."

She whines. "Fine. So tell me about Chase. He's not weird? Creepy? He's not an Odd Bob, is he? Lock your door while you sleep, just in case. You're too hot for your own good."

You think I'm hot? I snort.

It occurs to me that I've never discussed what Chase looks like with Calista, aside from the grainy picture she saw of him online. Initially, avoiding his looks in conversations was intentional. My head was spinning. But since I've known who he was —Diesel Man—I haven't brought it up. Sure, it helped that she was in New Mexico for the weekend and busy with work, but I've managed to avoid the question every time we've interacted.

I won't get away with that for the next month.

"Chase?" I ask, taking another bite. *How do I downplay this but get the point across?* "He's cute."

"*Cute?*" Her voice is thick with curiosity. "Define cute."

"You know what cute means. He's … cute. Good bone struc-ture." *Amazing body.* "He has a great smile." *The hottest hands.* "Nice … teeth." *Lips that I can imagine ravaging me.*

Calista grins. "Nice teeth, huh?"

"Yeah," I say, looking at my food and avoiding her stare. "Nice teeth are important."

She stifles a laugh. "*Megan.*"

"What?"

"If you look at *that* and all you see is nice teeth, we have a problem."

What?

I stand up straight, my fork falling to the countertop. My heart bursts into production.

Noooooo. This can't be happening …

Behind me is a shirtless and smirking Chase Marshall.

CHAPTER 15

$\mathcal{M}$egan

I DON'T WANT TO TURN AROUND.

Chase stands within arm's reach of me. A pair of black sleep pants makes his legs look longer. They dip on one hip, hanging in a way that highlights the muscles pointing at his groin.

As if I need a map to remind me of *that*.

My lips part, and I drag in a lungful of air. *Shit.*

"Wanna know what I see?" Calista asks, leaning toward the screen. "Because I'm making quite a list."

"Calista, I gotta go."

"No. *Wait.*" She waves. "Hi, Chase! I'm Calista, Megan's best friend. I hear you have nice teeth."

My cheeks heat. "*Calista …*"

"I'm just thrilled to hear she has a best friend." He bumps my shoulder with his, sending a spark coursing through me. "She's kind of irritating."

I bump his shoulder back. "I am not."

"She can be. I know," Calista says.

Chase looks down at me, his smirk growing. "Did Megan tell you that you have competition?"

"With whom?" Calista demands.

"Don't rile her up," I say, grinning. "You don't know who you're messing with."

"*With whom?*" she repeats. "You've been there not even three days, Megan. You can't replace me already. I *will* come to Mayberry."

Chase's brows pull together. "Mayberry?"

"Let it go," I say, laughing.

He slowly pulls his eyes from mine and turns to the phone. He places his forearms on the counter, leaning against the cabinets.

"Holy shit, Chase," Calista says. "You are *gorgeous*."

He snorts.

"Calista, *please*," I say, my cheeks burning. "Please stop it."

"Nice teeth, my ass. Speaking of, turn around, Chase," she says. "Let me see your ass."

"*Enough*," I say, making Chase laugh. "Act like you have some damn sense."

My admonishment is met with laughter—from both of them.

"So who is trying to replace me?" Calista asks. "We're not acting like that wasn't brought up."

"My brother Gavin."

"Does he look like you? And, if so, is he single?" she asks.

Chase grins. "No. He's not nearly as good-looking as I am."

"Fact check, Megs?" Calista asks me.

Fuck it. I lean against the counter too. My arms line up beside my boss's, our shoulders nearly touching.

He smells fresh and clean—like soap and wood. Out of the corner of my eye, I notice he hasn't shaved. *No one deserves to be this hot.*

I pull my thoughts together as I realize they're waiting on me to respond.

"Is Gavin as good-looking as Chase?" I ask, my chest tightening. "Well, he's much better-natured, I will say that."

"That wasn't the question," Calista says.

Slowly, Chase turns his face toward mine. His eyes snag my gaze before I can look away.

Amusement dances across his features. The shield I usually find snapped into place is missing or, at least, isn't as secure. He almost looks playful in the late-night hour. In fact, had I met *this* Chase instead of the grumpy cat version, I would've seen the family resemblance between him and Gavin right away.

But Chase still has more sex appeal. *Why? Why does he have to be so ridiculously appealing?*

My stomach tightens, and my heart begins to pound again. I could lose myself by staring at him, dreaming up situations and realities far from the truth.

"You see, Calista," I say, my eyes still locked with Chase's. "Chase and I have a deal."

"What's that?" she asks.

His lips twitch.

My brain races, trying to find the best way to handle her question. Obviously, he's wildly attractive. Sexy. *A catch.* But none of that matters at present because he's made his priority clear: Kennedy.

"She's my priority," he says. "If I'm open to messing around with you, that leaves room for mistakes."

I force a swallow and turn toward the phone. Calista has her phone on her makeup table as she brushes her hair. She winks at me before going back to the mirror.

"It doesn't matter how we feel. Our priority is Kennedy," I say.

My statement is met with silence. Calista remains quiet while Chase shifts his weight beside me.

"Can I call you tomorrow?" I ask, feeling the heftiness of Chase's gaze on the side of my face.

"Yeah. Sure. Call me tomorrow, toots. Love you."

"Love you. Bye."

"Bye. Bye, Chase. Nice to meet you and your great teeth."

I roll my eyes.

"Nice to meet you," he says.

I end the call swiftly.

My body is hot. The temperature in the room rises every second that it takes me to get the nerve to look at Chase. That doesn't stop a surge of chills from snaking down my spine.

"That wasn't awkward at all," he says.

I force myself to turn to him. "Not at all."

His shield is back, but a twinkle remains. "So you like my teeth, huh?"

His simple question breaks the tension. I burst out laughing and pick up my food. I carry it to the island, needing some space from him.

"You know, I've never had someone compliment my teeth before," he says. "Odd but satisfying. My parents have a lot of money in my teeth, so I'm glad that paid off."

"You know what's satisfying?"

He grins.

I roll my eyes. "The fact that you had teeth that needed braces."

"That's cold."

"That's … *just*. You can't have everything, Chase. It's not fair to the world."

He moseys toward the refrigerator. "Did you leave any leftovers?"

"Yeah. There's some left."

He takes out the containers to make himself a plate of food.

"Just so you know," he says, pressing the buttons on the microwave. "I don't have *everything*."

"Huh. That's good to know."

"I mean, my teeth are great." He turns and smiles. "And my … what did you say? Oh, my bone structure." He lifts his chin and tilts his head side to side. "I think I got that from my dad."

"It's not nice to sneak up on people, you asshole."

"What are you mad about?" He takes his dish out of the microwave. "I could've caught you talking shit. At least you were being complimentary."

"Oh, I was talking shit. You just missed that part."

He shakes his head and carries his plate to the table. I grab mine and follow him, sitting to his right. Instead of sitting, he goes to the refrigerator and brings back two water bottles.

"Thanks," I say, taking one from him.

"What kind of shit were you talking?" he asks, dropping into the chair.

I sit back and yawn, stretching my arms overhead. "I was just telling her what a dick you are."

"Oh." He scoops a forkful of rice into his mouth. "That's reasonable."

"And how I think that your *real* problem is that you want to be my friend, and you're mad that Gavin got to me first."

"*I* got to you first. You met Gavin later."

"Yeah, but Gavin established himself in my life well before you."

He twists the top of his bottle, narrowing his eyes.

Something about that gives me immense pleasure.

"Speaking of the devil," I say. "Does he come around here a lot? Or was me running into him a complete fluke?"

Chase takes a long drink. "I see him all the time. I helped him build that fence yesterday. He went fishing with us. I probably see him and Luke a few times a week."

"Don't you have another brother?"

"Yeah. Mallet." He takes another bite. "He lives out West. He fights for a living, so we don't see him much. He comes home now and then."

"Oh."

"What about you? Do you have siblings?"

I pull a leg up and wrap my arms around it. "Nope. It's just me. Well, me and my mom. That's the only family I have."

"I'm sorry. That sounds … lonely, I guess."

"It's okay." I shrug. "It's probably better like that. Mom has quite the history of sordid love affairs."

Chase grins. "Oh, really."

"Not in a romance novel kind of way. In a *she's been married multiple times and none of them last more than two years* kind of way. And I can't think of one of them that I wish would walk back into her life, either. They wanted her to pet their ego, wash their laundry, or, in the case of Rick—they wanted her pain pills after she had back surgery. He was a fun one."

"Yikes."

"Exactly."

He makes a face like he's thinking. "So no siblings, but no aunts, grandparents, or cousins either? No one at all?"

"My mom's mom and dad died when she was twelve. Her mom didn't have any family, and her dad's family were all … They were found undesirable to raise a child. Let's put it that way. So my mom floated between people until she was eighteen."

Chase settles back in his chair, his food forgotten. His forehead wrinkles as he studies me.

I fidget with the hem of my tank top. His heavy curiosity has me fighting the urge to get up from the table. It would be easier to walk away from this conversation. After all, it's what I do. But I can't deny the desire to stay right where I am. *For better or worse.*

"What's wrong?" he asks, his voice lowered.

"Nothing. Why?"

"You look like you don't know whether to crack a joke or run away."

Impressive, sir. I shift in my seat. "I just get antsy when I talk about my family. That's all."

"Can I ask why?"

My anxiety gets the best of me, and I can't take it any longer, so I get up. "Do you like talking about your family?"

"Yeah. I don't mind."

Good for you. I gather my plate, take it to the sink, and rinse it. Then I place it in the dishwasher.

"If you don't want to talk about it, it's okay," he says.

"No, it's fine." I brush a strand of hair out of my face. "I just …"

He stands and crosses the kitchen, stopping in front of me.

I haven't seen this side of Chase yet. It's softly curious. Kind. Concerned. It reminds me more of the way he is when his daughter is around—but now he's this way with me.

A warmth floods my body, heating me from head to toe. He's not rushing the conversation so we can get to the next part. It doesn't feel like a box to be checked so we never have to discuss it again. That's what it's felt like every time I've had the courage to open up to a man about these things before. Instead, his patience is surprising. It throws me a bit, but his genuine interest in me, in my story, makes my heart swell.

"This isn't a topic I love to talk about," I say, my voice teetering.

"Then we won't talk about it."

I smile at him.

"But sometimes when we don't love talking about things," he says carefully, "it's because we've never had the opportunity to do so safely. I'm just letting you know I'm willing to listen."

My heart fills with gratitude, nearly overflowing with the wave of emotion.

I'm afraid talking about this with Chase will make me look

silly. I am, after all, an adult, and the things that happened to me happened when I was a child. I should be over it by now. *Why should their churlishness still bother me? Am I that weak that the nastiness spewed at me by ignorant children affected my psyche for decades?*

Apparently.

But as I watch him across from me and absorb the kindness and consideration he's projecting, I don't want to clam up and walk away. So I talk.

"Before we lived in Dallas, we lived in a tiny town in West Texas," I say. "We moved from there when I was sixteen—partially because the kids were awful."

"Makes sense. Kids can be cruel."

"Yeah. They can." I take a deep breath and try to harness the words and courage to keep going. With every second that passes, the more time I have to let the self-doubt slip in. "I don't know … this feels so stupid."

"That's funny."

I quirk a brow. "Funny? Why?"

"It's funny because it's impossible for you to *feel* stupid. If you *feel* something, it's justified. It might not come from a logical place—maybe it comes from anxiety. But that doesn't make it stupid."

I grin. "There you go, being all logical again. I thought we said no romance."

He chuckles.

However, his explanation and demeanor resonate in my soul. He's right—something I'm slowly learning is typical. And the more I consider this, and the longer I stand in front of him, the more I want to share my truths.

Not for him. *For me.*

"My mom …" I exhale sharply, an anxious energy bubbling in my stomach. "She had no one to help her, to watch out for her. And anyone that she did have was gone as soon as she turned eighteen. She had nowhere to go, you know?"

Chase frowns but doesn't say anything.

"She participated in some … questionable behavior," I say, choosing my words carefully. "Illegal behavior unless you're in Nevada, and we weren't."

"I see."

"Yeah. And we lived in a small religious town that was quick to judge her. A young woman with no money, no family, no one who gave a shit. No food, no shelter—no anything. None of them offered to help her, mind you. They just wanted to make sure she knew she was a terrible person for doing what she had to do to survive."

Chase's jaw tenses.

"I was born," I say, my voice wavering. "By the grace of God, she got herself together. And she was a *damn good mother*. She was there. Present. She loved me every day of my life, and we might not have had much, but I never once had to question if I was the most important thing in the world to her." I blink back tears. "But that didn't matter because she'd already been deemed fit for hell by the saints in town."

"And you inherited that."

"And I was shamed and dirty because of it."

Tears wet the corners of my eyes as I remember the terrible things I was called. The jokes made at my expense. The pranks pulled on me because I wasn't popular. The parties I wasn't invited to, the girls who couldn't stay all night at our house, and all the friendships that failed as soon as their parents realized who I was.

And how horrible that must've been for my young, struggling mom—to watch the child she loved more than the world be bullied because of her choices. *That she had to make.*

What did those people want from her? Would they have rather she died? Was she supposed to afford housing, food, and medical bills from the money she received from the jobs no one would hire her to do? How was she supposed to leave town with a bag of ratty clothes to her name?

When I think about what I experienced, it hurts. But it breaks my heart when I think of what my mother *endured*.

Chase goes to the table and gets his plate. He cleans it and places it in the dishwasher without saying a word. Then he pops on the light above the stove and flips off the main kitchen light.

"We better get to bed," he says. "Morning comes fast."

I dip my chin, slightly embarrassed that I might've delayed his bedtime with my sob story, and head to the doorway. But before I can walk past him, he reaches for my arm.

His hand easily encompasses my bicep. His grip is gentle yet firm. It's as if he wants me to know that I could pull away if I chose to, but also that *he's here*.

It's the intentional part of the gesture that gets me.

My breath halts in my lungs as I peer into his eyes.

"I'd love to see what those girls would say about you now," he says, his tone husky. "You're successful and intelligent. Funny and a bit irritating. *And beautiful as hell.*"

I gasp, I know I do, but I can't stop it.

"Can I tell you something?" he asks quietly.

I nod. It's all I can do.

"I'm glad I walked in on you talking to your friend, and it wasn't you walking in on me talking to one of my brothers," he says.

"Why?"

He grins. "Because I would've been talking about a whole lot more than your fucking teeth."

I snort, pulling my arm away. A rush of relief exits my body. How natural was his transformation from an attentive listener, which is what I needed, to a borderline jerk. Somehow, I'm extremely grateful for that.

"My fucking teeth? Or fucking my teeth?" I ask, making him

laugh. "Your response will really dictate how the next few weeks go."

He continues to chuckle and heads down the hallway. He motions for me to follow.

I watch his back flex as he heads to the stairs in front of me. The muscles are glorious—enough to make me pant. But now I know for certain that Chase Marshall has a sweet layer inside. And I think that might be even better.

We get to the top of the stairs, and he stops. He speaks but catches himself before shaking his head.

"What?" I ask.

He sighs. "We gotta go to bed, Megan. We made a deal."

That we did.

I take a long, deep breath and commit his scent to memory. "Night, Chase."

"Night, Megan."

I head to my bedroom and don't look back.

CHAPTER 16

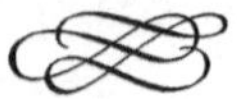

hase

BOOM!

"Damn these roads," I grumble, stabilizing the truck as it recovers from a direct hit to a pothole.

I circle my right shoulder and wince as a blast of pain shoots down my back and across my neck.

The sky glows half orange and half a deep, inky black. Work was long and hard. I wondered all day if time was slower than usual or I was just anxious to go home.

Because *I am* anxious to get home. It's pointless to pretend I'm not.

I've been on edge all day, and it's pissed me off. I was short with the crew. I nearly got fired for telling the superintendent he was a dipshit—even though it's true—and when Luke texted me that he thought Alyssa might be pregnant, I had less sympathy than the situation required.

Because sympathy *was* needed. Neither are ready to be parents.

I regrip the steering wheel and ignore the new blast of pain shooting down my back.

My phone rings as I pass Cotton's. When I see it's Gavin, I answer. *Thank God it's not Luke.*

"Hey," I say.

"What's up, lover boy?"

"Gavin, this isn't the day, and now isn't the time."

"Sounds like you've had a bad day."

I roll my eyes and turn up the volume on the speakers. "Have you talked to Luke today?"

"Yes, and that dumb motherfucker thinks he knocked up Alyssa." He pauses. "I'm assuming he told you that."

"He did."

"What in hell's bells was he thinking?"

"Clearly, he wasn't. Typical Luke shit, you know? Do what feels good now and worry about the consequences later. Well, buddy, later is now, and the consequences are hitting hard."

Gavin chuckles. "I hate it for him, but, man, does it make me feel better about myself."

I grin.

"So is *this* a better time because I want to talk about that dime living in your house," he says cheekily.

She's a ten, all right. I wipe my hand down my face.

I expected to struggle with this setup. Hell, it's why I refused it in the first place. There was no getting around being distracted by Megan. She's a dime. She's a ten. *She's fucking perfect,* and just like I figured, the more I get to know her, the more I want to know.

My stomach forms a knot. It pulls tighter and tighter the closer I get to home.

The real problem—one of them, anyway—is that it's easier

being around her than not. When she sits across the table or walks next to me through a muddy field, I don't think about how it could go wrong. I'm just sucked up in her world. I'm listening to her laugh, waiting for her next joke. I'm watching her smile and feeling it warm the inside of my cold, black heart.

I've reasoned with myself. I'm probably this way because I haven't allowed myself to get to this point in so many years. Women have served a particular purpose. That purpose can occur at their house, a motel, or on a blanket in the back of my truck if the situation requires it. For no reason—absolutely none—have I allowed a woman in my house who didn't share my blood or wasn't fucking one of my brothers since Kennedy was in first grade.

And here we are.

"Are you okay with Megan being there?" Gavin asks. "I've given you hell about it, which you probably expect. But it occurred to me this morning that I've never asked you if it's what you want or if you just agreed to the whole thing because you don't have a choice."

"Yeah, well, I don't have a choice."

"But you're okay with it?"

I exhale. "It's fine. Things are fine."

"Dammit, Chase. I know things aren't fine. I've seen her, remember?" He whistles. "But fuck if *she* isn't fine."

I half laugh, half groan. *Thank you for stating the obvious.*

That's the thing, though. She's more than fine.

I meant everything I said to her last night. *If those girls could see her now* ... But what stayed with me after we said good night was the pain in her eyes. The raw despair. The tears forming. *"And I was shamed and dirty because of it."*

That has rolled around my head ever since. Each time I recall those words, my blood pressure rises. *Fuck.*

I hate that she had to go through that, but I truly hate that she still carries the weight of it. That a part of her still connects to those disgusting words. That they still affect her.

I would dismantle anyone who ever said anything remotely close to that to Kennedy. Because, perhaps, her mother had been forced into a similar situation. And I didn't know. *I don't know.* And that slices me open too.

At least Monica left my identity with someone so they could relay it to the authorities. Thank God I was given Kennedy to love and raise. I'm also thankful that Megan was the one who showed up to help this month. *Megan—the bewitching woman who's entirely more than a hot nanny.*

"We've all heard about people who were just meant to be," he says. "And when—"

"*Whoa.* Gav." The hair on the back of my neck stands on end. "What in the hell are you talking about?"

"You don't think this whole thing is … I don't know—*fate?*"

My eyes go wide. "No, brother, I abso-fucking-lutely do not."

"Well, I abso-fucking-lutely do." I can almost hear his smile through the phone. "But maybe I have my signals mixed."

"Yeah. Maybe."

"Maybe she's in Peachwood Falls for me—*not you.*"

I chuckle. The sound houses an angry edge that amuses Gavin. He laughs, not bothering to hide his entertainment with my reaction.

"Would that bother you?" he asks. "Would it be a problem if I, say, ask her out? Buy her flowers? Bury myself in her hot little body."

I grit my teeth. "Can you not complicate this?"

"How would it be complicating it? You don't want her, so I'll occupy her for you. I'll distract her—dazzle her. She won't be able to stop talking about me, which will irritate you so much that you'll forget how much you want to fuck her."

I pull into the driveway. We picked up Mom's car yesterday,

and she's parked it on the right side of the gravel—the side I usually park on.

"Gavin," I say, killing the engine. "You talk about fucking her again, and I'll throttle you. Cool?"

"Why do you care?"

"I know you're joking and trying to get a rise out of me, so stop it. Okay?"

"Dude, I thought about her sweet little—"

"I'll demolish you."

Gavin bursts into a fit of laughter. Even though he's frustrating, I can't help my smile.

"Fine," he says. "Women can buy their own flowers these days. That's what I keep hearing, anyway."

I grab my Thermos and phone and step into the cool evening air. The light in the kitchen is on, and shadows dance along the walls.

Excitement takes over me like a little kid at Christmas. Except that present has to stay wrapped.

I sigh. *But at least I can look at it.*

"I'm home," I say. "I gotta go."

"Hey, Chase?"

"What?"

"I'm just kidding with you. I mean, I'd totally fuck her brains out. But there's one reason I won't even try."

I start slowly to the house. "Why is that?"

"Because from the moment she came into the bar the other night, she was all about *you*. She's a nice girl. She's fun. So you should just relax a little—let things work out however they do."

"Oh, I know how they'd work out." *With my cock halfway down her throat.* "That's the problem, Gav. That's the problem right there."

"Hardheaded motherfucker."

"It is what it is. Talk to you tomorrow, all right?"

"Later."

I enter the mudroom and drop my shit on the floor. The distinct smell of Mexican food wafts through the air. My stomach growls, reminding me that I skipped lunch.

Once my boots are off, I open the kitchen door.

Oh shit.

Post Malone is playing through Kennedy's phone on the table. She's at the island with a spoonful of what appears to be brownie batter dripping into her open mouth. Megan stands at the oven with mitts on, laughing at my daughter.

I've come home a thousand times to see my mom and Kennedy busy in the kitchen. But never like this.

"Hey," I say, barely loud enough for them to hear.

They both jump, twisting their attention toward me. Kennedy smiles brightly. *Super weird. Where's the combative teenager refusing to do algebra?* Megan waves an oven-mitted hand.

"You two look like you're having fun," I say.

"Enchiladas and brownies," Kennedy squeals. "I'm licking the bowl. Want some?"

"No. Not with your spit all over it."

She scoffs. "Oh, like that stopped you from stealing my Dr Pepper the other day."

"It was hot out, and you had good ice." I tap her on the head. "This all smells amazing."

"It's Megan's recipe," Kennedy says. "Well, it's someone's recipe from Los Angeles who Megan used to know. We were both starving after school, so we ran to the store and picked up the stuff to make it."

"I hope that's okay," Megan says.

Her face is glowing. Shiny eyes, rosy cheeks. She looks prettier than ever before.

"Yeah, that's fine," I say. "I should've left you money. I didn't think about it. I'll pay you back. How much was it?"

"It's fine," she says, running a hand through the air. "Don't worry about it."

I give her a look not to fuck with me, but she winks. *Naturally.*

"Got all of my homework done," Kennedy says, stopping Post Malone. "I have a piece of paper for you to sign from Ms. Falconbury, but it's not a big deal."

"*Ken ...*"

"It's not."

"Get it. I want to see."

"It's in my room."

I point at the hallway. "Then go."

She groans, huffing out the room and glaring at me the whole way. *Ah, there's the girl I know.*

Megan holds her hands out. "I didn't know anything about that until now. I have no idea what she's talking about."

"It's probably a detention," I say, making my way closer to the stove. "Kennedy has this habit of skipping Ms. Falconbury's class, and Ms. Falconbury has a habit of handing out detentions."

"Well, she can't skip class."

"No, she cannot."

I stop next to Megan and inspect her enchiladas. "And you said you could cook ... what did you say? Decently?"

"Yeah."

"This looks great, Megan."

She beams. "Thanks. I didn't want to oversell my abilities. I try really hard, and I'm pretty good with recipes. But what if I make something, and you hate it, and I've led you to believe I'm amazing? That would suck."

"Or maybe you need to stop worrying about what people think of you and be confident in who you are."

I didn't mean it as a throwback to our conversation last night, but it does apply. And she applies it.

Her eyes twinkle with something—gratitude? Hope? I don't know. But I do know that I could stand here all day and take it in.

Get away from her, Chase.

I head to the sink and wash my hands under hot water. Twice. Just to take up more time.

"How was your day at work?" she asks.

"Same shit, different day. How was your day here? Did things go okay?"

"Yup. I did the laundry in the bathroom and mudroom. I folded it all and sorted it for you and Kennedy, but I didn't want to put it away. It felt like an invasion of your privacy."

I grin.

She leans next to me, the soft scent of jasmine taunting me, and grins too. "Wanna know something?"

"What?"

"I wanted to be nosy. I wanted to go in your room and put your things away so I could snoop around."

I turn the water off and flick the water from my hands at her. She squeals as I grab a towel. My plan is to head to the table and wait on Kennedy. But like I'm on autopilot, I find myself at the sink again to be next to her.

"What do you think you'd find?" I ask.

"Something good, I hope."

I chuckle. "Like what?"

She bites her lip. It takes everything in me not to pop it free and sink my mouth against hers.

But I don't.

"Like what?" I ask again. "Whips? Chains? Handcuffs?"

Her eyes go wide.

I laugh. "I'm kidding."

She sighs, and I'm unsure if she's relieved or disappointed.

"Or am I?" I ask.

She shoves me, knocking me off balance. My chest bounces as I try not to laugh too loudly at her.

"You and I had an agreement," she says, checking the doorway for Kennedy. "We were pretending this didn't exist."

"What didn't exist?"

She looks at me like I'm ignorant.

"What are you talking about, Megan?" I grin mischievously, lowering my mouth to her ear. "Oh, right. We were pretending I don't want to taste your pussy."

She bats at my arm. I pull away, laughing way too hard.

"You just brought that up," she says, pointing at me. "Not me. I've not broken our deal."

"Semantics, sweetheart."

She blushes at the term of endearment—the one I didn't mean to say. Instead of recanting the word, I act like I don't realize I said it.

She tucks a strand of hair behind her ear. "Semantics, my ass. I didn't say a word."

"Oh, come on. Like you weren't thinking it."

"But I didn't *say it.*"

You didn't have to. I roll my eyes. "I just came home from work. You're the one speculating about what's inside my bedroom. I won't see an imprint of you on my bed, will I?"

She looks surprised. Slowly, the surprise turns into a mischievous grin. "No, but that would've been a damn good idea. Make you lie in bed all night wondering what I did on your blankets."

Well, that would be a slight deviation from wondering what I'd do to you on my blankets.

"Here it is," Kennedy says loudly, marching into the room. "Don't be pissed."

"There's always tomorrow," Megan whispers before returning to the enchiladas.

I want to say something back and deal with the heat building in my groin, but a detention notice is thrust into my hands. *Nice cock block.*

"Here's the thing," Kennedy says, hands on her hips. "I was there. I didn't skip class."

"Ken, please. Don't lie to me."

Her jaw drops. *"I was there, Dad.* I mean it. I was as shocked as you are when I got that today."

"After this exact conversation last week, I find that hard to believe."

"Dad."

"I thought we were getting somewhere. I thought you were going to do better."

"I am doing better. Why don't you believe me?"

Suddenly, my exhaustion from the day settles back into my bones.

Arguing with my daughter isn't going to help. If it would, one of the last sixteen hundred arguments about this would've cured the problem. And if that were the case, I would also know what the problem is—why she's testing every nerve I have left.

Megan smiles softly. I imagine she's grateful she doesn't have to deal with this longer than a month. I can't blame her. It's a lot.

But, *it's also everything.*

I exhale and turn back to Kennedy. Her eyes plead with me, her bottom lip beginning to quiver. She looks like the little girl she once was, and I remind myself she's still her. She's just bigger, and her life is more complicated.

Glancing at Megan, my insides twist.

Maybe my life is a bit more complicated too.

"Let's eat," I say, putting an arm around Kennedy's shoulders. "Then we'll talk about it."

"Really?"

I kiss the top of her head. "Really."

Kennedy wraps her arms around my waist and hugs me.

"Whoa, wait. I'm filthy," I say, pushing her back. "I need to grab a shower."

She hugs me even tighter.

Megan smiles and turns back to the oven.

The feeling of contentment catches me off guard. And it scares the shit out of me.

This is something I could get used to.

Get over it, Marshall. She'll be gone before you get used to anything.

And that's the way it should be.

CHAPTER 17

egan

"Look at you," Gavin says, dropping into the seat across from me. "You're one week in, and you're alive."

"It was touch and go there for a while, but I seem to be surviving."

The lunch rush at The Wet Whistle isn't much of a rush at all. Customers wander in as if they have nowhere to be and casually order their sandwiches while chatting up Tabitha. It's the most low-key establishment I've ever seen—even more so than a lunch I had in Spain, where the patrons could bring their own lunch to the restaurant and enjoy the atmosphere.

Gavin runs his hands down his jeans and tosses me a killer smile. "How are things going with my brother?"

I look down at my phone to keep him from reading my features.

Whatever I expected this job to entail, this wasn't it. Five days in, we're coming together in a routine that feels too natural.

I *just happen* to come downstairs while Chase is getting ready for work. He packs his lunch and gathers his things while I sip a cup of coffee. Some mornings he's almost chatty; others, he hardly says a word. But even those mornings, I'm pretty confident he likes me sitting at the table while he preps his day. He steals glances when he thinks I'm not looking. And every morning, without fail, he thanks me for being there. Then he flashes a smile, as small as it may be, that fuels my day.

It feels good to be appreciated. It feels even better to be wanted—both as the nanny and a woman. Because even though we've agreed that's not in the cards, it doesn't mean the urge has gone away. *For either of us.*

"Megs?"

"Oh, it's going pretty good," I say, tucking a strand of hair.

The knowing look on his face causes my cheeks to heat.

"Pretty good, huh?" he asks.

Before I must respond, Tabitha slides up to the table next to Gavin.

"Hey, cutie," she says to him, snapping a piece of gum. "What can I get ya?"

"Don't you look pretty today, Miss Tab," he says.

"You're such a flirt, Mr. Marshall."

He grins. "It's impossible not to flirt with someone as beautiful as you."

She swats him with her order pad. "What do you want? Anything?"

"Nah, I'm just here to harass Megan." He looks at me and winks. "Did you order already?"

I nod.

"Well, all right," Tabitha says. "I'll have your food out in a few, Megan."

"Thanks," I say.

Once we're alone, Gavin leans forward and laces his fingers on the table.

"What?" I ask.

"What, *what?*"

"What's that little smirk about?"

It grows deeper. "Oh, nothing."

"Dammit, Gavin."

He laughs. "You and Chase are two peas in a pod."

Tabitha returns with my grilled cheese and fries. She places the plate and a fresh Sprite in front of me before jetting off to help a large table of hunters who came in.

My bracelets jingle against the tabletop as I reach for my drink.

"My job as Chase's brother and your new best friend," he says, "is to ensure you're both ... you know ..." He searches for the right word. "I'm here to *facilitate* things."

"Do I look like I need a facilitator?"

He slowly blinks. "Yes."

I put my straw in the new glass and take a quick sip. *Ignoring his implications.*

"What have you been up to?" I ask, refocusing the conversation on Gavin.

The sly smile he gives me makes it clear he knows what I'm doing but is willing to play along.

"I've been working," he says.

"Looks like it."

He laughs. "I work here at night part-time—mostly because I like it, and if I have too much time on my hands, trouble seems to find me."

"I believe that."

My sandwich is buttery and cheesy—grilled cheese perfection. The first bite leaves a trail of oil down my chin.

"During the day," Gavin says as I dab a napkin to my face, "I work at Cotton's."

I put the napkin on the table. "I have heard about Cotton's many times this week, and I have no idea who the guy is."

"He's a farmer," he says. "He owns half of this county. His farm isn't far from where you broke down last weekend."

"What do you do for him?"

"A little of everything. Tend to the animals. Work on equipment. Bale hay. Seed, fertilize, harvest. You know—farm work shit."

"Sounds like you're a real Renaissance Man."

He leans back in his chair and nods. "That's me. Jack-of-all-trades."

I take another bite. *Oh my heavens. This is delicious.*

Gavin studies me for a long time. If he's waiting on my cue, he'll have to wait until the cows come home because I'm not leading this conversation. Not when I think he wants it to go in a particular direction I'm trying to avoid.

"Do you know what's funny?" he asks finally.

"What's that?"

"Here we are, best friends and all, and I don't know anything about you."

"That is funny."

He narrows his eyes, making me laugh.

I take another drink and settle in. "Fine. What do you want to know?"

"What do you want to tell me?"

"Nothing."

He laughs. "Wrong answer."

"Gavin, really—what do you want to know? My birthday? Favorite color? Favorite Paula Abdul song?"

He sits up like we're about to square off. "Birthday?"

"July twenty-eighth."

"Color?"

"Vermilion."

"Fancy," he says.

"It's color perfection."

He nods. "Noted. Paula Abdul song?"

"I'd say 'Straight Up,' but the video for 'Opposites Attract' is perfection," I smirk. "You have no idea who Paula Abdul is, do you?"

"I'll YouTube it later."

"Cool."

We stare at one another like we can't decide if we're friends or enemies. Our eyes are narrowed, brows furrowed. It stays that way until the corners of Gavin's lips begin to pull to the ceiling. They bring mine up along with them.

"Your turn," I say. "Birthday, color, and ... Aerosmith song."

"February first, cerulean, and 'Cryin'' is the best Aerosmith song of all time."

I make a face. "Wrong answer."

"How can it be wrong? They're *my* favorites."

"Everyone knows that Aerosmith's best song is 'Rag Doll.' Maybe I'll agree with 'Dream On'—*maybe*. But it's not 'Cryin'' in any way, shape, or form."

He grins. "Have you seen Alicia Silverstone in that video? I rest my case."

Together, we laugh.

Gavin stretches his legs out, much like Chase does when he's itching to get up after dinner but is polite while Kennedy and I chat.

"Do you need to go?" I ask.

"No. Why?"

I shrug.

"I saw Patti this morning," Gavin says. "We were getting gas at the same time. She asked me for your number, and I told her that I didn't have it. She thought I was lying."

"Why would you be lying?"

"Well, you know," he says cockily. "I usually end up with women's numbers."

I scoff.

"You think I'm kidding?" he asks. "I don't know who ninety percent of the people are in my phone."

I believe that wholeheartedly.

"You don't have mine," I say. "That says something."

"I don't have yours because you're … *you.*"

"What does that mean?" I ask, trying not to be offended.

"You're *my friend.* I'm not trying to hook up with you."

"Should I take that personally? According to your brother, you try to hook up with everyone."

He chuckles. "Well, according to my brother, I'm not allowed to try to hook up with you."

Gavin holds my gaze, letting that sink in.

Chase has banned Gavin from trying to hook up with me? What the fuck?

"Not that I want to hook up with you," I say, making that clear. "But why does Chase give a shit about who I hook up with?"

Gavin gasps. "You wouldn't hook up with me?"

"*Gavin.*"

"What's wrong with me?" He looks hurt. "And don't say I'm not your type because I'm everyone's type."

I burst out laughing.

"You're killing me here, Megs."

"If we were in another time and place, I'd totally consider you doable," I say. "You're cute."

"*Cute?* Kill me now."

I continue to laugh. "Stop it, Gav."

Tucker walks by the table. "I think you're cute, Gavin."

"Fuck off, Tucker."

He walks away, his belly bouncing as he chuckles.

"Fine." He sits up and straightens his shirt. "I'm still offended, but I'll let it slide."

"Thanks. Now, why does Chase care?"

Gavin's antics stop, and a coyness creeps across his features. I'm not sure if that's better or worse for me.

My heart beats faster the longer Gavin goes without talking. He becomes more smug. More arrogant. More entertained by this line of conversation. And while that worries me, I can't back out now because *I want to know the answer.*

I'm well aware that Chase is attracted to me. He's outright admitted it. But he's also been clear that it doesn't matter and has maintained a distance between us like it's his job. Ensuring that nothing happens between us.

If that's the case, why would it bother him if I hooked up with his brother?

"You know, I like the power I wield in this chat," Gavin says.

I wad up a napkin and throw it at him. He catches it quickly and laughs. Then he tosses it on the table.

"Let me ask you a question," he says. "How is a girl like you even available in the first place, anyway?"

"Oh, there are many reasons."

"Such as ..."

I mirror his posture and rest back in my chair too. "Well, the last guy I dated continued to use the dating app I met him on well after we were supposed to be exclusive."

"Yeah, I'm not into dating apps. It feels like you're auditioning for a role. Like, '*Hi, here are my stats. Am I good enough to fuck, date, or marry?*'" He snorts. "I don't need that kind of pressure."

"Same."

"What about the guy before that?" he asks.

I sigh. "Let's see. The guy before that worked all the time. I don't mean long hours. I mean, seven days a week, twenty-four hours a day. If he wasn't at the office, he was thinking about being at the office. And the guy before that was a jealous bastard. That didn't last long."

A parade of the men I've dated marches through my head.

Each of them leaves a bad taste in my mouth, and I can't remember being in a relationship with any of them where I felt comfortable. None of them felt like they were made for me.

Which is probably why I dated them.

"I have this nasty habit," I say.

"Like what? You're scaring me."

I giggle. "Not like that. I just have this habit of choosing to date men I know are bad for me." I try to find an example to help him understand. "Okay. There was this guy named Peter. In retrospect, he probably could've been a decent match. He had a good job, was sweet, and loved what I did for a living. And I refused to date him."

"*Why?*"

"It's a character flaw of mine," I say. "If something has long-term potential, I run like the wind."

"You make absolutely no sense, my friend."

I take another drink. "Oh, I know."

"What is your reasoning? What makes you the way you are?"

I cross my arms over my chest and exhale.

Why am I the way that I am? What a damn question.

My mouth goes dry. *What is it with these Marshall men and their ridiculous questions?*

"Is it one of those self-loathing things?" he asks.

"No, not really," I say slowly. "It's more of a … it's more of an unsettledness in my soul, if that makes any sense."

His forehead wrinkles. "So you want to be secure before you build a relationship? You want the job and house and to do all of that on your own first? Is that what it is?"

I sigh. "Not really. It's hard to explain."

"They say if you can't explain it to a child, then you don't understand it yourself."

"That might very well be true."

He grins. "No, it's not. Tell me."

"*Gavin …*"

I groan, trying desperately not to get sucked into the vortex surrounding him—the whirlpool that strips you of your defenses and makes you vulnerable to his charm. *Dammit.*

Like I have no choice—because I don't—I find myself trying to make him understand.

"I don't want to commit," I say. "I don't want to put myself out there."

"Fair. But why?"

"I don't know." My skin suddenly feels too tight. The room is too small. I tug on the bottom of my shirt to get more air against my body. "I guess it's that when I commit, or anyone commits, for that matter, you're trusting them not to hurt you."

My words fall between us. I don't know what Gavin assumed I was going to say. But I don't think this is it.

His playfulness melts away, and soberness replaces it.

These Marshall men are damn good men.

When I first met Chase and Gavin, I thought they were opposites. Chase was a grumpy cat. Gavin was a goofball. But now that I've spent more time with them, I see them more clearly. Sure, they're still broody and carefree, respectively, but they both carry a heavy sense of responsibility. Kindness. They may wear it differently, but they wear it—impressively—nonetheless.

My throat is raw, as if the words scratched the thin lining of my esophagus. My body tingles like it's suspended in time, and I'm waiting for something to break me out of the spell.

"I've never believed that anyone wouldn't hurt me," I say, my voice falling away.

His jaw clenches shut. "Has someone hurt you?"

"No, not like that," I say, grinning softly, touched by his concern. "I've just not had many reasons to believe that the love you read about in books is real. And if it's not, I'd rather save myself the time and energy." *And heartache when they cast me aside.*

Tabitha places my bill on the table. "Do you need anything else?"

"I'm good. Thank you," I say.

Gavin whisks the bill off the table and hands it back to the server. "Put it on my tab, please, Tab."

"No. I'll pay. Please."

Gavin gives me a look like Chase—the one I know not to bother arguing against.

"Thank you," I say.

"Yeah, well, I owed you one. I promised I'd buy your dinner after you went to Chase's if it went bad, but he raced up here and got it before I could."

I grin. "It's not a competition."

"Oh, I know."

He stands and waits for me to get to my feet too. I grab a final drink of Sprite, leave a tip, and follow him outside.

"What are you doing today?" I ask him.

"Going back to work. You?"

I glance at my phone to check the time. "I'm heading to the school to pick up Kennedy in a little bit."

"All right. Have fun. Tell my niece I said hi."

"Will do."

I turn toward the parking lot when Gavin calls out.

"Hey, Meg."

Looking over my shoulder, I pause. "Yeah?"

"Do you know why it's not a competition?"

"Why?"

He smiles. "Because Chase has already won."

"Hardly," I say, chuckling.

"You asked me why Chase wouldn't want me asking you out. It's because he's trying to figure out how he feels about you— just like you're doing the same with him."

"Again, hardly."

He shrugs.

"Didn't you hear a word I said?" I ask, laughing. "I'm trying not to set myself up for failure anymore. I'm trying to outgrow that specific behavior."

He walks backward toward his truck, his hair bouncing with every step. "Suit yourself."

"Goodbye, Gav."

I head to my car, leaving him behind me.

If only his words would stay back there too.

CHAPTER 18

$\mathcal{M}$egan

I HIT THE SPEAKERPHONE BUTTON. "HELLO?"

"Hi, Megan. It's Dorothy from Iyala. How are you?"

I stare at the screen. Sure enough, the number printed in white is one of the Iyala Nails office numbers. *What in the world do they want?*

Sure, the company and I parted ways without bad blood. They gave me a glowing reference as a going-away present, and I know they were disappointed to let me go. I was disappointed to be let go but also relieved to get out of the city in a strange way. Nevertheless, it was clear that there was no room for me at Iyala. *So why is she calling now?*

"Hey, Dorothy," I say, looking through the window over the sink. The sky darkens over the treetops. "How have you been?"

"Honestly, I'm a mess over here." She chuckles. "We just finished an audit, and you know how stressful those are."

"Yeah. I don't miss that."

She sighs. "I was hoping that maybe you did."

Huh?

I spin around and rest my back against the sink for support. Surely, I misheard her.

My brain kicks into overdrive, working hard to make some sense of the vice president of operation's sentence. *"I was hoping that maybe you did."*

What does that mean?

"Our summer line didn't hit our goal," Dorothy says. "To be honest, it didn't come close."

My spirits sink. I can imagine how the team felt when they got the final season reports. We always knew when they were coming in and would practically make ourselves sick for the couple of weeks leading up to it. The report numbers affect everything—how the next budget is divided, who gets bonuses, and who does not. And, in my case, who gets fired.

Despite having been let go from the company, my heart still hurts for them. I understand why I was let go. At the end of the day, it felt right for me anyway. But I can't help but be bummed for my former colleagues.

"I'm so sorry, Dorothy. I know that's extremely hard."

"Yes, it is. And we're looking for ways to make up the difference in the spring campaign. Unfortunately, it's already too late for winter."

"What's the winter theme?"

"Frost." She pauses, letting that sink in. *"We went with Frost."*

"That's …"

"It's uninspired, that's what it is. It's basic and unoriginal."

The oven timer beeps. I shut it off and remove a sheet of cookies. "I can't disagree. We ruled out Frost as a concept nearly every year. Why did you choose to go that direction now?"

"Oh, I don't know anymore. Our creative team struggles to fine inspiration. They have virtually no ear to the ground, so to speak. They're flat and one-dimensional. I don't know if you saw the marketing materials for winter, but they were absolutely boring, Megan."

I jump at a sound behind me. Chase walks through the door holding two pizzas. He gives me a sideways smile that makes my knees weak.

"Dorothy, can I put you on hold for a moment, please?"

"Of course."

I tap the mute button.

"I didn't know you were on the phone," Chase says, putting the pizzas on the table.

"It's fine. My old job is calling me to tell me how much they miss me, I think."

Chase's eyes darken.

"Did you pick up Kennedy?" My chest tightens. "She's still at Neve's. She told me you would get her on the way home."

"I did tell her that," he says, running a hand over his head. "But I forgot it was Neve's birthday today, and she's having a few girls stay the night. I already told Kennedy she could stay."

My brows shoot to the ceiling. *You mean, we're alone?*

He holds my gaze so long that I shiver.

"I'm going to grab a shower," he says. "And whatever you just baked smells great."

"Cookies."

He grins and walks to the mudroom. The lock clicks in place.

A breath of air rushes from my lungs as I hit the mute button again. "I'm sorry, Dorothy. I'm back."

"I won't take up much more of your time. But I'm calling to gauge your interest in coming back to us."

I still.

"This is probably the moment that I admit we were wrong to let you go," she says. "You have a knack for this industry that is dreadfully missing from our team, and we need you, Megan. We need you desperately."

What?

"Well," I say carefully, "I'll admit I wasn't expecting this. And I have a lot of questions and … wow. This is just very unexpected."

"I understand. How about this—would you like to email me a list of questions so you can sit down and pull your thoughts together?"

I nod. "Yes. That would be helpful."

"You have my contact information, and I look forward to hearing from you."

"Sounds like a plan."

"Oh, and Megan?"

"Yes?"

"I'm serious. If you have competing offers or have taken another position, I'll match salaries. I need you."

I slow blink, blindsided by her admission. "Okay. I'll email you next week."

"Have a good weekend," she says.

"You, too. Goodbye."

"Goodbye."

I end the call and stand frozen in place. "What just happened?"

The door swings open, and Chase walks in clad in a pair of gray sweatpants sans shirt. If I didn't know better, I'd say he knows exactly what he's doing.

I turn away before I drool and take out two plates, glasses, and a Sprite. I hold up a beer, offering it to Chase. He nods and picks up the pizzas.

"You know," I say, following him into the living room. "I thought we said no lingerie."

He puts the pizzas on the ottoman. "Huh. I don't remember that one. Why? Do you want to break out something sexy tonight?"

"Uh, no. Maybe I lumped it in with no cleavage."

He looks at his chest. "Yeah, well, I don't have any of that, so I'm good."

"Gray sweatpants are men's lingerie. Everyone knows that."

He snorts, opening the boxes. "Who made up that bullshit?"

"Not me, but I concur."

Slowly, he stands and runs a hand down his abs. He smirks. "Want me to change?"

"I do not." I put a slice of pizza on my plate, not looking at Chase, and then sit at one end of the couch. "Fridays are pizza and movies. Is that right?"

He chuckles. "Yeah. That's right."

"We don't have to do this, you know. I can go to my room and hang out—give you some space. Or I can even take your mom's car and—"

"Respectfully, hush." He grins. "You're not going anywhere. Eat your pizza and relax."

"Yes, sir."

He rolls his tongue around his mouth but doesn't say anything.

After grabbing a couple of pieces of pizza and his beer, he sits on the other side of the sofa. He hands me the remote, giving me a look not to argue with him, then gets comfortable.

I have no idea what to watch. So instead, I decide to talk.

"Guess who I had lunch with today?" I say before taking a bite.

"Who?"

"Gavin."

Unamused Chase is amusing.

"I was at The Wet Whistle before I was supposed to get Kennedy at school—"

"Yeah, I'm sorry for not telling you she was going home with Neve. It slipped my mind."

I shrug. "It's fine. No harm, no foul."

He grimaces and goes back to his dinner.

"Anyway, I was eating," I say, "and Gavin walks in. We had an interesting little chat."

"What about?"

I grin. "Gavin stuff."

He scoffs. "That sounds like a headache to me." He takes another bite. "Did Luke come by today?"

"Not while I was here. You know, I've yet to meet the infamous Luke."

"You're not missing much."

"I don't know. You and Gavin are two-for-two on the interesting level." I open my can of Sprite. "Apparently, I'm interesting too, though, because my former boss, Dorothy, just offered me my job back."

"*Oh?*" He chews slower. "You gonna take it?"

I sigh, falling back against the pillows. "Honestly? I don't know."

"Did you like working there?"

"Well, that's tricky. On the one hand, I loved it. I got to travel all over the world and attend events and meet all kinds of people. But, on the other hand … no. I didn't. Not really—not thoroughly."

Chase places his beer on the end table. The sound of the can hitting the wood dings through the room.

The light overhead is dim—something I haven't noticed about the living room until now. The room is pretty dark without the television's light, the sun's rays from the window, or the lamp by the fireplace.

"What was the worst part of the job?" he asks.

"Well, I guess it was just the loneliness of being on the West Coast alone. Mom won't leave Dallas—which is ridiculous on so many levels. But I get it. Her life is there; she shouldn't have to uproot all that for me."

Although, I wish she would.

"But you liked California?" he asks.

"It was lovely. I don't think it's for me, per se. So many people. So much garbage. Never a dark sky or a quiet evening—two things I didn't know I loved until I came here."

We exchange a grin.

"So what did you love about your job?" he asks before taking another bite.

I set my plate on a box and then curl my feet up under me.

"My favorite thing was the traveling," I say. "I saw so many incredible places—Morocco, Greece, Peru. Iceland was amazing. Maine and New Hampshire and Vermont in the fall were stunning."

"Is that something you still want to do?"

I laugh. "Strangely enough, *no*. It's odd because it was my favorite part, but I'm … tired, I guess. There's nothing left that I'm chomping at the bit to see and so much else that I'd rather do."

"Like what?"

"Fuck if I know. I just know that I feel like I've completed that part of my life. So another part has to be open, right?"

He grins before wincing. He rolls his shoulder around, holding it with his other hand.

"What's wrong?" I ask.

"I whacked my shoulder off a bucket last week."

"Did you go to the doctor?"

"No, I didn't go to the doctor," he says like it's a harebrained idea. "They'll just tell me to take an over-the-counter pain reliever or an anti-inflammatory. I don't need to pay a fifty-dollar co-pay for that."

"So you sit and suffer. Got it. So smart."

He gives me a look while continuing to move it in circles.

I start to offer to rub it but stop short of speaking.

If I get my hands on that man …

My stomach clenches. *Hard.*

It's suddenly darker in the room. Quieter. The air is thicker

—hotter. I watch the way he cups his shoulder with his hand and wonder, not for the first time, what it would feel like on me.

Fingertips pressing against my skin. The heat of his body radiating into mine. The coarseness of his palm biting against me.

He winces again—this time, closing his eyes and exhaling harshly.

I shift in my seat, trying to ignore the way heat builds in my core. I try desperately not to imagine his face twisted—eyes closed, breathing roughly—as he climaxes.

It's been a while since you got laid. Relax, Megan.

"Fuck," he says again before resting his head against the front of the couch. Pain is written all over his face. He sets his plate down beside mine.

You can control yourself. He's not willing to do anything with you anyway, so what could it hurt to offer to help him?

I tingle all over at the prospect of having Chase Marshall in my hands—of finally getting to touch him, even if it's innocent. And it would have to be innocent. I promised I would respect his boundaries.

"Let me help you," I say.

His eyes pop open, but he doesn't move. I can do this. I can help him and help myself at the same time. Like I said earlier—no harm, no foul.

"Sit up," I say, getting to my feet. I swallow hard. I'm committed now. The ball is in his court.

"What are you doing?"

"Let me help you feel better."

He chuckles, the sound low and rough. It strums a taut chord in my belly that I try to ignore.

"I took a massage class in India," I say, not mentioning that it was one-half hour of instruction five years ago. *I remember virtually nothing.* "There's no reason to sit in pain when I might be able to assist."

Good. That sounded virtuous. He doesn't need to know I'm so wet that I can feel it on my thighs.

"Having your hands on me feels like I'm asking for trouble," he says.

"What are you saying? That you can't control yourself?"

His eyes hood as he watches me stop in front of him. Slowly, he drops his hand, giving me the okay to touch him.

"I can control *myself*." Much better than I knew I could. "Besides, I'm an employee doing my job."

"How's that?"

"I'm here to make sure that Kennedy is taken care of," I say. "And what happens if you can't go to work next week and then can't afford food? I would've failed at my job."

He chuckles.

"Sit on the floor," I say. "Let me sit on the couch behind you."

Chase does as he's asked. My breathing is ragged as I sit, placing one leg on either side of him. I block out the proximity of his head to my sex. *Don't go there, Megan.*

He leans his head to the side, offering me access to the area that hurts. It's slightly swollen.

"You should probably see a doctor," I say.

"I'll take another anti-inflammatory. It'll be all right."

Holding my breath, I reach for him. Blood races through my veins as I drape my hands over his shoulders. I slide my hands all the way down until my thumbs rest on the top of his trapezius muscles.

Holy shit.

The contact causes an explosion inside my body that settles in the apex of my thighs. My brain screams that this is a very bad idea. *What am I doing?* But my body doesn't stop touching his.

He sucks in a breath, and his head tilts back as if he's absorbing the same hit of adrenaline as I am. It gives me a full view from his Adam's apple to his lap. I'm convinced he was crafted by God, and God knew this would punish me someday.

Because I can't *really* touch him.

I draw his muscles upward with gentle pressure, hoping my hands aren't shaking. Pressing the tips of my fingers into his shoulders, I squeeze and lift the muscle toward his collarbone. I find a rhythm, scaling the length of his shoulders. Kneading and pulsing against his skin, I focus on the areas that seem to get the most response.

"Damn, Megan," he hisses. "That feels fucking good."

"You're tight. No wonder it hurts."

"Right there." He groans, moving his neck around as I work on him. "Maybe now I can sleep tonight."

I ease the pressure. My palms skim across him and take in the dips and ridges of his muscular body. I allow my fingertips to drift from the side of his neck and down his shoulder, breaking contact just before his triceps.

My mouth goes dry, and my chest constricts. Having him in my hands makes it terribly hard to remember where the line is drawn. Or if there is a line because the longer I touch him, the more uncertain I become.

I want him. I want him so freaking bad that it hurts.

My sex throbs, begging for contact—*for relief.* I need to be *touched.* I need to rid myself of the swell of lust that's been building since I saw him climb out of his truck almost a week ago.

Chase leans back and rests his head against the couch. The sides of his head press into my inner thighs moments before he tilts his chin. He looks up at me.

His eyes are filled with the same feeling, the same desire—*the same need* filling me. It's raw and unfiltered. It's *hot.*

I force a swallow and stare down at him, my hands resting on the top of his chest.

He doesn't say anything. Still, he manages to ask me a question—the one I want him to ask, but the one he shouldn't. *Do you want to take this further?*

I'm torn. I want to say yes. I want to lose myself in him for as long as it takes to get this merciless need out of my system. But I know why we agreed not to. *I need to make sure that he's thought this through …*

My breathing grows ragged. "There are a hundred reasons we shouldn't."

"No. There's only one."

Right. "Well, that one reason is bigger than a hundred others could be."

My heart slams against my ribs, and I wonder if he can hear the raucous. I wonder if he can hear the rush of my blood or the way my lungs fill and release quicker than usual. *Can he feel the heat of my body?*

"I knew this is how we would end up," he says, his long lashes blinking.

"How's that?"

"With me fighting myself about you."

I force a swallow, knowing he's right. This was his concern, and it was obviously justified. I don't want to look like I'm pressuring him or trying to wiggle my way into getting what I want.

But as I shift my weight, his head wiggles against my thighs, and I think I might die.

"We agreed not to go there," I say, forcing the words to come out of my mouth. "Yes, I initiated this tonight, and maybe I overestimated my ability to touch you and walk away. But I can't let you forget why this is a bad idea."

He turns his head to the side. The friction is enough to make me want to whimper.

I need a release. For heaven's sake, *I need relief.*

My brain scrambles to think of a way out of this so I can get to my room and end my misery. My vibrator isn't what I want, but it'll suffice.

"Well, here's the thing—I'm distracted anyway. Whether we get up and walk away or not, I'm going to think about fucking you every minute you're here. I can't get around that."

I hold my breath.

He grins. "So what good is it really doing to stay away from you? You're here. The damage is already done."

"*Hey*," I say, slapping his chest with my right hand.

Before I can do anything, his hand covers my wrist. He attempts to pull me around him—to guide me to his lap. But the movement causes his shoulder to tense, and he yelps in pain.

"Clearly, you need me back here," I say, testing the waters. "Maybe that's a sign."

He pivots around, grabs me by the waist, and moves me until I'm astride him.

"Clearly," he says as my sex moves against his rock-hard cock, "I need you right fucking here."

I gasp, my body on high alert. I can't think clearly—I don't want to think clearly. I want to give in and let him have his way with me.

But, unfortunately, I'm a responsible woman.

"You better think this through," I say, circling my hips. "We had an agreement for a reason."

But please throw it away. *Please. Throw. It. Away.*

I move harder against him, realizing it's not helping my attempt to give him time to think. But also not caring enough to stop.

I'm soaked, my body dampening my jeans. He sinks his hands into my hips and presses me down harder against him. *Oh shit.*

I bite back a moan, the denim's resistance against my flesh better than nothing.

"Change in the agreement?" he asks.

"What do you propose?"

He smirks, his fingers dipping under my shirt and pressing

so hard into my skin that it nearly burns. "We satiate this *thing* between us."

"And you think that will help things how?" I ask, struggling to keep a clear mind. "Because I'm pretty sure we agreed when we weren't alone, and I wasn't on your lap, not knowing how the other person tastes is our best route to success."

"Respectfully, I think we were wrong." He leans so close that his mouth almost touches mine. The heat of his breath takes mine away. "Because how you taste is all I can fucking think about."

I whimper as I sag into him. It takes everything I have not to grab his face and drag his mouth onto mine. But I don't. Because somewhere in my almost thirty years of life, I've gathered some form of self-control.

Who knew?

"I leave in three weeks," I say. "I guess giving in once can't hurt."

"Oh, sweetheart. If I give in once, there's no way I'll be able to keep my mouth off you."

"Except when Kennedy is around?" I ask, almost panting.

He nods, lifting his hips against me. *Easy, Chase, or I might come from this.*

"Then I have one question, Mr. Marshall."

"What's that?"

"Why aren't you on me already?" I ask with more confidence than I possess.

He bucks against me harder. *Ooh.*

"Ask me nicely." He smirks. "I need to know exactly what you want."

I lift on my knees so I'm kneeling over his lap. Holding his face in my hands, I grin. "Fuck me, Chase."

His smile is sinful. "My pleasure."

CHAPTER 19

egan

"It better be my pleasure, too," I say moments before his mouth crashes on top of mine.

I moan against his lips. He smiles against mine.

One hand goes to the back of my head, holding me against him. The other slides under my ass and rocks me back and forth over his dick.

A flurry of explosions rips through me, and I feel like I might actually combust.

His kisses aren't frenzied. They're slow. *Deliberate.* Each swipe of his tongue, every press of his lips, is intentional. It's as if we have all night.

Because we do.

My fingers wind through his hair. My nails dig roughly along his scalp. He sucks in a hasty breath but then kisses me harder.

His hand cups my jaw, holding me to him when I try to

pull back. His eyes open, staring into mine with an intensity that I feel pooling inside me until he gets his fill from my mouth.

Finally, he nips my bottom lip and lets me go.

I pull my head back, desperate for a breath of air. He kisses across my jawline and down my neck.

"We're really doing this?" I ask, grinding my pussy against him. He lifts his hips, and I grind harder.

The contact is a double-edged sword—giving me the promise of the relief to come but keeping it out of reach.

"We're doing this," he says as his hands go to my chest, "until you tell me to stop."

"For the love of everything—*don't fucking stop.*"

He chuckles, dragging my shirt over my head with a flourish. His eyes sparkle with dark mischief. "Don't worry. I have no intention of stopping anytime soon, sweetheart."

"Chase Marshall, for the first time since we met, I can't argue with you."

His smile grows wider as he pulls me into his chest. He works quickly to unfasten my bra. When I lean back, his eyes are glued to my darkened nipples pointing through the white lace fabric. Slowly, I shimmy the straps down my arms and let the material fall between us on our laps.

The cool air licks at my exposed skin. It's a stark contrast from the heat building in my core, and the juxtaposition makes me shiver.

Chase palms my breasts and then rolls my nipples in his fingers. Each flick of a thumb against the sensitive flesh sends another wave of need between my legs.

He lowers his head, gaze holding mine, and sucks one sensitive bud into his mouth. My head falls back, my hair dusting my shoulders, as I moan his name into the night.

"*Chase,*" I say, gasping as the tip of his tongue swirls around my nipple.

He chuckles against me. The vibrations reverberate in every inch of my overwhelmed body.

"You're being awfully quiet," he says, nipping my other breast. "You usually won't shut up, and now you only know my name."

"Are you complaining?"

"Strangely, I might be."

"Oh, do you like me now?"

He grins. "I'm beginning to like your mouth more and more."

I hold his face in my hands and kiss him. This time, I'm in control. I explore his mouth with my tongue and nibble on his lip. I suck his tongue and make him react by digging his hands into my hips.

I slide off him and get to my feet. His eyes go wide as I urge him to stand. He complies without a fight, although he's obviously confused by my abrupt change in plans. Once he's standing, I slowly slide my fingers into the waistband of his sweatpants and push the fabric down his legs. His confusion abruptly switches to all-out desire.

Holy fucking hell.

He palms his thick cock and sits on the edge of the couch. A bead of pre-cum already dots the top. "Get on your knees."

"Yes, sir."

His roguish and wicked smile is nearly enough to make me orgasm.

I take his length in my hand, wrapping my fingers around it one by one. Holding his gaze, I drag my tongue roughly across the top, taking the dots of pre-cum away with it.

"Good girl," he says.

Good girl? I laugh, flicking my tongue against the underside of his cock. "Do you want to be a good boy and come in my mouth?"

"Keep talking like that, and I'll flip you over and come in your pussy right fucking now."

"That would be a tragedy." I wink, hoping I appear more in control than I really am. Internally, my muscles clench. Temperature soars. I'm trembling—my body screaming for him to touch me. "I haven't even gotten to suck you yet."

"Megan—*fuck*," he hisses.

I sink my mouth over his cock, wrapping my lips around the velvety shaft as I slide back up. A rush of air escapes his lips as I swirl my tongue around the tip.

"Yes," I say, sucking my way down the side of his cock. "We're going to fuck. Later."

Licking back up to the head, I watch his eyes burn. *It's so fucking sexy*.

I sit taller. Wrapping one hand around his shaft, the other cupping his balls, I take him down my throat and back up again.

His hips flex, and his Adam's apple bobs as he tries to contain himself. He reaches between us and squeezes one of my breasts, playing with the nipple as I find a rhythm.

"That feels so good that I could just lose it right now," he says through clenched teeth.

Seeing him on the precipice of losing control because of me is one of the most powerful moments of my life.

I hum. The rumble makes him moan.

My panties are soaked. Wetness coats my thighs, and the denim of my jeans sticks to my skin. I clench my legs together, hoping for relief.

Relief that doesn't come.

The need only gets worse.

I swirl the head again before taking him deep down my throat.

"Stop if you don't want me to come in your mouth," he warns.

His balls swell. The base of his cock shakes, and his thighs tense.

"Megan ..."

My eyes water as I continue the pace, not about to stop without tasting him.

He thrusts into my mouth, his hands digging into my hair and holding my head in place. A shot of cum finds the back of my throat. Another hits the roof of my mouth. By the third splash of cum, I'm swallowing as fast as he's emptying himself into me.

"Motherfucker ..." He moans, his hips off the couch and the back of his head buried into the sofa. *"Motherfucking hell, Megan."*

Finally, he collapses. His fists ease in my hair, and I can pull back. Then, after a final lick across the head of his cock—to which he trembles—I rock back on my heels and wipe my mouth with the back of my hand.

Tears run down my face from the experience. But my sense of satisfaction outweighs any discomfort.

I made him come. He came like that for me.

He pants, chuckling in disbelief. "That was the best blow job I've ever had."

"Really?"

He laughs and sits up. "I've been lying in bed every night this week, thinking about fucking you. Hell, if I'd known you could suck a cock like that, I'd have been dreaming about that."

"I aim to please."

"Your turn."

"What?" I ask, my sex quivering.

His gaze is dark. "I believe I promised to return the favor."

Of course, he did. Of course, I want him to. *I need him to.* But I'm afraid I'll fall apart as soon as he touches me.

Chase stands, careful not to bump me, and pulls his pants up. I memorize every line in his body, every ripple of muscle, before it's hidden.

He reaches for me. His fingers nab the belt loops, and he yanks me toward him. My button is freed. Zipper dragged down in one quick motion. The fabric over my ass and to the floor before I can gather my thoughts.

He grabs the pizza boxes and tosses them on the floor.

"Hey, that's perfectly good pizza," I say.

"And it's fine. It's in a box." He steps back and takes me in like a fine piece of art. "My lord, you're beautiful."

The compliment makes me self-conscious. I cross my arms over my stomach—or try to. Instead, he grabs each wrist and pulls my arms back.

"Don't hide from me," he says. "Why would you do that?"

I shrug.

He drops my arms but gives me a warning look not to move. Then he makes a show out of looking at me inch by torturous inch.

"Smooth skin," he says. "Big, heavy tits. Curved hips. Nice, round ass. Thick thighs."

I half laugh. "Careful with your adjectives, buddy."

He lifts a brow. "Megan, your body is a fucking wonderland. Look at what it does to me." He nods toward his groin, and I see him getting hard again.

Wow.

"When I look at you, I want to mark you all over," he says. "Suck those big titties. Grip those hips. Smack that ass. Get between those fucking thighs."

Oh. My.

"Lie on the ottoman," he says, the tone no-nonsense.

I walk backward until the backs of my knees hit the edge of the furniture. Then I sit.

"Lie. Down," he says.

I scoot on my behind until I can lie flat.

He growls. "Knees up and spread your legs."

My chest pulls tight.

"Now," he says.

I pull my knees up and then let my legs fall to the sides.

"Thatta girl," he says, dropping to his knees.

He grabs my waist and pulls me closer to the edge. When I look down, his face is framed by my knees.

"Let's see if you're ready." He smirks as he drags a finger through my slit. I shake, and my legs tremble at the simplest of touches. "I'd say you're wet enough."

"You think?"

He pops his finger in his mouth, sucking off my juices, and then pulls it out.

"I'm going to need more than that." My clit throbs with each heartbeat. "I didn't torture you."

He settles in, his mouth hovering over my soaked opening. "I'm not going to torture you either."

One hand goes on each thigh, and he spreads me wider. The air hitting my wetness, his hands on my skin, and his breath against my pulsing mound are almost too much.

And when his face buries against my swollen flesh, *it is too much.*

"Chase!"

I buck against him as he licks and sucks, lapping my desire like he's dying for it. One hand holds my hips in place. The other presses circles and applies pressure to my nub.

"Oh my gosh. *Chase,*" I almost scream.

The words come out wobbly. It's hard to scream when your teeth are grinding together. I can't open my eyes. I can't think. I can't do anything *but feel the buildup.*

"I. Can't. Do. This," I say, the words bouncing like I'm on a gravel road.

The sensation is too much. The touches are too intense. The flicking of my overstimulated clit so much that it almost feels like it's zapped with electricity.

I dig my fingers into his scalp as deeply as his fingers are buried in my hips. He slides a finger, then two, then three into my body and pumps them over and over again.

His tongue flattens against my clit, and I grind my body against his face.

It's just too good. The rise is too fast. The pressure building is too much.

He pulls his face away at the same time that he twists his hand and then pulls his fingers out of me.

The ride to the top of my orgasm hits its peak. I moan, unable to hold my legs up anymore as I hand all control over to my climax.

I'm no longer in control.

"I can't," I cry out, bracing for the moment when the rush hits.

"Yes, you can. Come for me, baby. Let me watch your pussy come for me."

He presses a kiss to my clit, and that does it. Then coupled with the vigor of his fingers working their magic, I fall wildly apart.

The pressure building in my core breaks.

A stream of wetness rolls down my inner thigh, and a deep, *deep* sense of letting go overtakes me. The level of satisfaction, of pleasure, crashing over me is unmatched.

I've never felt anything like this before.

Everywhere tingles. The tension in my body dissipates. It's as if a button has been pushed, and my stress has been reset to zero.

It. Is. Fabulous.

"Chase," I say, struggling but managing to prop myself up on my elbows to look at him. "That was …" I gasp a breath. *"Incredible."*

He looks … surprised. "Do you always squirt?"

"Huh?"

"You just squirted."

I scramble off the ottoman and look at where I was lying. *It's soaked.*

My cheeks heat. "I … I'm so embarrassed."

He laughs and looks at me like I'm talking out of my head. "Embarrassed? Megan, that is the hottest thing I've ever seen."

I just look at him. *I can do that?*

Before I have time to wrap my brain around what just happened or get my legs sturdy beneath me, Chase takes my hand.

"Let's go," he says.

"Let's go? Where? Where are we going?" I look over my shoulder as we walk out of the room. "My clothes. The ottoman. *The pizza …*"

He tugs me toward the hallway. "We'll clean up down here later."

"But where are we going?"

"Condoms are in my room."

Condoms?

He stops at the base of the stairs and turns to face me. His eyes are lit up—almost as bright as his smile.

"I warned you that I would want you all the time," he says.

"So you still want me after you just saw that?"

He pulls me into him and looks down into my eyes. "I think I just opened a hell of a box of problems because I want you more right now than I've ever wanted you. And I've not slept since you got here."

I flush. "Oh. Well, okay, then."

"Will you let me inside you tonight?"

I run my fingertip over his lips and smile. "Only if you make me do that again."

He laughs, grabbing my ass and picking me up. I wrap my legs around him, and he carries me, his mouth on mine, to the bedroom.

And to a number of orgasms I didn't know were possible.

CHAPTER 20

hase

Moonlight filters through the curtains that weren't properly closed in my haste to return to bed. Megan was worried about the mess on the living room floor. She feared that if Kennedy came home unexpectedly, she would look at the pizza boxes and discarded clothing and think someone had broken in. So while Megan soaked in my bathroom after I thoroughly ravaged her, I disposed of my condom and cleaned up the mess downstairs.

"Do you think I should go to my room?" she asks, her voice sleepy. Her arm drapes across my bare chest as she snuggles into my side. "I mean, the answer is yes. I should. But do you want me to go now or wait a little longer?"

I stare at the ceiling and imagine watching her climb out of bed.

No. I don't want you to go now—or later, for that matter. This is ... nice.

I stroke her arm with my fingertips. "It's not hurting anything for you to stay here."

She smiles against me.

I don't fight the grin that twitches along my lips, but I struggle with the lie I just told.

None of this is surprising to me. When Megan stepped out of her car, I knew she had the potential to cause me a lot of trouble. Hell, I might've known that when she was still a stranger giving me shit from the other side of a foggy window.

I want Megan in my bed. I want her lips wrapped around my cock again, my mouth exploring every piece of her body. I want to hear her laugh, watch her smile—come home from work, and see her in my kitchen with my daughter. And that's all kinds of screwed up.

It's a setup for pain. This is going to hurt—badly, I'm afraid.

And if I don't play this right, it won't just hurt me. It'll hurt Kennedy too.

"What's the matter?" she asks, yawning.

I pull her closer to me if that's possible. "Nothing. Why?"

"You just tensed up."

"Oh." *Did I?* "My shoulder is still sore."

"Want me to massage it again."

I chuckle. "Only if you want to repeat what happened the last time you started rubbing me."

She tucks her face against me and laughs. The sound pleases me—too much.

Chase, you've fucked up.

Megan slides a leg over mine. I rest my cheek against her head and appreciate the moment. It's been too long since I've had a moment like this.

Have I ever had a moment like this? The question stirs something deep inside me.

"Can I be honest with you about something, Chase?"

"I hope you're always honest with me."

"Good." She exhales as if she's struggling to accept whatever she wants to say. "I feel a little guilty."

I pull back, tipping her chin up so she's looking at me. Her eyes are bright and vulnerable. My first instinct is to kiss her—to kiss away the vulnerability and show her I'm still here. But kissing isn't what she needs. Not right now. She needs words and communication to work out whatever plagues her.

"What in the world do you have to feel guilty about?" I ask.

She smiles softly. "I knew when I offered to massage your shoulder that it probably wasn't going to … end there."

Fair enough. "Okay, well, if I'm being honest with you, I probably knew that too." I wait for her to continue, to draw the line between her admission and her feelings of guilt. But her response doesn't come. "I'm not following you, sweetheart."

She slips out of my grip and nestles against me again.

"Hey," I say, chuckling. "You're not leaving me hanging. So what do you feel guilty about?"

"I … Did I just, you know, complicate this?"

"You mean, did *we* just complicate this?"

She shrugs, her narrow shoulders slipping against the sheets.

"I was an active participant in tonight's activities," I say. "Do you think I should feel guilty for something? Because if you do, I don't."

She presses a kiss to my side, and it melts my insides.

"How is a woman like you single?" I ask. "It boggles my mind."

"Gavin asked me that today too."

"Did he now?"

She laughs. "As I told him, it's pretty simple."

"So explain." *Tell me everything you told him and more.*

She sits up, and the sheet pools at her waist. The moonlight shines behind her, illuminating her figure with a soft, muted glow. Her heavy breasts hang like teardrops, and the roundness of her stomach is utter perfection.

I rest my hand on her thigh, my fingers dangerously close to her pussy. I press them lightly into her soft flesh and will myself to listen. Ensure she knows I'm interested in more than just her body.

"I think I have a character flaw," she says pensively. "I intentionally choose men I know aren't a match—ones I know won't work out. I think I told you this on the road when I broke down."

"You did. I still don't understand why, though."

She shrugs, staring off into the night.

As I watch her, my thoughts return to the night on the road. *"I choose to have relationships that I know won't work out because it's my comfort zone—which is odd because there's nothing comfortable about it."*

Okay ... "Do you pick out men who won't work because you're not ready to settle down? Or is it something else?"

A vague smile touches her swollen lips. "Maybe both."

I roll over on my side, propping my head up with my hand. "It's smart not to settle down until you're ready because, let me tell you, kids are a pain in the ass."

She laughs softly.

Though the words are easy to say, the reality isn't as easy at all. The truth is, it doesn't matter to me if she wants to settle down or why. Still, her admission feels like I've just lost something important, and I can't shake that.

"I don't know if it's that, really." She slowly faces me again. "I'm not averse to marriage and children in theory. Actually, the idea of creating a family excites me. I just don't know if I would be good at it."

I chuckle. "What does that mean?"

She grins shyly. "I don't know what that means. It means ... *what it means.* How do I know I would be a good wife or mother?"

I stroke her thigh and wonder how on earth she'd second-guess herself on that. She's a natural—and that doesn't come easily to everyone. I know.

The moment Mom and I met Kennedy in the cramped offices at CPS, my whole life changed. I went from a proverbial bachelor to a single dad with no idea how to raise a daughter. It took a minute to wrap my head around things.

And Kennedy? She was thrust into a big, loud family with a league of adoring people waiting to dote on her hand and foot. It took a while for her to acclimate, to trust us—especially as she grieved the loss of her mother.

The tears my baby shed. Night after night, sitting in bed and crying for her mom. I didn't know how to make that better, how to get on her level. How did I sympathize with her when I've never lost someone, and I, sadly, didn't really even know Monica?

But I sat beside her every night and told her it would be okay. Hell, I cried with her sometimes because watching her devastation devastated me. It took some time, but we formed a bond. We figured out our new life together. And little by little, she accepted her new family—except Luke. He was nearly immediate. *That should've been an onus of what was to come with that kid—always preferring the troublemakers.*

Despite Kennedy's initial reticent and sullen reaction to Megan's presence, she quickly warmed to her. My daughter has a natural skepticism of new people. I attribute that to how she made her way to me. But Megan's genuine affection, humor, and equally no-bullshit meter meshed beautifully with my daughter, and they've created a special friendship.

I suspect Megan would be an amazing mother.

"It's scary to consider," she says.

"It scared the hell out of me. Well, let's cut the shit and admit that it *scares* the hell out of me every day. You've met my child."

"Did you want to be a dad?"

I roll on my back and sigh. "No. Kids were the last thing on my to-do list—if they appeared at all. I wasn't like you. I knew I'd be a shitty dad. I didn't even like kids." I turn my face to face her. "I still don't like kids. Only mine, and I only like her sometimes."

She smiles like she doesn't believe me.

"You're great at it, you know," she says. "You're an excellent father."

"Thanks." I blow out a breath and stare at the ceiling. "I try, you know. I try hard to do the right thing for Kennedy. Sure, she has my parents and siblings, but I'm her only parent." *And I feel tremendous guilt for that.*

"I didn't know Monica, but I know she'd be proud of what a good dad you are. I'm sure she rests easier knowing you're taking such good care of her baby."

My heart grows heavy as I think about my daughter's mother—a woman I barely knew. Why did she try to go it alone? Did she struggle? Was it hard for her?

Was she going to tell me?

"You know," I say around the frog in my throat, "a lot of people think I should be angry with Monica."

A long, quiet moment passes between Megan and me.

"Are you?" she asks finally.

"I get it. I mean, she withheld my child from me. That's cruel. I missed so much of Kennedy's firsts. I was deprived of all the excitement of having a kid." I look at her and grin sadly. "And I think I would've been excited … after the shock wore off."

She smiles back, stroking my leg tenderly.

"But how can I condemn Monica?" I ask. "I don't know what she was going through. I don't know her situation. All I know for sure is that she kept our daughter healthy. Ken was happy when I met her—all things considered. Monica kept Kennedy safe." I blow out a tired breath. "I'll never get answers about why she made her choices, so I choose to feel grateful for everything she did right."

"That's an amazing way to look at it."

"Well, that's really the only way to look at it, right? I mean, I want Kennedy to grow up and know that so many people love her. I want her to feel supported. To know her worth and value. If I have a chip on my shoulder about her mother—someone who I know Kennedy's going to have questions about and be curious about—that defeats the purpose."

"Does she ask about her?"

I move my shoulder and wince. "No, not a lot. But it'll come. And when it does, I want to look at her and tell her how much her mother loved her, how she was the center of her world. But how can I do that if I'm secretly pissed at Monica? That doesn't serve Kennedy, nor does it serve her mother's memory. The stories I tell her about Monica are the only things Kennedy will ever know about her, and I'll be damned if she thinks anything other than the best."

Megan crawls across the bed and lays beside me once again. This time, she holds me tighter than ever before.

The peace that comes with having her in my arms is dangerous. But I can't deny that if time were paused right now, I wouldn't be upset about it. It feels pretty damn good with her by my side.

"You're a good man, Chase Marshall. Even if you are a grumpy cat."

The memory of her calling me that in front of my mother makes me chuckle.

"Now, enough of this sad shit," she says. "How are we going to handle this now? I mean, we have to be respectful of Kennedy."

I kiss her head again. *I love that you consider my child.*

"The ball is in your court," she says.

"Well …" I contemplate my options. "I guess the only thing I want to avoid is Kennedy thinking that something is happening between us. You and I are adults, and we know what this is." *And that you're leaving.*

The thought is a punch in the gut, but I move on.

"So I guess if we can keep our distance in front of her," I say, thinking quickly, "and make sure she stays our priority, then we can figure out how to get time together."

Her hand slides down my stomach, resting on my cock. "I think that's a good plan."

"One more thing. I will have to go out of town overnight for a couple of nights this week. Probably Thursday or Friday. Just giving you a heads-up."

"Okay. No problem."

"Oh, there's a problem," I say, ripping the blankets off us. I take her hand in mine and wrap it around my hardening cock. "You touched it. Now it's your problem."

She looks up at me with a devilish grin. "That's a problem I can solve."

Thank God.

Megan

"WHERE ARE YOUR CONDOMS?" I ASK, THEN LICK HIM FROM BASE to tip.

He hisses through his teeth. "Drawer to your right."

I tease him, swirling my tongue around the head. He watches me with a heated gaze as I pull him out of my mouth with an audible *pop*.

Leaning over the bed, I slide the drawer open. Chase's hands cup my ass before his fingers slide down my slit and dip into my opening.

"*Shit*," I gasp, looking desperately for a condom. I lift my hips and spread my knees to offer him better access. *That feels so fucking good.*

He plays in my wetness while I search in the darkness.

"Chase, I can't find any," I say. "Are you sure they're here?"

"Yeah. Dammit." He draws his fingers slowly away from me

and then leans over me, flipping on a lamp. He peers into the drawer. "Oh, fuck. I think I'm out."

I glare at him. "Tell me you're joking."

He falls back on the bed and covers his face with his hands.

My pussy throbs. My breasts are engorged. He's flipped a switch to my libido, and I can't turn it off. Only he can satiate me.

And he's going to have to.

His cock stands tall, sharing my body's refusal to give up. I take it in my palm and slowly stroke it while considering an alternative.

"Chase ..."

"Yeah?" he asks, his voice hoarse.

"This is the unsexiest conversation I've ever had, but I'm on birth control. And I just had my yearly exam a couple of months ago, and it came back fine. I'm disease-free."

He chuckles. "And you haven't fucked anyone since?"

"No."

His eyes flare. I'm on my back, and he's hovering over me in a split second. "You went from the unsexiest thing ever to the sexiest."

"It's sexy that I'm in a dry spell?"

"*Were.*" He grabs my legs and wraps them around his waist. "You *were* in a dry spell."

I reach between my legs and wink. "You're right. I am pretty wet."

He growls. The low and guttural sound coalesces in my core.

"I'm clean. I have an app thing from the doctor on my phone if you want to look at it," he says.

"You'd just hand me your phone?"

"No." He slides a finger into me, making me moan. "But you can go over there and get it if you want. I'll unlock it for you."

I suck in a breath and close my eyes, absorbing the waves of pleasure from him touching me.

"Are you going to get it?" he asks. "Or *are you going to get it?*"

"The phone or your dick? Is that what you mean?" He twists his fingers and pulls them out slowly. "*Shit, Chase.*"

"That's what I mean."

It would be easy to say I trust him without thinking about it. That would be the hedonistic answer, and I'm on a quest to pursue pleasure.

But it seems I've turned into a responsible adult.

"I'm happy to make you come on my fingers or face," he says. "I don't want you to feel pressured, sweetheart."

Damn this man.

My heart swells, and I open my eyes. A set of bright-green eyes that holds no secrets peers down at me. There's no shield, no sense of manipulation to get what he wants—only a man who genuinely cares about me. Who wants to do the right thing … even if it's uncomfortable.

He eases me back to the bed and lies beside me. My chest rises and falls as I try to make sense of the riot of emotions inside my head.

"I trust you," I whisper.

"Come here."

I roll over, facing him. My lips are met with his.

He holds my face in his hands as if he's holding something valuable. His mouth is soft, and his movements slow. He kisses me like he has all night.

He kisses me like he means it. *Like he wants me to know that.*

It takes me aback. The tender and sweet surprises me and throws me for a loop.

Shouldn't this be expected? Shouldn't this be something I've felt before? Shouldn't it always be like this?

He continues to press kisses lazily along my jaw, down my throat, and across my collarbone. There's no rush. There's no frenzy to get down to business. Maybe that's because we've already done this tonight.

Or this could be something new altogether.

My throat is raw as I roll Chase onto his back. The light is bright, and I prepare to climb on top of him. I'm suddenly self-conscious. I move to turn the light off when he stops me.

"Where are you going?" he asks.

"I'm going to kill the light."

"Why?"

"Because …" I don't finish the sentence. I can't. If I thought telling him that I don't have an STD wasn't sexy, telling him I'm nervous about him seeing my body when I'm on top of him is worse.

He holds my gaze and gently guides me until I'm straddling him. My breathing is ragged; my heart thumps a mile a minute.

I can only imagine my appearance in this light and from this angle. This isn't the living room with the hazy lighting and friendly shadows. This isn't the moonlight that's just as forgiving. This is a bright LED light whose job seems to be pointing out every roll, each stretch mark. *Fuck that light.*

"Hey," he says, rising and kissing me. "You're beautiful."

Oh, my heart. I smile at him but quickly look away.

"*Megan.*"

His hands clamp my thighs.

"*Megan,*" he says again. "Look at me."

I take a deep breath and gaze up at his chiseled abs, over his hard chest, and at his gorgeous face.

"You have no idea how lucky I am to be here with you right now," he says softly. "Every time I remember that you've allowed me to be inside you tonight, I can't believe it."

I blush. "Chase, stop."

"I can't stop. Apparently, no one has told you how beautiful you are, and you need to know."

"This isn't happening," I say, starting to move off him.

He presses down on my thighs. If I struggle to move, he'll let me up. I can see it in his eyes. But in the depths of the green, I also see him asking permission to hold me on top of him. *I let him.*

"What don't you like about yourself?" he asks softly. "What are you worried about?"

I shrug.

"Tell me. Point out the things you want to turn off the light over."

"Why?" I ask, my cheeks reddening. "This is embarrassing."

He grins. "What's embarrassing? These sexy thighs? Your perfect tits?" He holds them in his palms like he's weighing them. "This makes my dick hard just thinking about them."

My shoulders fall, releasing a bit of tension.

"This curve right here …" He runs his hands down my sides. "For fuck's sake, Megan. This is every man's dream."

"Well, thank you," I say, face flushed.

"How do you not know this?"

"It's hard to turn thirty and not have a reason to have cellulite and a round stomach, you know? Well, *you* don't know, but it is."

He snorts. "You mean the fact that you're healthy? You eat? You enjoy food? Why do you need an excuse for that?"

I can't believe I'm sitting naked on top of Chase Marshall having this conversation, but here we are. *Could my life be any weirder?*

"It's hard, Chase. Every magazine, every online picture, every—"

"Are photoshopped." He smiles. "Every fucking one of them. And even if they're not, you're not competing with those women. Hell, you're not competing with anyone. Don't have a fucked-up beauty scale because let me tell you …"

He runs his hands over my stomach. I start to pull away as he touches the most self-conscious part of my body. But the look in his eyes keeps me from it.

The longer he touches it, the more comfortable it becomes.

The stretch marks and added weight to my belly feel seen—like the need to keep it hidden is futile. And the way that makes me feel wholly accepted is like nothing I ever imagined.

"Let me tell you," he says again, "that I'm one lucky mother-fucker getting to touch you like this. That you would allow me the privilege. And anyone touching you should feel that way, or you should tell them to fuck off."

The longer I live with his words, the more I believe them. *The more comfortable* I *become.*

"Okay," I say, grinning. "I'll remember to tell the next guy that."

He lifts a brow. I don't know what that means, but it makes me laugh.

"I'm not laughing," he says, lifting me.

He pauses, and I nod. Then he positions his cock against my opening, and I slide down slowly, sinking onto him.

Oh. My. Fuck.

I'm full—so incredibly full, and the fullness threatens to burst me wide open.

"Give me a minute to acclimate," I whisper, rolling my hips gently.

Without the condom, he's even harder. The friction between us is a total turn-on. Every move is more electric. Each tilt of the hips is sharper. Every contraction of muscles feels like an energy exchange from one body to the other, and there's some-thing so intimate, so hot about it that I moan.

"*Holy shit,*" he says, groaning and fighting not to thrust into me. "Your body is so hot. You're burning up."

"I'm on the edge already."

He chuckles. "Good, because I can't last long inside you like this."

"I'm going to try to move," I say, holding my breath.

Hissing as I rock against him, the thought of his body inside mine is a mindfuck. No condom. No barrier. Just him and me.

"Slow down," he says, squeezing my hips. "Let me enjoy you."

He holds my gaze as I ride him slowly. The reverence and the sweetness in his features, coupled with the desire written all over his face, is something I'll never forget. Every future sexual encounter will be compared to this.

And it'll fail.

Because this is it, this is everything. This is being wanted. Desired. This is me giving up control because he asked for it. He didn't demand it or expect it. He requested that I trust him.

I thought I told him no romance.

Grinning at the memory, I rock against him again. He lets me pick up the pace and gives me free rein to take control. It doesn't take long before I'm ready to again fall over the edge for this complicated man.

He sucks in a breath and smashes the back of his head into the pillows.

"I'm going to come," I say, the pressure inside me building.

"Good timing then. I'm trying to hold it back."

I rise up and then press down, grinding on his cock. He gasps and drives his hips into me.

"I'm coming, Chase," I groan as the flood of my orgasm breaks through my body.

"Me too."

He grits his teeth as I ride out the waves of pleasure. Watching him come apart for me, under me, with me, is the biggest high I've ever felt. *I have the power to make this man lose control.*

It's downright spectacular.

Once he's emptied himself inside me and my orgasm has crashed, I roll off him.

"Hey," he says.

"Yeah?"

"Where are you going?"

I smile. "Bathroom."

He sits up and presses a quick kiss to my lips. Then he hops off the bed.

"Come on," he says, going to the bathroom. "Let me give you a bath."

"You don't have to do that."

He stops in the doorway and looks at me over his shoulder. His eyes shine. "I know I don't. But I want to. Okay?"

I want to argue with him and tell him it's unnecessary—that I can clean myself up. But the longer I look at him, the more I decide not to.

Let him take care of you, Megan. What can it hurt?

"Okay," I say, climbing off the bed. When I reach the doorway, he takes my hand in his.

As I look up and into his eyes, I grin.

I know exactly what can get hurt—me. But that's a risk I'm willing to take.

CHAPTER 22

egan

"It's kind of weird not having Gram and Pap around," Kennedy says, sipping her butterscotch milkshake.

She sits across from me, next to Chase, inside Melvin's, a little sandwich shop in Brickfield. They brought me to the town next to Peachwood Falls to get a pair of muck boots. Apparently, it's a sin not to have good rubber boots in the country.

Who knew?

"Gram called to see if I went to church this morning," Kennedy says.

"What did you tell her?" Chase asks.

"I told her no." Kennedy laughs. "I'm not lying to save you—especially about church."

Chase rolls his eyes. "Oh, come on. You're going to throw me under the bus like that?"

"Better than me getting thrown in hell." She slurps her milkshake again. "Sorry, Dad."

Chase stretches his legs under the table. His eyes hold mine as his foot settles against me. I smile at the contact, and he grins back.

We've managed to keep our hands off each other and play it cool. Kennedy came home from Neve's yesterday shortly after we got out of bed—*Chase's bed.* Thankfully, she called before she arrived, and we jumped in the shower and got ourselves sorted before she came through the door.

We spent the beautiful, if not chilly, Saturday watching movies and doing chores around the house. I made cheeseburgers for lunch, and Kennedy wanted a chicken and rice casserole that Maggie makes. She called her gram and got the recipe, and we gave it our best shot.

It didn't turn out too bad.

After dinner, we took a walk down by the lake, where I managed to slide down the bank and into the water—hence, the need for boots. Because, apparently, I can't go too long without embarrassing myself around Chase Freaking Marshall.

Chase strokes my leg with his foot. "Do you go to church, Megan?"

"No," I say, screwing up my face. "I have off and on in the past. I mean, I believe in God—a greater being that created the world. I don't think I need to sit in a pew one day a week and listen to someone tell me what's wrong with my relationship with Him." I pause. "Or Her. Why does everyone assume that God is a *him?*"

"Right?" Kennedy huffs. "That's so sexist."

"What about you?" I ask Chase. "Do you go to church?"

"Not enough to make Gram happy," Kennedy says, bumping shoulders with her father. "But she picks *me* up every Sunday. She sits in front of the house and honks her car horn at precisely eight thirty. And if I don't come out, she comes in and gets me."

Chase smirks. "You're getting no sympathy from me. I survived my years with your grandma. It's your turn."

"She's *so* old-fashioned. I love her more than anything, but she doesn't get me sometimes."

"If that means Gram doesn't understand your need to go to a high school dance at fourteen, then maybe you don't get her. Because she and I are on the same page."

Kennedy sticks her tongue out at her dad. He gives her a look that hits its target because she quickly turns back to her drink.

I smile at their interaction. It's so sweet and honest, yet I can see Chase's concern. Kennedy is at an age where she behaves just enough to remind you that she's still a child. Then she wallops you with an attitude, request, or insight that scares the shit out of you.

Kids know way more than I did at that age.

"What about you, Megan?" Kennedy asks.

Her tone for the question tips me off—she will try to rope me into supporting her point.

"What about me?" I ask.

Chase's gaze is trained on me, probably to warn me about what's to come.

"Were you allowed to have fun at my age?" she asks.

Chase starts to respond, most likely to bail me out, but I got this. I answer before he can get a word in.

"Yeah. I was allowed to have fun," I say. "I wasn't going to high school dances until I was in high school, though. Come to think of it, I don't even know if you're allowed to attend high school events until you're a student there."

"Well, at Peachwood High, no one cares about that," she says like she knows everything. "My friends go all the time."

"Do you want to know what my friends did at fourteen?" I ask. *Not that I had many, but she doesn't need to know that.*

"What?"

"They snuck out to meet boys. They told their parents they were at one place, and they'd stay the night somewhere else. They drank alcohol at parties they weren't supposed to attend and pierced their belly buttons using rubbing alcohol and needles."

Chase coughs. "Don't give her any ideas."

Kennedy grins, and it's full of mischief.

"Want to know what happened to them?" I ask.

"Sure," Kennedy says.

I start to tell her a bunch of baloney to scare her straight. But as I form the stories to share, I realize Maggie probably already did that. I bet Chase has done the same, and it's not working.

Glancing at Chase, I will him silently to be patient. Then I turn to Kennedy.

"They went on to graduate, get a job, and have families," I say. "Well, most of them, anyway."

Kennedy grins smugly. "Shocking."

"Really, Megan?" Chase asks.

"Kennedy," I say, sitting back in my chair. "When your dad, or your grandma, gives you rules, it's not because every single thing you do is going to ruin your life."

She grins at her dad out of the corner of her eye.

"You might sneak out and not get caught," I say. "Or you might get in the car with someone you shouldn't and make it back just fine. But all it takes is for something to go wrong one time. *One single time.* Your whole life might be over before it's even begun."

"But what's the odds that it happens to me? Like you said, nothing happened to your friends."

I lift a brow. "I didn't say that."

"But you said they went on with their lives like normal."

"Sure, they did. But one graduated with her baby boy in the crowd. She missed prom because she just gave birth."

Kennedy's smile wobbles.

"We took our senior trip," I say. "And a boy in my class was on probation and missed it. He couldn't leave the county. There was a car accident on Christmas Eve during my junior year. A bunch of kids from my chemistry class were out having fun in the middle of the night and wrecked the car. Killed one of them. Another still walks with a limp, and a third, the last I heard, was traumatized over being the car's driver that night and watching his friend die. He's had to live with that every day."

Her face pales as she listens. Her eyes widen.

"My senior year," I say, "there was a big party before the last day of school. Each class had done this for decades before us. My mom didn't let me go."

"At all?"

I shake my head. "I was so mad at her. Everyone was going, and this was the party of the year. I'd waited for this thing since August. I remember pacing my room and crying, fighting with my mother about how mean and strict she was and why she had to be such a tyrant. It was really easy to hoist all of my anger on her. How could she do this to me, right?"

Kennedy stills.

"A whole bunch of parents had to pick their kids up at the police department that night ... but not mine," I say.

She looks at her dad. Chase crosses his arms over his chest but doesn't say a word.

"You see, Kennedy, I get it," I say. "I understand how it feels to be the only one not getting to do stuff. I was that girl. I sat at home while everyone was out having fun, and I was the one that had to listen to all the stories on Monday morning about the events of the weekend. It didn't feel good. I wanted to be a part of that so badly. And trust me when I tell you that I understand how left out it can feel when your classmates are doing things and you can't." *Because your mom wouldn't let you ... or more often because you weren't invited.*

"Yeah ..."

"But I get it now. She was protecting me. Was she overbearing? Sometimes. Did she make all the right choices? Probably not. But she was trying to keep me from the situations where that one thing—that one life-altering event that I couldn't come back from—might happen. She had to weigh the pros and cons of each situation and make a game-time decision, knowing that if she made the wrong one, it would be her fault. Or she'd feel like it was, anyway." I smile. "And now? I have a great life. I've traveled the world and had important jobs. I get to have experiences now and, I promise you—the experiences as an adult are head and shoulders better than anything you could have as a teenager. I swear it."

I don't have to look at Chase to know he's grinning.

His foot taps the top of mine before he slides it back and sits up again.

"Well, now that both of you are against me ..." She sighs and looks at the door. "Hey! There's Uncle Luke."

Our attention turns to a younger version of Chase and Gavin walking to the table.

Luke is a touch shorter and thinner than Chase but carries the same playfulness I associate with Gavin. His hair is styled to the side. His legs are clad in denim, and a flannel shirt sets atop a white T-shirt. *Is that a gold chain around his neck?*

"Fucking great," Chase mutters just loud enough for me to hear.

"What do you know?" Luke says, sitting beside me like we're long-lost buddies. "It's like I saw your truck out there and came in to see what's happening."

"What are you doing in Brickfield?" Kennedy asks, clearly smitten with her uncle.

"Well," he says, narrowing his eyes and earning a giggle from his niece. "You are entirely too young and innocent for me to divulge such things."

Kennedy makes a show of rolling her eyes.

Luke turns to me and smirks. His chin hosts the same dimple as Chase's. There's a hint of mischief in his eyes that I'm familiar with—Gavin has the same one.

"You must be the woman everyone is talking about," he grins.

"*Luke …*" Chase warns.

"I am the woman everyone is talking about," I say, feeling him out. "My name is Megan, and it's nice to meet you."

Luke seems impressed. "

"I've heard a lot about you," I tell him.

"Is that so?"

"Yup."

"It was all good, right?" he asks. "My brothers have a habit of making me look bad because they're so intimidated by my good looks."

Chase snorts.

"It was mostly good," I say. "Gavin talked a little crap, but it wasn't too bad."

Luke's jaw drops. "That bastard."

Everyone at the table chuckles, and I'm relaxed once again.

"Dad," Kennedy says. "Can I get a cookie?"

"You just had a milkshake. Do you need more sugar?"

Luke huffs and pulls out his wallet. He takes out a five-dollar bill and hands it over to his niece. "Yes, she needs more sugar. What kind of question is that?"

"Don't tell Uncle Gav, but you're my favorite," Kennedy says.

Luke winks at her. "If he starts pulling on me, let me know. I have to stay ahead."

Kennedy gives him a thumbs-up and leaves for the ordering counter. As soon as she's gone, Luke leans in.

"I have news," he says. "Alyssa isn't pregnant."

"You better go buy a fucking box of condoms," Chase says, shaking his head. "Tell me you learned something from this."

"I learned something from this." Then he tilts his head toward me and whispers, "I did not learn anything from this."

Despite Chase's unamused stare, I laugh.

"What are you guys doing here, anyway?" Luke asks.

"We came to get me boots because apparently boots are required clothing for Peachwood Falls," I say.

Luke snorts. "From what I hear, I'd have thought my brother would require no clothing from you."

"Mind your business," Chase tells him.

"You're a bit of a shit starter, aren't you?" I ask Luke.

"Oh, just a bit. I like to keep everyone on their toes." He yawns. "I just left Alyssa's."

"The woman you thought was pregnant?" I ask.

He nods. "Yup. That's her. And it took us all night and all morning to decide to take a break. At first, she was pissed at me over a joke. Then I was pissed at her for being pissed at me. Then she thought she was pregnant, so we were both panicking. But now that's behind us ..." He shrugs. "We've maxed out my emotional reserve."

"That's understandable," I say.

He waves at Kennedy. "I'm going to get going. I just wanted to come in and give Chase some crap."

"Gee, thanks," Chase says.

Luke gets up. "I'll call you later, Chase. Nice to meet you, Megs. You're everything Gavin said you were."

I laugh, mainly at Chase's reaction. "Well, I hope that's good."

"It's great." He walks backward toward the door. "Bye."

"Goodbye, Luke," Chase says. Then he sighs. "Well, that's Luke. See? You weren't missing much."

I lift my foot until it's in his lap. His eyes go wide as I rub his crotch.

"I think he's funny," I say. "A nice mix of you and Gavin. What about your other brother? Mallet? Is that his name?"

Chase holds my foot against him. His fingers slip beneath

my jeans, and he grips my ankle. I don't know what's hot about that, but my temperature spikes.

"Mallet's an asshole most of the time," he says. "He's a good guy. I probably like him better than Gavin and Luke. But he's … always pissed off."

"Who? Uncle M?" Kennedy sits down with her cookie.

Chase grins, letting go of my leg. "That cookie is as big as your head."

"I know. And I still have two dollars."

I giggle and drop my foot back to the floor.

Chase looks at me. "You girls ready?"

"Yup," Kennedy says, spraying cookie crumbs across the table.

I nod, even though I'm not.

Sure, our lunch is over, and there's no reason to take up a table. But sitting here with the two of them, chatting about random stuff and making each other laugh—it's one of the breeziest, most relaxing Sundays I've had in a long damn time.

At least I get to go home with them.

"Let's go," I say.

We get to our feet, and Kennedy leads us to the door. Chase walks behind me, pressing his hand into the small of my back.

"Thank you," he whispers in my ear.

Kennedy skips off to the truck.

I stop as Chase walks around me to hold the door. "For what?"

He doesn't give me enough room to step outside without running against him. I don't mind.

"Thanks for trying to talk some sense into her," he says. "I appreciate it."

"You know what I appreciate?"

"What's that?"

The door swings shut behind us, and we head to the truck too. I dip my chin so no one can read my lips.

"I appreciate how freaking sore I am today," I say softly. "You stretched me out."

He growls and takes a step to the side, away from me. "Behave."

I stop in front of his truck. "Or what?"

He watches me with hooded eyes.

"Or you'll spank me?" I pout. "Oh, what a shame."

"Get in the fucking truck before I bend you over that bench over there."

I laugh, wishing I could kiss him but knowing I can't. Then I climb in the truck, and off we go.

CHAPTER 23

*M*egan

The house is so quiet without anyone home.

I pitter-patter around the kitchen, sipping a cup of coffee I have no business drinking in the afternoon. My sleep is interrupted enough by Chase or thoughts of Chase. I don't need another element to get in the way of rest.

I grin. *Not that I mind the recent disruptions.*

My email pings. I sit at the table and pull up the message.

Dear Megan,

I'm circling back to our conversation from the end of last week. I sincerely hope you've given my offer consideration. The marketing department knows I've contacted you, and they're just as excited about the prospect of having you back as I am.

Please feel free to ask questions and inquire about any hesitations. I'm here to assure you that Iyala is your home. We believe that, and we believe in you.

Best,
Dorothy Kaziwell
President

I sip my coffee and stare at her words. "If you believed in me, you wouldn't have let me go."

Instantly, I feel bad for thinking that way. They didn't treat me poorly. They made a business decision. *But why is the situation so different now?* If it was so easy to lose me, how could I be that important to them?

My mind drifts to California and what life would look like if I went back. The people. The noise. Sitting in traffic for hours to go five miles.

But it is money—good money. And with the position comes so many opportunities that most people would kill for.

I try to make myself excited about it. I remember the disappointment of being let go. Even though I was ready to go back to Texas or to do something different wherever that was, it still felt like a loss. *They didn't need me.* And if they had changed their mind before I left, I probably would've stayed.

But now that I'm not there, *now that I'm here*, none of that is tempting.

Except I'm not *here* either. Not for much longer.

"Why does life have to be so damn hard?" I ask as rain begins to pelt the windows again.

I set my mug down and pick up my phone. I scroll through my texts from Chase. All week, he's habitually sent me selfies throughout the day. In his truck. Next to a power pole. Beside a swiftly flowing creek. I return the gesture with pictures of myself on his bed, doing laundry, and making dinner.

The pictures might get more provocative when he leaves town tomorrow morning for a couple of days. I hope so, anyway.

I stare at the last picture he sent me and zoom in on his face.

He's exhausted and filthy, but a twinkle in his eye makes my heart squeeze. Beneath the picture is a text that he'll be home late.

Home.

I awaken my computer and re-read Dorothy's email. *I'm here to assure you that Iyala is your home.*

Out of all the words in Chase's message and that email, those stick out.

It's such a simple word—just four letters. *Home.* But there aren't enough letters in the alphabet in the world to capture the meaning of it.

I stand, picking up my coffee and wrapping my hands around the mug.

"Where is my home?" I ask aloud.

I wander around the room as I wander around life, looking for an answer. Looking for a place where I belong.

Looking for my home.

I've always imagined that I would live in a place full of love. My life would be bursting at the seams with people, PTA conferences, and neighbors dropping by for no reason. It would be somewhere I didn't wake up and feel like an impostor living in someone else's life.

There wouldn't be a fear that it all might end abruptly—that the rug might be pulled out from under me when I least expect it. Like every time one of my mom's marriages ended. And when things at school seemed to be settling down, I thought I was making friends, only to wake up to our front yard with a million forks stuck in the ground. Or when we moved to Dallas, I left behind everything I'd ever known.

When I lost my job.

I pick up my phone and call my mom. She answers on the third ring.

"Hey, honey. How are you? Is everything okay?" she asks.

"Hi, Mom. I'm good. Everyone is gone, and it's nice and

quiet, so I thought I would check in." *And I needed to hear your voice.*

"Well, I don't have a lot to report. The pain in my leg is getting better, thank goodness. I've watched every movie on the Hallmark Channel. I'm tired of ordering takeout, and I think I've gained twenty pounds just sitting here."

I smile. "You're tired of takeout?"

She laughs, and the sound soothes my soul.

"How are you liking Peachwood Falls?" she asks.

"Oh, it's … fine."

She hums. "How is Chase? Are you two getting along?"

"Yeah. We're getting along swimmingly."

"Okay, that sounds suspicious."

I take a sip of my coffee. "I don't know what to tell you. We're managing just fine."

"That's good. Maggie called last night and said they're having a ball at Kate's. Apparently, Kate's roommate moved out, so they've been patching, painting, and getting ready in case someone else moves in. You know how much they love a project."

"I didn't know they were project people, but I can see that."

"Maggie bought the house they live in now because it needed so much work," Mom says, chuckling. "Lonnie wanted another place closer to town, but Maggie was desperate to get her hands dirty in that old farmhouse. She thinks you can't make a house a home without putting in elbow grease. I don't know that I agree."

I mosey down the hallway, past the stairs, and into the living room. The wind picks up outside, and sheets of rain pour past the windows. I pick up a blanket off the couch and put it over the back where it belongs.

"I can see what she's saying," I say.

"You can?"

Shrugging, I sit on the ottoman—and grin. "Yeah. Think

about it. Think about my apartment in LA. It was a box that I came to after work. I slept there. Ate there. But it was essentially the same box someone else occupied before I arrived. It wasn't *mine*. It never felt like mine."

She hums in agreement.

I take a deep breath. "Iyala called and offered me my job back."

My statement is met with silence.

"I told them I wasn't sure," I say. "They asked me to email them my response, but I haven't."

"*Oh.*"

"They called on Friday."

"And it's Wednesday, and you're just telling me?"

I stand, prickled by her defensiveness.

"Are you going to go?" she asks.

Sighing, I close my eyes. "I don't know, Mom. I don't know what to do."

"Do you want to go back to California?"

"No," I say cautiously. "I don't. I mean, it's a job, and *I need a job*. I can't live with you forever."

"Well, you could."

Her response makes me grin. "I know I could, but I can't. I don't want to."

"I'll try not to take offense to that." She laughs. "I understand what you're saying, and you're right. You shouldn't want to live with your mom."

My hand slides along the mantel over the fireplace as I view the framed pictures on the ledge. All the Marshalls are present, and most are with Kennedy. But my favorite one of all is Chase with his brothers.

I pick up the silver frame and inspect it closer.

Gavin and Luke flank Chase. A taller, darker, tattooed version of them stands on the other side of Gavin. Someone must have told a joke seconds before the picture was snapped because all four are laughing. Gavin points at Luke, Luke's head is thrown back, and his eyes are squeezed shut. Mallet is smirking as if he's fighting his amusement. And Chase? He's smiling from ear to ear, displaying a pure happiness I've rarely seen since I met him.

And I love it. I love that look on his handsome face.

I set the picture down.

"Mom?"

"What, honey?"

"Is Dallas your home?"

"Well, I live here."

I perch on the arm of the sofa. "But living there doesn't mean it's your home. Do you know what I mean?"

She hesitates, pulling in a breath as she considers my question.

"I've been thinking about that a lot lately," I say. "How can I be thirty years old and still feel like a vagabond? Shouldn't I be settled by now instead of avoiding serious relationships and only dating emotionally unavailable men?"

"That's probably my fault."

"I'm not bringing this up to make it your fault, Mom."

"Oh, Megan, I know. But that doesn't change the fact that I haven't set a very good example for you over the years."

My insides still.

We don't talk about this much, and we talk about it in depth even less. I don't want to make her feel bad for anything she's done. I'm sure she doesn't spark a conversation about this because she doesn't want me to feel inadequate about my choices. So we tiptoe around the topic like we're walking on ice, afraid it'll crack and we'll fall through.

Neither of us wants to freeze to death.

But maybe now is the time we address things.

"For what it's worth," I say softly, "I think you've set a great example. You're strong and smart, and don't let anything bring you down. Look at the life you made for us. Think about all the memories we have together."

"I appreciate that more than you know. But I … I'm responsible for the way you feel about relationships. You don't want to let anyone in because you don't want to wind up like me—old and alone with a string of men behind you. So instead of settling down and having a family—beautiful babies that I know would be the sweetest thing for you, honey—you stay on this island where you feel safe." She sighs. "I can't blame you for that. But I hate it."

I stand, my chest shaking with trepidation. "Well, maybe … you know …" I glance around the room again. "If I could find the right person someday who would treat me well—someone I could trust not to take a sledgehammer to my life—maybe I could consider settling down with someone."

"That's my hope for you."

That's my hope for me too.

It scares me to admit it. My heart pounds, and my underarms sweat. Considering letting someone in my life in a way that matters is terrifying.

What if it starts a chain of men in and out of my life? What if they get close enough to hurt me like I've seen many men do to my mother in the past? What if I end up feeling like an impostor in my personal life?

I've never met anyone I implicitly trusted. There's never been a man who I looked at and believed wholeheartedly was a good man. I haven't met the country song version of a man who drives a truck and holds open doors. Someone who takes me to Applebees on a date night and is just as happy with a beer on the back porch as anything after supper.

My throat burns.

I've never met anyone like that until recently.

Adrenaline trickles through my veins, and I have to move. I walk into the kitchen and pace the room as my head spins.

Am I losing my mind? Am I losing touch with reality?

What am I thinking?

I've known Chase for almost two weeks. *Two. Weeks.* How do I rationalize this?

The longer I think about it, the more confusing it gets. Yes, he's a great guy. The sex is phenomenal. He's fun to be around, which is a surprise.

But I'm leaving here in two weeks. His teenage daughter is his top priority—as she should be. I'm not even certain I want to be involved with a teenager full-time.

I cringe. *What are you thinking, Megan? You aren't staying here. You don't have a role or the opportunity to have a role in Kennedy's life long-term. Get yourself together.*

"Dallas is my home because this is where I raised you," Mom says. "I'm happy here. My friends are here. My life is here." She pauses. "I'm safe here."

I exhale harshly.

"You'll find your home, Megan."

"I'm starting to wonder if that's true."

"One day, you'll wake up and realize that a piece of your heart resides outside your body. You'll feel a draw to that place no matter where you are in the world. You'll only feel whole and content when you're there—and that will be your home. That's where things make sense. That's where you're meant to be."

I lean against the counter and glance around the kitchen. I can hear Kennedy's laughter and Chase's sighs as she prods him for a reaction. The smell of dinner wafts through the air.

And I smile. *This place is a home.*

"My doctor's office is calling," Mom says. "Call me later, okay?"

"I will. Love you."

"Love you, Megan. Goodbye."

The call ends. I'm holding the phone in the middle of the

kitchen as a myriad of emotions rolls through me. The biggest feelings scare me because here, in this room—in this house, my life makes more sense than ever.

I look at my screen.

Chase: What are you doing?

Me: Figuring out dinner. You?

Chase: Trying not to punch my supervisor.

Me: Sounds like a solid plan. 💪

Chase: I have another solid plan.

Me: Do you?

Chase: I want you to sleep with me tonight.

Me: What about Kennedy?

Chase: Once she's in her room, she doesn't come out. I'll be gone from tomorrow morning until Friday night. I need to get enough of you to hold me over.

Me: You're insatiable.

Chase: Are you complaining?

Me: Not even a little. 😊

Chase: I should be home around seven.

Me: I'll be here.

Chase: See you then.

Me: See you then.

I set the phone down and stare out the window. The rain continues to come down in buckets.

"You'll only feel whole and content when you're there—and that will be your home. That's where things make sense. That's where you're meant to be."

I march to the table and open my email. My fingers go to the keyboard.

Hi, Dorothy,

Thank you for your email.

While I appreciate you reaching out, I don't believe Iyala is a good fit for me at this time. I didn't take this decision lightly. There have been a few opportunities available to me recently that I would like to explore.

I wish you the very best.

Sincerely,

Megan Kramer

I hit send.

And hope I don't regret it.

hase

"Slow down, Marshall, or you'll get a ticket."

I ease my foot off the accelerator and watch my speedometer fall. *If only my anxiousness would fall along with it.*

The night is dark, and the rain is unrelenting. My windshield wipers squeak as they struggle to keep up with the onslaught pouring out of the sky. Unfortunately, the weather does nothing for my mood; I'm already irritated.

I've never been irritated about going home before. What's odder is that while I'm frustrated about going home, I want to get there. I wish I were already there. I wish this drive were over.

Megan Kramer is turning out to be a double-edged sword in my life.

Each day that passes, I find myself falling harder for her. I enjoy being with her a little more. When I watch her with Kennedy—cooking together or figuring out how to sew a button on a jacket together—I find myself playing the what-if game.

What if this was a thing? What if Megan stuck around? What if Megan and I gave this a try?

In a vacuum, this would work. I have zero doubts. But I don't reside in a vacuum.

"It's been two weeks, Chase. You're outta your mind," I groan, the words barely audible over the wipers.

The cab of the truck fills with the sound of my ringing phone. I see it's Mom and accept the call.

"Hey, Mom. It's pouring here, so I can't hear very well."

"Oh. Do you need to go?"

"Nah, I have a ways to go yet. Talk to me." *Distract me from my thoughts.* "How are things with Kate?"

Mom laughs. "They're good. Her new apartment is darling. Of course, she let me pick out her curtains and some rugs."

"I bet she did."

"What does that mean?"

"It means you probably paid for them, didn't you?"

"I can hear you, asshole," Kate shouts. "How are you, brother?"

I stop at a light in Bricksville just as the rain tapers off. *Thank God.* "I'm good. How are ya, Kate?"

"Living and loving life. Being a badass like usual."

"Well, I see you still have your humbleness. That's good."

She laughs.

"How is Kennedy?" Mom asks. "Does she miss us yet?"

"Of course, she misses you."

"Good. I don't want to become obsolete."

"Don't think that's happening anytime soon," I say, hitting the accelerator again. "How's Dad?"

"He's out golfing with Kate's neighbor. They've golfed almost every day we've been here."

"Hey," Kate says. "I heard you have a … what did Luke call her? A dime?"

I roll my eyes.

"Her name is Megan," Mom says.

"Right. *Megan*," Kate says, giggling. "How is Megan?"

I grip the steering wheel and cross the city limits.

Fields extend from the road on either side. There's no light to be seen—no streetlamps or houses lit up. Not a damn thing. Somehow, it's fitting.

"Megan is good," I say. "She and Ken are like two peas in a pod."

"What about you?" Kate asks.

"What about me?"

"Are you two peas in a pod too?"

I shake my head. "What have you done, Mother?"

"I haven't done a damn thing," she says. "I simply showed Kate a picture of Megan and let her draw her conclusions."

"Right. You didn't guide her to any particular conclusions. Sure. I believe you."

"Give me the phone, Mom," Kate says. The line gets muffled before Kate's voice becomes clear once again. "Hey, it's me. I walked into my bedroom for a little privacy."

I sag against my seat.

"Are you doing okay?" she asks. "I know how Mom can be. And she left you there with Megan and Gavin and Luke. Good grief, Chase. How are you surviving? Do you have to fend the boys away with a stick?"

My jaw sets. "No. I just told them I'd break their necks if they do anything stupid."

"Ah. So you do have a thing for her."

I think about lying and saying I don't. I consider ending the conversation and telling Kate to go play games with Mom. But then I remember it's Kate who I'm talking to, and if anyone will hear me and understand what I'm trying to say, it's probably her.

"Talk to me, Chase. What's going on?" she asks.

I exhale. "I don't know, Kate. I'm fucked, I think."

"If you weren't, I'd be worried about you."

"Why is that?"

"I saw her—that's why. She's freaking pretty. And from what Mom said—and I realize I have to take that with a grain of salt —she's sweet and smart. What more could you want?"

Not much. Maybe not anything.

I roll my shoulder around to keep it loose. "For starters, I could want someone who lives near me."

"I hear she's unemployed. That's helpful."

"For two, I could choose someone who wants to live in the middle of nowhere. Megan is a city girl, Kate. She didn't even own a pair of boots until last weekend."

Kate chuckles. "So? Get her some. Problem solved."

"I did get her some." *Then I gave her some.*

My cock hardens as I remember her slipping into my bedroom Sunday night. I bent her over the edge of the bed and sank so deeply inside her that I was afraid I'd lose myself forever.

Unfortunately, I didn't.

"Kate, I would never admit this to anyone else, so keep your mouth shut."

"You got it."

I groan. "I'm fucked up over this woman, and I don't know what to do about it. It's been two weeks. She's all I think about. I'm already dreading the day she leaves. Tell me this is normal behavior. That I just haven't had someone at my disposal like this in so long that I forgot what the convenience felt like."

"Yeah, but I don't think the convenience is bugging you."

Of course, it's not.

"Let's break this down," she says. "What are you worrying about? What's your holdup? Your hiccup, so to speak?"

"Well …" I run a hand over my jaw. "She's going to leave soon."

"And you can't ask her to stay?"

"No, I could, I guess."

"Solved. What else?"

I flip my turn signal and pull onto the gravel road leading to my house.

"I'm worried this isn't the right move for Kennedy," I say, my voice void of levity. "She's never had to share me with another woman. And she's at this stage of her life where she needs to be the only thing I focus on, but here we are, and I'm thinking about Megan just as much as I'm thinking about my daughter. Hell, probably more. Am I fucking this up?"

Kate laughs. "No, you're not fucking anything up—except maybe Megan, and I'm pretty sure she's enjoying it."

"No. Hard limit. We aren't discussing my sex life."

"Fine, fine." She sighs. "Look, maybe you need someone in your life. Kennedy needs a woman figure, Chase. A role model. And it would be healthy for her to watch you in a solid relationship with someone. Stop looking at it from a pessimistic angle. You're allowed to have a life, too, you know."

Relief washes over me.

"And I know what you're thinking," she says.

"What's that?"

"You're worrying that things won't work out, and you're going a million miles a minute and wondering what that looks like. You're wondering if it makes you irresponsible."

I grin. "How did you get so wise?"

"Well, that had nothing to do with you. Or Gav. Definitely not Luke or Mallet."

"Speaking of Mallet, have you heard from him lately? I haven't talked to him in a while."

"Briefly. We talked briefly last week. He's good, I think. Sounded happy for once. Well, happy in Mallet language."

I laugh. "I feel you on that."

"Right? But, no, he's okay. He finally seems to be coming around again. You can talk to him about things now that don't always wind up being about the divorce, so that helps."

I frown.

"But back to you," she says. "Do you like Megan? Like really like her?"

"Kate, I don't know. I mean, yes. I do. But I've known her for less than a month, and it's ridiculous that I feel this way. I don't even know her. I sure as hell don't know her well enough to wonder if it's realistic or ludicrous even to consider the shit I'm considering."

"Only you know the answer to that."

"Nah, you know. Tell me. Am I being ignorant? I mean, she either leaves in two weeks, and I never see her again." *My stomach clenches.* "Or she leaves, and we try some long-distance thing." *That will never work.* "Or she leaves, and we see how it goes. Or she stays here and …" I sigh. "*Fuck.*"

Kate chuckles softly. "I love seeing you like this."

"How?"

"I don't know. Living a life, maybe. Having something for yourself. It's nice."

Yeah, it's nice. For now.

Mom's voice echoes in the distance.

"I gotta go. I promised Mom pedicures today," Kate says. "So we're off to get pampered while Dad golfs. Again."

"I didn't even know Dad likes golf."

"Me either."

"Okay, well, I'll talk to you later. Tell Mom I love her."

"I will. And Chase?"

"Yeah?"

"You're allowed to have a life. You should have one. Everyone will be better for it—Kennedy included."

I pause. "But what if it doesn't work out? What if Kennedy is attached and Megan takes off?"

"Then Kennedy becomes more resilient. You, of all people, know how strong that little girl is. She lost her mother and somehow still became this happy, spirited, tenacious young woman."

My heart warms. *That's true. She has.*

"I think you're overthinking this a little, Chase. You're not giving Kennedy enough credit. I mean, sure, if things get serious between you and Megan and they don't work out, Ken might be upset. But Chase ..." She pauses. "What if they work out? I know you, big brother, and you would never even consider letting someone into your life who wasn't an amazing person. So if this is even on your radar, that means something. And maybe it means that Megan could not only be good for you, but she might also be very good for Kennedy."

Fuck.

"Kennedy might get heartbroken. But what if you push away a woman who might bring things into her life that you can't give her? And, Chase?"

"Yeah?"

"Maybe this isn't just about Kennedy. Maybe you're afraid of getting your heart broken too."

What the hell? "I think you just dove into the deep end, Kate." *Or not.*

She might be right. Not getting into a relationship is much easier than dealing with the complications of having another person in my life. Am I using Kennedy as an excuse? Not really. She is my main point of concern. But is that also fortuitous? Yes.

She sighs. "I gotta go. Call me anytime but wait a couple of hours first."

Laughing, I shake my head. "Fine. Thanks, Kate. Love you."

"Love you, Chase. Bye."

"Goodbye."

I end the call and watch my house come into view.

It glows softly in the darkness, light radiating from the kitchen and living room windows. Just knowing Kennedy and Megan are inside makes my entire body warm.

This is what coming home should feel like.

I put the truck in park and cut the engine.

You have time. Just enjoy the next couple of weeks and see what happens.

Trust in yourself.

Megan looks out the kitchen window and grins. I smile back.

All the worry I have when I'm not here is gone as soon as I'm with her.

That has to mean something.

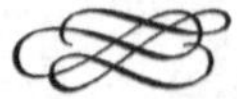

egan

"I win. *Again*," Kennedy says, yawning. "That's seriously pathetic."

"How is that pathetic?" Chase asks.

"Because you both are way older and have played rummy a lot more than I have. Yet I still kick your butts."

I hold out a hand. "Hold up. I didn't grow up playing rummy, so that's not true."

"Were you raised in a barn?" Chase shakes his head. "*Didn't grow up playing rummy*. What did you do with your time?"

Come to think of it, I'm not sure.

I scramble around in my mental trunk full of memories and try to remember how I killed time in my childhood. "I rode bikes. I made sandcastles. Swam. Built forts, climbed trees … played with dolls. But I didn't play card games."

Kennedy yawns again, resting her chin in her hand. "Where did you learn how to play, then?"

"My best friend, Calista, was my next-door neighbor in LA. When I first got there, I had an apartment the size of your bathroom, Kennedy."

"Really?"

"Yes. It was tiny. And I paid out the nose for it, which is wild now that I think about it. Anyway, Calista lived next door, and because of the rent, we couldn't afford to go out. So she showed me how to play rummy."

Chase gets up from the table and grabs Kennedy's snack plate.

"Do you know how to play euchre?" Kennedy asks.

"What?"

"Euchre. Do you know how to play that?"

"I have no idea what euchre is," I say.

Kennedy looks at her dad and sighs. "We're gonna have to teach her. She can't possibly go to Sunday dinners at Gram's and not know how to play euchre. Luke will never let her live it down."

Chase puts the plate in the sink. His shoulders are tight as he turns on the faucet. "Yeah, we'll have to teach her."

His tone is hollow. Uncertain. And after he shuts the water off and turns back around, he's watching me warily. I understand why.

I shift in my seat. "Well, thank you for thinking of me. But when Maggie gets home, I'm going home. So no euchre for me."

My breath stalls in my chest as I wait for one of them to say something.

It's the truth. I won't be here for Sunday dinners. They know that.

So why are the three of us acting so weird?

"I got some ice cream today." My chair screeches across the hardwood. "Anyone want a bowl?"

"Nah, I think I'll go to bed early," Kennedy says. "My head hurts a little. Is that okay, Dad?"

"Sure. Go on, and I'll come up and say good night in a little bit."

Kennedy smiles at him. Her gaze slides past mine. The only acknowledgment she makes that I'm in the room is a slight nod before she disappears down the hallway.

Chase dries his hands while I sit, holding my breath. Something just happened, and I'm not sure what it was. But the room reads differently now. It's stale, stuck as if it's holding its breath too.

He walks by me toward the mudroom. "Come on."

Huh? I'm confused, but I do as he asks. "Where are we going?"

"Let's go for a walk."

We're quiet as we put on our jackets. I smile at the memory of picking out the calf-high rubber muck boots as I slide them on. Chase opens the door for me, and I enter the chilly evening air.

Mud slops around our steps as we round the side of the house. The breeze bites at my face, and I pull the top of my jacket over my mouth.

"I have to be out of here early. Earlier than usual tomorrow," he says.

"Well, don't expect me up then." I look up at him and grin. "Five o'clock is my limit, and I barely make that."

He cocks his head to the side. "Yeah. I thought you weren't a morning person."

"I'm not."

"You've been up every morning since you got here."

"Well, drinking coffee and watching you putter around shirtless is my reward."

Chase's fingers flick my knuckle. I open my hand, and he slides his palm against mine, his fingers lacing through my cold digits.

I tingle at the sweet, innocent contact that feels as intimate as anything we've done.

"I thought I'd be worried," he says. "I've never left Kennedy overnight with anyone besides my parents since I got her."

"Well, I'll take good care of her."

He squeezes my hand. "I know you will."

Really? I peer up at him through the misty night and take in his sharp jaw and dimpled chin. His eyes crinkle at the corners when he's thinking, and it's adorable.

"I'm at a strange place in my life," he says, his breath billowing.

"How so?"

"Well, on the one hand, I'm trying to hold on to my daughter. Maybe too much. I don't fucking know. She's a teenager now, and I'll have to give her more rope, but that's terrifying. It's like her future relies on the decisions I make. I've already failed her once."

I rub his knuckle with my thumb. "You haven't failed her, Chase."

"If I hadn't been so careless or self-centered, maybe her life would've been different. Maybe she wouldn't have been in the car with her mom in a shitty neighborhood and gotten carjacked. I could've helped them, you know."

My chest tightens. "But you didn't know. That's not on you. And I'm not blaming Monica either because I have no idea why she didn't tell you. I'll give her the benefit of the doubt and say she had her reasons. But, Chase, you did the right thing as soon as you knew Kennedy existed. You can't blame yourself for the rest."

He shrugs like he's not so sure I'm right. "The other side of the coin is …" He exhales. "I'm ready to have a life again."

I try to release his hand, but he clamps down on it. He refuses to let go.

"I talked to Kate today," he says. "And she told me I'm not irresponsible if I want more for me."

My palm sweats despite the cold. The heat of my breath puffs into the air like a train. But the more I try to regulate it so Chase doesn't notice, the more noticeable I think it becomes.

What is he saying? He wants more? More ... what? More who?
More me?

"What do you think?" he asks.

"I think ... this is your choice."

"That's a non-answer."

I laugh. "It was a reply, so it counts as an answer."

Chase leads me to a wooden swing beside the lake. We sit on the damp surface, and the cold bites into my backside. He notices, lifts me, and sets me on his lap with his hands around my stomach.

We swing gently for a long time, enjoying the cool breeze. I rest my head against his shoulder and let the rhythm lull me into a false sense of security.

"Do you find it hard to trust people?" I ask.

He hums. "No, not really. That's pretty surprising, now that I think about it. But I'm not generally a distrusting person unless Luke is involved."

I grin.

"Why? Are you?"

"Surprisingly, I am. Or maybe not surprisingly. I don't know."

"Why do you ask?"

I turn my head so I can see his face. "Because of this."

It takes him a few moments to understand what I'm saying.

He pulls me tighter against him and kisses the top of my head. The gesture feels like a million butterflies in my stomach —as if someone took the world's stress off my shoulders and handled it for me. *It's nice.*

"Do you think it's weird that we're sitting here like this?" I ask, playing with his fingers. "I mean, not that long ago, I didn't know you existed."

"It is funny, isn't it?"

"Yeah."

He moves beneath me, adjusting his position. "But maybe it's not weird, Megan. Maybe this is ..." He chuckles. "Forget it."

"Forget what?"

"Nothing."

I pry his hands off me and stand. "Remember our agreement?"

He grins, amused. "We shredded that thing a long time ago."

I climb onto the swing, straddling him. He wastes no time wrapping his arms around my bottom and scooting me as close to him as I can go.

His face is animated as he watches me. *My lord, he's so damn handsome.*

I cup his cheeks in my hands, the scruff scratching my palms. My thighs tense at the sensation—and the memory of what it feels like between my legs.

"Forget what?" I ask again.

"Maybe this is what two people do who want to fuck."

I snort, my core clenching. "That's not what you were going to say."

He leans his head back arrogantly—like he knows he's in control. "What do you think I was going to say?"

"If I knew, I wouldn't be asking."

"What did you want me to say?"

What I wanted you to say is ridiculous for two people who barely know each other. My face flushes with embarrassment, and I start to extricate myself from his lap. But he holds on.

"How about this," he says, his tone low. "I'll tell you what you wanted me to say."

"Chase—"

"You wanted me to say that maybe our connection isn't so weird after all." His eyes shine under the moon. "You hoped I would tell you that I can't stop thinking about you and that you're wrecking my life. That I want to come home and see you. That I wait for your texts during the day. That I'm so fucking unsure what this all means, but I'm also so damn certain that this is different from anything I've had before, and I can't imagine ever finding it again."

I lean forward and press a kiss to his lips. His words sink into my psyche, but I pivot away from the seriousness of it all. "Are you saying you have a crush on me, Mr. Marshall?"

He rests his arm along the top of the swing and laughs.

I rest my cheek between his collar and jaw, smiling from ear to ear.

He refastens his hands around my ass and sighs. "So that's it? I say all that, and you accuse me of having a crush?"

"Not just a crush. *A big crush.*"

"Yeah, well, here's the bullshit—I knew this would happen. As soon as you climbed out of that rental car, I knew you were my weakness. That you'd be trouble."

I hum against his chest.

We swing back and forth. I know I haven't said anything in return, but I'm afraid it'll be wrong if I say too much. But as I nestle against him and hear his beating heart, I know I have to say something.

I can't pivot forever. And really—I don't want to.

"This isn't like anything I've felt before either," I say, wading into the conversation slowly. "And that scares me a little."

"Why?"

I sigh, wishing the answer was as simple as the question.

"Logistics, first of all," I say. "I can't do a long-distance relationship, and I'm not going to find a job in Peachwood Falls. I can't afford to move here and support myself."

He nods slowly.

"And even if I could …" I raise and look at him. "We don't even know each other, Chase. You can't make big life decisions over something you've only known for a few weeks."

"*Someone*, you mean."

"Either way." I frown, taking in his frustration. "Whenever I see or talk to you, I fall harder. I get more comfortable. But every day is a day closer to when I go home."

He studies me in a way only Chase can. His grumpiness reminds me of the day I met him. It settles over his features, and he narrows his eyes as he navigates his thoughts.

"So," he says, pressing his lips together. "You're telling me you're falling for me."

I smack his chest. It cracks his demeanor, and he chuckles.

"Do you know what I think?" he asks, swinging us again.

"What's that?"

"I think it might have something to do with logistics, and that's fair. And it might have something to do with us just getting to know each other, and that's fair too. But I think you're out of your comfort zone with this, and that scares you."

Asshole.

"I'm not a clown, and you don't know how to navigate without a circus," he says, echoing our first interaction.

"Oh, *you're a clown.*"

He rolls his eyes, making me smile.

My stomach knots as I feel how he touches me. It's tender and with respect. But there's an underlying strength that reminds me that he'll protect me and, by the feeling of his cock hardening under me, that he'll fuck me too. *And I think I'll love one just as much as the other.*

Chase is everything I've never allowed myself to have. And I can't rid myself of the nagging voice that reminds me why I haven't ever had someone like him. That voice worries how I'll feel when this ends between us.

If it ends.

When it ends.

I sigh. "Can we stop talking and make out instead?"

He laughs. "I'll compromise."

"Do I get your cock at the end?"

"Always."

I kiss him quickly. "Then let's compromise."

He shakes his head, entertained by my antics. "Let's make a new agreement."

"Fine. What do you want it to say?"

"I want it to say," he says, looking me in the eye like I'm not listening, "that I want you in my bed. I want to kiss you whenever and wherever I want. I want you, and you're important to me. Okay?"

Oh my gosh.

No one has ever said that to me before. I'm not sure I've ever been important to anyone besides my mother. *And Iyala Nails, if I believe that—but only when it benefits them.*

"It's time that I start factoring myself in my life for a change," he says. "I don't think I ever would've bothered or even noticed until I met you."

It would be wonderful to grab his words and let him prove that he means what he says. But I can't lose touch with reality … and why we weren't doing this.

"But what about Kennedy?" I ask.

"We'll take it slow. She likes you, and I think you're good for her. Kate has lots of opinions and most of them favor me getting to know you."

I grin. "I think I like Kate."

He squeezes my ass cheeks and kisses me not-so chastely.

"You're such a fucking distraction," he says against my lips.

"You knew that when you met me."

He swipes his tongue through my mouth. "That wasn't all I knew."

I hop off him and start to unbutton my pants. His eyes glimmer with mischief as he pulls his pants down too.

"No one can see us down here, can they?" I ask.

He spreads his knees while I climb on. "Nope."

"Good. Because I'm going to make you come inside me so hard that there might be fireworks."

He laughs. But the laughter turns into a prolonged hiss as I sit down on his cock. Finally, he grips my waist before I can move.

"Um, Chase? I want to ride you."

"I know. But before you rock my world, I want to hear you say you're my girl."

My cheeks blush. "Really?"

He seems to be as surprised as I am that we're having this conversation but also … not. It's as if he's resolved that this is the way things are, and he's cool with it. *Happy with it.*

That's good because I am too.

"I thought having you around would be the problem," he says. "Turns out that having you around and not having you locked down is the real distraction."

I swivel my hips, my body flooding with heat I can't extinguish.

I don't know what I'm doing with this—this man, this relationship, this life. It could all go wrong—he could change his mind—and there's little doubt it would break my heart. But instead of panicking and feeling like an impostor, I give in. I lean into Chase's smile. His sincerity. I let myself soak up his words.

"Turns out that having you around and not having you locked down is the real distraction."

How did I wind up here? How did I get so freaking lucky?

Chase nibbles at my bottom lip. "Tell. Me. You're. Mine."

"Okay," I say, breathlessly. "I'm yours."

He grinds me down on him and captures my lips with his. The force frazzles my brain.

Chase takes over, moving us together in a slow, easy dance. It's not the fucking I think it's going to be. It's sweet. It's intentional. It's something different altogether, and if I'm not careful, I might misidentify it as the beginning stages of something more than lust.

egan

I RUSTLE AGAINST THE SHEETS.

My head is foggy—heavy. The cloud of sleep is thick in my brain. I've partially woken, only to be trapped between awake and asleep a handful of times.

Dreams have been vivid since I drifted off shortly after midnight. Chase has been featured in all of them, regardless of the setting. That makes waking up a bit better. I get to remember our conversation on the swing, sharing a shower with him after, and then sneaking back to my room to avoid a walk of shame from Chase's room to mine in the morning and bewildering Kennedy. And having to answer a lot of questions I'm not prepared to tackle—especially not alone.

Frustrated by my inability to make sense of reality—*am I dreaming again, or is this real?*—I try to turn onto my side.

And can't.

What the …? I press off the mattress with my hip and realize I'm pinned to the bed.

Panic rushes over me. A tug-of-war starts in my brain of whether to scream or freeze or to start kicking and throwing punches. I gasp, opening my mouth to yell for help, when large, warm waves ripple through me—starting between my legs and radiating in all directions.

"*Oof,*" I gasp, forcing my eyes to open.

Oh shit.

Chase lies on the mattress, face in my pussy. He's watching me—eyes trained on mine—as he licks and sucks around my opening.

I force a swallow down my parched throat. *Good thing I didn't need to scream. I wouldn't have been able to anyway.*

My head is scrambled despite being acutely aware of the delicious assault on my sex. I wonder what time it is. But as I start to look at the clock on the bedside table, Chase flicks my clit with his tongue.

"*Ah,*" I moan, reaching for his head.

He chuckles against me, rocking my hips back to give himself more access to my bud. I let my knees fall to the sides. I grip the side of his head and soak up the pleasure.

Every pass of his tongue gets me closer to the end.

He slips a finger inside me and works it just how I like it. I press my head into my pillows and climb to the top to my orgasm.

"Don't be loud," Chase says, kissing my clit, which makes me shiver.

"I can't help it."

He chuckles against me again. "You better help it, or I'll have to gag you."

I raise my head and stare into his eyes. "How loud do I have to get to be gagged?"

He shakes his head before burying it against me.

I try to remember his orders not to yell, but the intensity of the impending explosion proves to be too much. I grab a pillow and cover my face.

Chase bites gently on my swollen nub, and I lose it.

My legs shake—my body trembles. A gush of desire rolls down my slit and pools on the bed beneath me.

The sound of Chase's tongue licking, caressing—delivering the pleasure coursing through me—only prolongs the delicious torture.

I grit my teeth and ride out wave after wave of intensity.

Finally, when I'm spent, I release the pillow and toss it to the side. It's just in time to catch Chase pulling away from me. My orgasm coats his face.

"That's one hell of a way to wake up," I whisper.

He grins, picking up the pillow I just had. He slips it out of the pillowcase and uses the fabric to wipe himself off.

"Come here and let me repay the favor," I say, scooting up.

"Can't." He tosses the pillowcase at me, grinning. "I've gotta go to work."

"What?" I glance at the clock. "It's three thirty in the morning."

"And I've gotta go."

I hold out my hands like, *what the fuck?*

He gets off the bed and walks around to the side. He sits and pulls me toward him. I nestle against his chest, breathing in his cologne and memorizing it for the next two days.

"I couldn't leave without something to remember you by," he says, kissing my head.

"Pretty sure I'm the one with the memory." I pull back and look into his eyes. "Be safe, okay?"

He nods. "If you need anything, call me."

"I will."

He searches my face like he's about to say something else but doesn't. Instead, he half smiles and kisses me. "I've gotta go."

"Are you sure I can't reciprocate?"

"I wish." He kisses me again. "Two days. When I get back, you're in my bed."

My stomach wobbles. "We'll see."

He grins wickedly. "Damn right, we will." He gets off the bed and heads for the door. "Go back to sleep. I'll call you later this morning."

"Okay."

He cracks open the door, gives me a final smile that lights me up from the inside out, and then leaves.

I fall back against the bed and giggle. *How is this even real?*

Sighing, I contemplate whether to go to the bathroom or go back to sleep. But the energy pulsing through me has me turning to my phone instead. Feelings I've never felt before roar through me, and I don't know how to keep them inside. *They need to be let out.*

I unlock the screen and find Calista's name.

Me: I think I just fell in love.

CHAPTER 27

$\mathcal{M}$egan

"WELL, THAT SUCKS." KENNEDY TURNS THE CORNER FROM THE stairs and moves into the living room. "I just wanted to take a shower."

I turn down the volume on the television. "And why can't you get in the shower?"

"Because it's storming."

As if on cue, a rattle of thunder shakes the house.

"And why can't you shower when it's storming?" I ask, not following her.

She shrugs and slumps into a chair by the fireplace. "I don't know. Pap always says not to shower or be on the phone in a storm. Doesn't make any sense to me, but he also texts me his name after every message, so there's that."

I snort. "He does?"

"Yeah. *Love, P.* Or *Call me back, P.* Or *Did you want some fried potatoes for supper? P.*" She shrugs again. "Like, yeah, Pap. I can

241

see the number and your face when you text me. It's on top of the screen. There's no need to identify yourself."

Something about that is ridiculously adorable, and I can't help but giggle. Kennedy, although not as amused as I am, laughs too.

She snuggles down into the chair. "What are you watching?"

"This woman went missing for fifteen years, and the only clue about where she went was a yellow bandanna next to her cell phone on the side of a road. Long story and I'm not sure if it's relevant yet or a red herring. I'm ninety-nine percent sure her husband did it, but the investigators seem to think it was the neighbor. So who knows."

She hums.

"What do you like to watch?" I ask.

"Nothing, really. I YouTube nineties music videos. Sometimes I'll watch something if everyone talks about it, but I usually don't like it enough to become obsessed."

"Nineties videos, huh?"

"Yeah," she says.

"Did you know your uncle Gavin hasn't seen the 'Opposites Attract' video by Paula Abdul?"

"What? *That's a classic.*"

"I know."

"I'm a big Paula fan. She doesn't get enough clout from my generation."

"Agreed," I say, impressed with her stance on this important fact.

We sit in silence for a few minutes before my stomach growls. Kennedy looks at me as I press my hand to my tummy.

"Hungry?" I ask her.

"I'm always hungry."

A kid after my heart. "Let's go make a snack."

"Who did your nails?" she asks as we walk to the kitchen. "That color is the bomb."

I hold up a hand and inspect the shitty job I did before bed last night. "I did them, and this is not my best work. Please don't judge once you see them in the light."

"What color is that?"

"Offset," I say, grinning at the memory of the night we came up with that name. "We named it after … Well, I can't tell you that because you're a minor. But someday, I will, if you want to know."

She slides onto a barstool on the island. "What do you mean *you named it?*"

I find the peanut butter, caramel, and mini cookies I bought at the grocery yesterday. Then I find the apples.

"I mean, I named it," I say, pulling out the cutting board they use for veggies. "Well, I can't say that. It wasn't just me. But the team worked late one night, and we might've had some wine in plastic cups, and we came up with Offset." I hold up a hand. "It didn't make the cut for fall last year, but I snagged a few samples because I loved it so much."

Kennedy's brows pull together, and the dimple in her chin, like her dad and uncles, shines.

I take out a knife and begin to peel the apples. "You do know that I worked for Iyala Nails, right?"

Her jaw drops to the counter. "*No, I did not know that.*"

I smile at her reaction. *This must be what it feels like to be a celebrity.*

"Are you joking?" she asks, still in disbelief. "You *did not* work for Iyala."

"No, *I did.* How do you think I got the pink tote from the spring collection?"

"I don't know. I just thought you were cool or something. *You worked for them? For real?*"

I laugh. "Yes. I promise. You can look at my email if you want. They got ahold of me last week to offer me my job back."

"Did you take it?"

"No."

"Why not?"

I slice the apples and set them aside. Then I smear a few spoonfuls of peanut butter on the board.

"It wasn't a good fit anymore," I tell her, relishing the peace that comes with those words. "I worked there for a long time and had a lot of great experiences. But I'm just not a California girl."

"Where do you live?" she asks, watching me drizzle caramel on the peanut butter.

"Well, I'm from Dallas. That's where my mom lives. So I guess I live there."

She looks confused.

"I'm between jobs," I say, snapping the caramel bottle closed. "Sometimes being an adult sucks."

She throws her chest onto the counter and sighs dramatically.

I laugh. "What's that about?"

"You think being an adult sucks? Try being a kid."

"I was one once, you know."

"Yeah, but a single dad didn't raise you."

Okay. Where are we going with this?

I place some cookies, chop a banana, and add it to the board's periphery.

"You're right," I say carefully. "But I was raised by a single mom."

"Yeah, but moms know about periods and boyfriends. Dads are just … cringy."

I grin and slide the board between us. She takes an apple and drags it through the peanut butter and caramel.

"Like, I know he means well, and he wants the best for me," she says, crunching down on the fruit. "But he has no idea what it's like to be a teenage girl."

"No, he wouldn't know that. But what about your aunt Kate? Can you talk to her about stuff?"

"Ha." She drags the apple through the board again. "Kate is busy. I love her and know she'd do anything for me, but I can't call her and ask her to buy me tampons."

Wow. I never thought about that.

I nibble a piece of banana and watch Kennedy pick out a cookie.

I've always looked at Kennedy and this situation as a child with a fantastic family. She has love out the ass. Her behavior, I've decided, is just typical teenage crap.

But is it?

I've never considered having to ask a man for tampons or help when starting your period for the first time. Or how to do makeup. Or wanting pretty bras and panties—how does she manage that?

What about boys? Dating? Oh my gosh—birth control?

"Do you have a boyfriend?" I ask, testing the waters.

She laughs at me. "Right. Like Dad is going to go for that."

"That doesn't mean you don't."

She smiles coyly.

"Look, Ken, I'm not naive. I know what it's like to be fourteen. You're getting attention from boys. But are you giving them yours?"

She bites a cookie and watches me curiously. "I don't know. Are you asking me as my friend or my babysitter?"

"I'm not your babysitter."

"Yeah. You kind of are."

I grip the edge of the counter. "Well, whatever you want to call me—I'm here. If you want to talk to someone, not your grandma or aunt, you can talk to me."

"But you'll tell my dad."

"Tell him what?"

She grins. "Nothing. There's nothing to tell."

I shake a finger at her before taking another piece of banana. "You're cute." I head to the refrigerator to get a drink.

She sighs behind me. "You know what would make me happy?"

"I have no idea." I take out two bottles of water and let the door slam shut. "Do you want to tell me, or do you want me to guess?"

She takes the drink I offer her. "It would make me happy if I could be seen just for me. Just Kennedy Marshall, a fourteen-year-old girl from Peachwood Falls, Indiana. A girl who loves beauty supplies and hates math."

"Okay. Seen for that and not as … what?"

Her face falls, and she looks down at the board.

My heart immediately hurts for her. I want to reach out and hug her, but I don't. I don't know how she would take it. Besides, I don't want to disrupt her from talking to me.

"Do you know about my mom?" she asks softly.

"Yes. Your dad told me."

The corner of her lips rises before her eyes do. "And that's what I am before I'm anything else."

She holds my gaze with a decade of pain and frustration floating through the green orbs. It's a shot to my soul because I know that pain. I've felt it too. Maybe differently, but I know what it feels like to carry a burden I did not create.

"Can I tell you a story?" I ask, hoping that if I open up to her, she'll feel more confident in opening up to me. *And hopefully trust me because I know what it's like to have few people to trust.*

"Sure."

I walk around the counter and join her at the island. I slide onto the stool next to her and get comfortable.

"When I was growing up," I say, "we lived in a tiny town in Texas. Literally in the middle of nowhere. My mother was born and grew up in that small town."

"What's her name?"

"Denise."

She nods.

"My mom had a very rough life. She was dealt a shitty hand from birth. A lot of unfair stuff happened to her, and it made her make many choices that she wasn't equipped to make—choices she shouldn't have had to make," I say. "I had a rough and lonely childhood. Do you want to know why?"

"Why?"

"Because I was the daughter of Denise Kramer before I was anything else. And that wasn't a good thing to be."

Kennedy takes a cookie and breaks it in half. "That's how I feel, sort of. I mean, I don't even know anything about my mom, so I don't know if she made good choices or not. But when my family looks at me, they see *that*. They see the little girl they picked up in the office with blue carpet and a big metal desk. They don't see *me*."

A lump settles in my throat, and I can't help it. I put an arm around her shoulders and pull her against my side. She rests her head against mine for longer than I anticipate and then sits back up again.

"I understand what you're feeling," I say softly. "I understand why you feel that way."

"I know they love me. How could I not? They practically love me to death." She grins. "But I feel like I'm stuck in a toddler's life, and they refuse to let me … I don't know—breathe. And no matter what I do or what happens, they feel this stupid guilt like it's their fault. Like, '*Oh, Kennedy got detention again. How did we screw her up?*' They never think, '*Oh, maybe Mrs. Falconbury is just a twat and says rude things to Kennedy, so instead of dealing with it, sometimes Kennedy just avoids it.*' It never occurs to them, '*Well, Kennedy couldn't tell us about the party because we wouldn't even have considered it, so she had to sneak out.*'"

"Okay, I see your point. But sneaking out isn't safe. Don't do that, okay?"

"I'm not ignorant, Megan. I know Dad tries to protect me from getting hurt, and I appreciate that. I love him. Some of my friend's parents don't care, and I'd rather have Dad going berserk over me sneaking out than not caring. But can't there be something in the middle?"

I sigh. "I'm not your parent, so I feel uncomfortable discussing what can and can't be possible. But I think that your dad can be a rational person."

"With you, maybe." She laughs. "Can you imagine me telling my dad that I want to be on birth control?"

Oh, I can imagine, and it's not pretty.

"Are you having sex?" I ask her.

She shakes her head.

"I know you think I will snitch you out to Chase, but this is important. This isn't whether you wear makeup at school or not."

"You don't care about that?"

"In the grand scheme of things, no. I don't. But I'm not your parent."

"Unfortunately."

I laugh. "But sex is a different thing, Ken. If you're having sex, there are conversations and precautions that you need to take. Woman to woman, this is nothing to play around with."

"So are you giving me your consent to have sex?"

"*No, I am not.*"

"Don't you say it's because I'm fourteen."

"Kennedy, *you're fourteen.*"

She glares at me. "That's not a reason. That's an excuse to give me more rules."

I sigh, twisting in my seat to face her directly. *God, help me. I have no idea what I'm doing here.* "Look, I don't know how to talk to you about this, and there are a few reasons maybe I shouldn't do it in the first place."

"Talk to me about this, Megan. I can't even breathe the word *sex* in front of Dad, and if I say it to Gram, she'll probably douse me with holy water."

I smile. "I doubt that."

"Then you don't know her."

"Okay," I say, exhaling. "Ultimately, it is your choice when you have sex. No one can stop you. Your dad, Gram, me—we can all tell you that you should wait until you're older. But the truth is that you will do it if you want to."

Kennedy smiles smugly.

"But let's back up a second," I say. "*It should be your choice when you do it.* If someone is pressuring you at all—if they're telling you some bullshit like if you love them, you'd do it, or all the girls are doing it, or if they threaten you that someone else will if you won't—*do* not *have sex with that person.* They don't want to have sex with you. They want to control you. They're forcing you to give them something you can never get back. That's not the person you want to have sex with, okay?"

She considers this. "Okay, fair. No one has ever said it like that to me."

Thank God. "Next is that having sex isn't like piercing your ears. You can't just wake up one day and think you'd like to make this decision, and then that's it. It stops there. Because sometimes it doesn't."

"Like if you get pregnant."

"Or an STD. Or many things. Sometimes you don't find out until years later, so you can't just trust people or be careless about it."

"Again, fair."

"Also," I say … I groan. *How do I do this?* "You shouldn't feel like sex is dirty. Or shameful. Or that something is wrong with you because you're thinking about it, okay?"

"*Wow.* You are *so* not my dad."

I cover my face with my hands. "And he might kill me if he heard this."

"Well, let him know—not really, don't tell him I asked you about this—that you're making much more sense to me than he would."

I smile at her. "Sex can be a great thing. It should be a great thing. And if it's not great, if you aren't safe and consenting, you shouldn't be doing it."

"Got it. Sex should be great."

Please don't repeat that to your dad.

We sit and stare at each other. The longer we sit, the harder it is to keep a straight face. Then finally, we both start laughing.

"Are we done with this conversation?" I ask, exhausted.

"Please?"

"How about you let me go upstairs and get my manicure stuff, and we can do our nails?"

"And not talk about sex?"

"That would be phenomenal."

She grins. "I'll find the remote so we can see who the bandanna man is."

I climb off the stool. "What?"

"Your show. We'll finish it while we do our nails."

I smile at the pretty girl in front of me. I see why Chase worries about her. He'd be wrong not to be concerned, but something tells me Kennedy will be okay.

She's a lot smarter and stronger than he gives her credit for.

I head toward the hallway when she stops me.

"Megan?"

"Yeah?"

"You'll be a really good mom someday."

All I can do is return her smile because if I try to speak, she'll hear the lump in my throat.

I walk toward the stairs with my head held slightly higher.

Perhaps she's right. Maybe I could be a good mom someday.

Will I ever trust someone enough to share a child with them?

CHAPTER 28

hase

"THREE HOURS OF SLEEP IS GETTING ROUGH," JASON SAYS, yawning as he climbs out of his work truck.

"You're telling me." *Imagine how rough it is when you're getting used to sneaking into a woman's room in the middle of the night and instead wake up in a shanty motel alone.* "I don't know how long I can do this shit."

"Well, I've got bills to pay and mouths to feed. I'll be doing this shit for the rest of my life."

"You just got spoiled, Marshall," Robbie says, clamping a hand down on my sore shoulder. "You got out of the habit of traveling since the front office let you stay close to home for so long."

I shove his hand off me.

The sun isn't up yet, and the sky is just starting to wake up. Our crew worked until two this morning before we returned to our hotel to catch a few hours of rest.

The storm that ripped through central Illinois was a doozy. Power lines and poles are down everywhere, and if locals stopped asking us when the power would come back on, it'd be on much faster.

And I could go home a lot faster, too.

"I'm gonna go call the office and check in," I say. "You guys good?"

Jason nods. "Yeah. I'm gonna down this coffee, and then we'll start prepping to restring this section."

"I'll be back."

I stomp through the tall grass and splash across the creek parallel to the road. The cab of my truck is still warm as I slide back into my seat.

"This sucks," I say, setting my hard hat on the seat beside me.

I stare at the horizon and watch the day's first sun rays begin to tease their way into the sky. Something is calming about the sun rising. Dad always said that the sun coming up was a sign that you get a new start. All of yesterday's mistakes were erased in the night. I liked that idea growing up, and I've kept it with me my whole life.

Despite my exhaustion and anxiety about getting home, peace is floating through my veins. I'm usually a barrel of nerves when I'm away. Even if it's Mom with Kennedy, I still feel like something is amiss if I'm not there. I keep waiting for that to come back—to encounter the rock in my stomach and the acid pit at the base of my throat. I'm so familiar with them both.

But they fail to appear.

I could get used to this.

My eyes close, and I sigh easily, thinking of Megan.

I wonder what she's doing and if she's enjoying her morning. I laugh as I imagine her stomping around the kitchen, pretending to be good with being up before the sun. She's so damn cute when she moseys into the kitchen like she's not there to see me—as if she needs coffee that early. Sometimes I want to laugh at or tease her, but I don't. I don't want to chance having her stop coming.

I grab my phone and find Kennedy's name. I recheck the time, ensuring she's still home before school, and then press the green button.

"Hey, Dad," she says.

"You sound chipper."

"Well, I'm not. I can't find my black Jordans, and I know I put them in the mudroom, and they're not there."

"Huh. Did you ask Megan?"

"Yeah. And you know what she said?"

I grin. "No, I do not."

"She said she didn't wear them."

I can't help it. I laugh.

"That's something you would say. You didn't tell her to say that, did you?" she asks.

"Although I don't wear them either, did you check in the dining room?"

"Why would they be there?"

I scratch the top of my head. "Because I think I remember you tossing them around the corner the other day so I wouldn't see them when I told you to take them to your room."

"*Oh.*"

"Yeah—*oh.*"

"*Anyway,*" she says above the sound of her feet trotting down steps, "are you working?"

I watch Jason talk to Robbie. He's pissing him off on purpose. *Why does he do that?*

I sigh. "Yeah. But good news—I'll be home tonight."

"That's good."

"If I can get these guys to stop bickering with each other, we should be out of here late this afternoon."

"I'm sure Megan will be happy to hear that."

My breath stills. "Why? You haven't been giving her a hard time, have you?"

Kennedy laughs. "Uh, no. She made me a peanut butter board last night. Ever had one of those?"

"Nope."

"It's delicious. She drizzled caramel on it and cut up apples and bananas—and had little cookie things. *So yum.*"

"That does sound good."

"Maybe she'll make it for you one day."

There's a hint of something in her voice—a tease, maybe, or a taunt—that I can't put my finger on. But before I can figure it out, she changes the subject.

"All right, we need to talk about my birthday soon," she says.

"You have a month before your birthday, Ken."

"Yeah, but Neve and I want to do a spa day at the new spa in Bricksville, and I heard they're booking out for about a month. So I need to get you on board so we can get on the books."

I chuckle. "You and Neve need to slow your roll."

"So I can go ahead and have Megan set up the appointment for me?"

"No. Why would you ask Megan to set up your birthday party?"

"I don't know. It just seemed like the easiest way to get it done."

Shaking my head, I sigh. "We'll talk about it when I get home."

"Cool."

"I hope you have a great day today. Be good."

"Yeah, yeah, yeah. I'm always good."

I hope that's true.

"Megan is yelling at me to hurry," she says. "So I gotta go. See you tonight, Dad."

"I love you, Kennedy."

"Love you, Daddy. Bye."

"Bye."

She ends the call like I'm an afterthought.

I hold my phone, staring at the screen. She's all right. Kennedy is perfectly happy there with Megan. *Everything is going to be all right.*

> Me: You up?

> Kate: Can you calculate time zones?

> Me: Sorry.

> Kate: I'm up now. What do you want?

> Me: Thank you.

> Kate: You're welcome. But what for?

I try to articulate what I want to tell her. Thank her for … being rational. Talking the truth to me. Getting our parents to her house so I could get Megan to mine.

> Me: For not being another brother. They just got worse as they went. Mallet, Gav, Luke. Can you imagine yourself as a boy? Fuck my life.

> Kate: 😀 😀 😀 😀

I LAUGH.

> Kate: Since you're here, I have a
> big meeting today with my boss.
> Whisper a little prayer or juju
> or whatever for me, okay?
>
> Me: Okay. Good luck.
>
> Kate: Thanks. 😊
>
> Me: Going back to work.
>
> Kate: Learn about time zones
> during your lunch hour.
>
> Me: 👍
>
> Kate: And also learn emoji
> etiquette. We do not thumb unless
> we want to fight.

I snort and swipe off her name. But I find another name before I put the phone down and return to work.

Megan's picture, which I saved from the lake the other night, is in her contact file. Her cheeks are pink from the cold, and her lips are swollen from my kissing them. She's a beautiful, wild mess, and seeing her smile fills me with hope ... for me. Something I haven't had for a long time.

> Me: I can't wait to see you.

Her response takes a few minutes, but it's worth the wait.

Megan: I'll be here when you get
back. Hurry. 🤍

Me: 🤍

"I'm such a fool," I say, laughing at myself.

I silence my phone and slip it into my pocket. Then finally, I get back to work.

CHAPTER 29

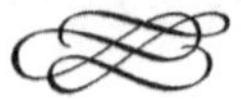

$\mathcal{M}$egan

"How are things going?" Maggie asks.

I put her on speaker and set the phone on the ottoman. "It's going great. I think we've found a rhythm." *No pun intended.*

"Is Kennedy behaving herself?"

"You know she is," I say, folding a blanket left on the couch this morning. "I haven't had any trouble with her at all. You painted her out to be this wild animal, and she's been nothing but an angel for me."

"I'm *so* glad to hear that. I've been checking in with Chase, and he's been giving me good reports, but I thought it was time to check in with you and get your side of things."

"No complaints here. How is Lonnie? Are you enjoying yourselves?"

Maggie laughs. "It's so much fun being with my daughter after spending every day with my rotten boys. Kate wants to shop, read books, and paint the dining room. I'm used to finding fishing worms in my refrigerator and mud tracked through the house."

I laugh too.

"Kate got some great news today," Maggie says. "She's being sent to a workshop in Miami and then transferred closer to home."

"Oh, *wow*. Maggie, that's great. I bet she's excited to be closer to you guys."

"She is, but not as excited as we are. I think Lonnie might burst at the seams."

I pluck a water bottle from between the couch cushions. Then a quart of blueberries. *Really, Kennedy?*

"So on that note," Maggie says hesitantly. "Lonnie and I have decided to head back home early."

My stomach falls to the floor. *What?*

"Kate will have to pack because she leaves for Miami on Monday. When she gets home, she will have a lot to do for the move." She giggles. "I can't believe I just said that. *Kate's moving home.*"

I can't believe you just said that either, Maggie.

The blueberries fall from my hand and smack the floor. Tiny berries scatter across the hardwood, rolling under the furniture. *Shit.*

"When will you be back?" I ask, getting on my hands and knees to gather the fruit.

"We'll hit the road in a little while. If I can keep Lonnie from stopping every mile, we should be home tomorrow afternoon sometime."

"*Oh*. Okay."

"I'll see you soon, sweetie."

I blink back tears. "Yeah. See you soon."

"Goodbye."

"Bye."

I roll onto my back and stare at the ceiling. *Breathe, Megan.*

What does this mean? Will Maggie come home and I'll need to go? Why would I stay at Chase's house with no good reason?

What happens between us now? Will reality settle in, and we'll acknowledge this was a lustfest? Or will we manage to figure something out?

I put a hand on my chest and practice breathing evenly.

"It'll be okay. Don't panic. He's given you no reason to think things will blow up in your face … *like everything always does.*"

I groan and roll back over and continue my berry search.

"No. Nope. This will be fine," I say aloud. "Everything has been going so well. There's no need to …"

My voice trails off as my phone begins to ring. A number I don't know flashes across the screen. *Huh.*

"Hello?" I say, sitting on my knees.

"Yes, is this Megan Kramer?"

"It is."

"Hi, Ms. Kramer. This is Principal Walding at Peachwood Hills Schools. We have a situation with Kennedy Marshall, and you are listed as the point of contact. Is that correct?"

Oh shit.

I get to my feet, the blueberries forgotten. "Is she all right?"

"I need you to confirm you're the point of contact, please."

"Yes. I'm the point of contact. Is she all right?"

He sighs. "She is. But we'll need you or her father or grandmother—I believe they are the other two on the list—to come to my office. We have a few things we need to discuss."

My mind spins. *What do I do?* "Okay. Well, I can be there in twenty minutes. Is that okay?"

"That'll be fine. Just let the secretary know I'm waiting for you."

"I'll see you shortly."

"Goodbye, Ms. Kramer."

I end the call. "*Fuck.*"

Holding my head, I pace back and forth. "What do I do? Do I call Chase? Do I call Maggie back?" I stop moving. "No, Chase asked you to take care of things. You don't even know what the situation is yet. It could be silly, and there's no need to worry him."

I groan, looking at the ceiling. I consider calling Gavin but quickly decide against it. Chase never insinuated that I should do that if something arose.

"Mom swears you're the right person to help with Ken, and honestly ..." A grin twitches against his lips. *"I might not disagree."*

"You might not, huh?"

"Well, in your favor, you seem like it'll be hard for Kennedy to steamroll."

I laugh. "That, I assure you."

"So we have a plan then?"

I race upstairs to put on clean clothes.

It looks like I have an appointment with the principal.

"Hi. I'm Megan Kramer here to see ... the principal." *I forgot his name.* "He called me a little while ago."

"Yes, Ms. Kramer. Have a seat, and I'll let him know you're here."

She eyes me over the top of black-rimmed glasses like I'm a stranger coming in off the street. *Nice.*

I sit under an oversized picture of *Principal Walding* and his big toothy grin.

My nerves have been frayed since I hung up the phone. I've gone back and forth over whether to call Chase. If it's an emergency, I'll have to let him know. But, in the end, it makes the most sense just to let him get his job finished so he can come home. He'll be home tonight, anyway.

Besides, he put me on the call list so I could take care of things.

This is *things.*

A door squeaks to my right, and the same man in the picture above me stands behind me, minus a few strands of hair.

"Come in, Ms. Kramer," he says, ushering me into his office.

Kennedy sits in a pleather chair with her arms crossed over her chest. Next to her is a woman in her forties with perfect hair and a button-down top tucked into a pleated skirt.

I make a point not to look at my jeans and T-shirt. *At least I found a blazer to throw on over my shirt.*

Principal Walding pulls in a chair from the waiting room for me to use. I sit next to Kennedy. When I look at her, she rolls her eyes and huffs.

Fabulous.

"Ms. Kramer, I'm Principal Walding, and this is Mrs. Falconbury. Kennedy is in her Health and Wellness class."

I fold my hands on my lap. "It's nice to meet you both."

"We've had a few situations lately where Kennedy decided to skip class," he says. "I'm sure you can understand why that's unacceptable."

"Yes. If she's not there, I can see why that's a problem."

I glance at Kennedy out of the corner of my eye. She glares at me.

"Here's the thing," Kennedy says, hands on her hips. *"I was there. I didn't skip class."*

"Ken, please. Don't lie to me."

Her jaw drops. "I was there, Dad. I mean it. I was as shocked as you are when I got that today."

"After this exact conversation last week, I find that hard to believe."

"Dad."

"I thought we were getting somewhere. I thought you were going to do better."

"I am doing better. Why don't you believe me?"

The principal takes off his glasses and places them on his desk. "She's had no fewer than seven detentions already this year."

"That feels excessive," I say.

"It is excessive," Mrs. Falconbury says from across the room. "And totally unnecessary. If she just showed up, I wouldn't have to punish her."

Kennedy's eyes are trained on the floor.

"What happened today?" I ask. "Did she miss class again today?"

"No," the principal says. "Today, Kennedy chose to have a verbal altercation with Mrs. Falconbury."

Kennedy springs up in her seat. "That's not true."

"I've already heard enough from you today, young lady," her teacher says.

"But I didn't choose to have any altercation with you. *You* chose it. You started saying—"

"Kennedy, lower your voice," Mrs. Falconbury says.

The principal holds up a hand. "Enough, Kennedy."

What the fuck?

"Well, I guess I should've skipped class today then," Kennedy says. "It would've been better than to have to go through this."

The principal sighs and looks at me. "Kennedy has been suspended for three days."

Kennedy glares at me. Again.

"Okay," I say, giving her a look to settle down. "I understand something occurred today, and you're sending her home. But I haven't heard her side of the story."

"Backtalking a teacher is never justified, Ms. Kramer," he says. "She's been on her third strike for quite a few strikes. This is the proverbial straw that broke the camel's back." He looks at

Kennedy. "Maybe you can go home, cool off, and return with a new attitude."

"Let's back up," I say, clearing my throat. "She backtalked a teacher. I got it. But that means we don't need to hear what started all of this?"

"Her attitude started all of this," Mrs. Falconbury snorts.

I turn to her slowly. "Considering I've been very polite, and you've dismissed me like a child, I sense that maybe Kennedy isn't the only one with an attitude problem. Respectfully, of course."

Kennedy's eyes go wide.

"Ms. Kramer," Mrs. Falconbury says, clearly placating me and doing her best not to lose her cool. "This is an ongoing issue with Kennedy. We'd like you to take her home and talk to her about her behavior. Someone needs to get through to that child."

I laugh, anger bubbling up inside me. "*Again*, I'd like to hear her side of the story."

Mrs. Falconbury sighs and throws up her hands.

"Kennedy," I say, looking at her and ignoring her teacher's antics. "What happened?"

"I got suspended for three days. That's what happened."

"Why?"

She just stares at me.

"Ken, level with me here," I say. "*Tell me what happened.*"

"You're just wasting our time," Mrs. Falconbury says.

That's it. I've had enough.

I slide my attention to the woman beside Kennedy. "Right now, *you* are wasting *my* time. I'm trying to get to the root of the problem, and you keep interrupting me. I'm starting to wonder if you don't want her side of the story told."

"That's ridiculous."

"It is, isn't it?" I ask, piercing her with my stare. "Now,

Kennedy, *what happened*? Ignore everyone else in the room and talk to me."

Kennedy sits up in her chair. Her eyes are wary, and she frowns. It's not a look I've seen on her before. It's filled with suspicion and alienation as if everyone is against her. A swell of emotion I haven't felt in a long time overcomes me and hits me right in the heart.

I reach over and take her hand in mine and give it a gentle squeeze. Tears form in the corner of her eyes. *Oh, sweet girl.*

"I can't remember," she whispers.

"Yes, you do. And your side of the story is just as important as Mrs. Falconbury's."

The teacher huffs again, and I remember that I can't act like the fool I want to be now. I'm the role model here. *Maybe the only one, it seems …*

Kennedy's chest shakes as she hiccups a breath. "She accused me of taking a cupcake—one of those little Hostess ones in the wrapper—out of her desk."

What? I look at the teacher. She pales.

"And I didn't do it," Kennedy says. "Why would I steal a cupcake? If I'm hungry, I have ten bucks in my backpack, and there's a vending machine in the atrium."

"Why did you think it was her?" I ask the teacher, still holding on to Kennedy's hand.

"Because the wrapper was at her feet."

"Because Frankie threw it there, and you know it," Kennedy fires back.

"Now, let's settle down," the principal says.

Mrs. Falconbury sighs again.

"You're *always* blaming me for stuff," Kennedy says, tears wetting her cheeks. "You always say that everything is me. *I* took your cupcake. *I* left my computer at home on purpose because I'm thinking of you when I get up in the morning, which would mean that *I* choose to make my day harder to spite you. You said *I* shared my notes with Hope so she could pass the test. I'll be honest—I didn't even take notes. I don't even like Hope! But you didn't care about that."

In. Out. I focus on my breathing.

"I'm already a bad person to you," Kennedy says through tears. "You just give me detentions left and right."

"Because you don't come to class."

"Why would I want to? You say stuff and have everyone laughing at me."

Excuse fucking me?

"Kennedy," Mrs. Falconbury says, fiddling with the edge of her skirt. "That's not true. We have fun in class. I don't treat you any differently than I do anyone else."

Yeah, no. I scoot to the edge of my seat, gripping the armrests so I don't launch myself across the room.

"If you're making any kid feel uncomfortable or accusing them of things or making a joke out of them—that's not *having fun in class*," I say, pinning her to the chair with my gaze.

"She's being dramatic."

"Really? What was it today?" Kennedy asks, wiping her nose with the back of her free hand. "If I had a mother, maybe I would know how to behave?"

My blood boils so hot that I think it will spew out of me. *"You said that to her?"*

Mrs. Falconbury flinches.

"Ms. Kramer, I'm going to need you to settle down," Principal Walding says.

I get to my feet and pull Kennedy into me. Her head buries in my chest. Her shoulders shake from the force of her tears, and it's all I can do not to cry too.

"Did you say that to this little girl?" I ask the teacher.

She dares to wave a hand through the air like she's discussing the weather. "This is getting ugly for no reason."

"I asked you a question," I say pointedly.

"I have serious doubts that it came out of my mouth. It was probably one of her classmates," she says. "But the shoe does fit."

My shoe will fit up your ass, too, lady. I don't say that, but I think she reads my mind. She leans away from me with a hand on her throat.

"So you don't argue with what Kennedy's saying?" I ask. "You're admitting that her version of events is correct, just that she's too … what? Sensitive?"

Mrs. Falconbury pales.

"We send this child to school every day for a safe place to learn," I say, my voice shaking with anger. "Not to be ridiculed by an adult who should know better."

Her eyes go wide.

I turn to the principal. "And you should be ashamed of yourself."

"Ma'am, I hear you. Some of this is new information to me."

"Have you ever asked?" I ask, my voice rising. "Have you ever listened to Kennedy to see what was happening? Have you ever *done your job* and thought that maybe it wasn't normal for a child to be written up constantly? It didn't trigger something in you that something may be amiss?"

He looks down at his desk.

"Kennedy isn't perfect," I say, running my hand over her head. "She's a teenager who is going to make mistakes. That's how she'll learn. That's what will teach her to be a responsible, strong, empathetic adult—*something the two of you aren't.*"

"Ma'am …" Principal Walding looks at me warily.

"I'm not sending her to school every morning so she has to sit in front of this woman," I say, jamming a thumb toward my new nemesis, "and be belittled. *Not happening.* I'll happily take her home for the next three days. That should give you time to figure out how you will fix your staffing issue."

Mrs. Falconbury snorts.

"Janice, please …" Mr. Walding says to her.

"Oh, look at you. You made a little girl cry." I grit my teeth. "You bully her so badly that she doesn't want to come to your class, and then you get another power trip when you give her detention. She either gets detention or is humiliated. That's so big of you. Do you feel like you won?" I glare at her. "She may feel helpless. I, however, do not."

I motion to Kennedy that we're about to leave. Then she picks up her backpack and slings it on her shoulders.

"Principal Walding, I'm going to suggest that you dig deeper into this issue and make some adjustments because I assure you, I will be doing the same."

He looks at the teacher with wide eyes.

"I'll be in touch. Have a good rest of your day," I say, giving them each a final icy stare to drive home my point.

I yank open the door, and Kennedy and I walk out. The secretary doesn't say a word as we march by her desk and into the afternoon air.

Adrenaline spikes inside me as the sun hits my face. But I'm almost knocked over by Kennedy before I can get my bearings.

Her arms go around my waist, and she hugs me tighter than I've ever been hugged.

"Thank you," she says, her words muffled against my clothes.

I pat her back.

I'm desperately holding back tears while my heart breaks. It reminds me of all the taunts and jabs I received growing up. "Do you want to talk about it?"

She shakes her head. *Good. It might make me go back in there alone, and I look washed out in orange.*

"Let's go home and have some ice cream," I say. "Then we'll figure out what to do. Does that sound okay?"

She pulls away and smiles a megawatt smile. "Sounds good."

"Let's go, kiddo."

I follow her to Maggie's car. We climb in and head off for home.

 egan

My ANTICIPATION GROWS WITH EVERY SECOND THAT PASSES.

Kennedy sits across the table from me, legs crisscrossed on the chair and hands folded in her lap. The look on her face mirrors the sea of emotions raging inside me.

My heart hurts for her.

All afternoon and well into the evening, we talked off and on about what had happened at school. She's told me how it feels to sit in a classroom and have her peers laugh at her. She talked about knowing her vulnerabilities and not being able to fix them, and much to my surprise, she's demonstrated a great deal of emotional maturity by acknowledging her part in the problem at hand.

She knows she can handle the situation better. She just didn't know how.

There's not much I can say to her because I don't know how she should've handled it either. But it's tough to be heard and listened to—two completely different things—if the audience doesn't want to listen. And, in this case, Mrs. Falconberry doesn't want any part of that.

"So how do you think Dad will handle this?" she asks, nibbling on her bottom lip.

I blow out a breath. "Well, he's logical and loves you more than the world. So you have that going for you."

"It's a *three-day suspension*. I think his logic will dissolve pretty fast."

"Well, I'm sure he's not going to be thrilled. But I'm sure he'll understand once we tell him what happened."

She grins. "When *we* tell him what happened? Does that mean you won't make me do it alone?"

"Were you trying to get me to say that?" I ask, pretending to be shocked.

"Maybe."

I smile. "Yeah, I'll help break the news."

As I look at her across the table, I notice she's sitting a bit taller. More confident. And I wonder if finally squaring off with Mrs. Falconbury and being heard helped her establish boundaries that make her feel safer.

I know it would've me. Because when I had to do it—when I had to risk more ridicule and draw even more attention to myself to be taken seriously, it helped.

Even if it was one of the hardest things I've ever done.

"Ken, I'm proud of you."

"Why?" She smiles mischievously. "Are you a rebel? Do you think I'm a boss because I got suspended?"

"Absolutely not."

She laughs.

"I'm not saying you handled this whole thing the right way," I tell her. "And I'm not condoning skipping class or getting into verbal altercations with the teachers, nor do I think getting suspended is great."

"Noted. Let's get to the *proud of me* part."

I make sure she knows I'm unamused. "It's not easy to confront people when they aren't treating you the right way because you don't always have to be polite. You don't have to—*you shouldn't*—allow yourself to be another person's punching bag. You don't have to pay for their bad days or moods. Stand up for yourself."

"That should be easy, but sometimes it's not."

"I know. As wild as it sounds, sometimes taking the beating in whatever form it's coming in is easier than putting up boundaries." I lean closer and look her in the eye. "But I don't give a shit if someone is your teacher, your boyfriend, a judge—whoever, if they are harming you—speak up. Because if you don't use your voice, you'll never be heard."

She grins. "Got it."

Great. "Want a drink?"

"Sure."

I get up, wishing I could pour a rum and Coke, but grab two glasses of water instead.

"Do you know what I don't get?" she asks.

"What's that?"

"Why is my teacher so mean? What did I ever do to her?"

I hand her a drink and sit back down. "Honestly? Who knows?"

"It's unfair."

I take a long drink, letting the water cool me down before I respond.

"You'll never be able to figure out why people act as they do," I say. "Mostly because it has nothing to do with you."

"Of course, it does. She acts that way *to me*. It's all about me."

"It's not," I say, chuckling. "Think of it this way—you say that I treat you differently than your dad. Right?"

"For sure."

"Okay. In each situation, what's different?"

She furrows a brow.

"You are the same person. The situation is the same. So what's different?" I ask.

"Well, it's you and Dad."

"Right." I point at her. "Your dad is a single dad. He must keep you alive and healthy. You are his whole, entire world. He worries about you every single second of every day. He's not just thinking about this event—he's wondering how it'll affect you a year from now. A decade from now. When you're retiring from your job and collecting Social Security."

Kennedy laughs. "No, he's not."

"I assure you that he is. But me?" I shrug. "You're a friend's kid, so I don't have the same concerns for you that he does. But I had similar situations growing up, so instead of worrying about how this will affect you in high school, I'm thinking about how you feel today. Same problem. Two different angles."

"*Oh.* Okay." She nods as if it makes sense.

"So how we react to what you do has nothing to do *with you,*" I say. "We react the way we do because of the things we've experienced. Do you see what I'm saying? How people act comes from a place of fear, pain, or worries you could *never know* because you haven't lived their life."

"I'm using that in reverse. *'You don't even know my life.'* I'm going to say that to the next person who suggests I should be a morning person or that a party isn't the place for me."

She watches me with a twinkle in her eye. Something about it makes my stomach tighten.

"What?" I ask.

"Do you think there's any way that you'll stick around when Gram comes home?"

"We'll hit the road in a little while. If I can keep Lonnie from stopping every mile, we should be home tomorrow afternoon sometime."

Maggie's words from earlier today, before I was summoned to the school, roll through my brain. *She's coming home tomorrow.*

"Do you want to?" she asks me.

It's such a loaded question—*do I want to stay here with her and Chase?*

A large part of me wants to remain in this house and see if it could be my home. *I think maybe, possibly, it could.* But saying that out loud is equivalent to putting a bull's-eye on my back. It feels like standing on a rug and giving someone the corner, taunting them to see if they can pull it hard enough to knock me off.

"But maybe it's not weird, Megan. Maybe this is ..."

I gulp.

My hand trembles as I tug on the end of my shirt.

"We'll take it slow."

I grin. We took it anything but slow. Things with Chase were hard and fast. He hated the idea of *me*. I didn't love the idea of *him*. But we couldn't stay apart.

There's no reason I should've landed in Peachwood Falls, yet here I am. And not only does this town, this house, and *this family* feel like my new comfort zone, but it also feels like an end zone. This is where I catch the last touchdown.

"Maybe," I say, answering her question. "I can't promise you anything."

"But you want to stay?"

I grin. "Maybe."

She laughs. As she speaks, headlights shine through the kitchen. Kennedy looks at me and blinks.

"Who's telling him?" she asks.

"This is your thing. If you want me to help break the ice, I will. But I think you need to take the lead on this."

She groans. "But if I say something, he'll blow up. There won't be a chance for me to explain. But if *you* say something, he'll at least pause before he yells at me."

"He's not going to yell at you."

She doesn't look convinced.

"Fine. Does it make you feel better if I say something first?" I ask.

She nods emphatically. In the distance, Chase's car door slams.

"Hey, Megan?" Kennedy asks.

"Yeah?"

She glances out the window and then babbles. "I want you to know that I know that you and my dad are … I don't know what you call it when you're old, but I know you're … kissing." She makes a face. "So if you need to kiss him to make this work out better for me, I won't freak out. I already know. So lay one on him, and I'll stand back here and smile like an angel."

I burst out laughing as my cheeks heat. But the laughter is short-lived. It dissolves as the mudroom door opens, and Chase steps into the kitchen.

"Hey," he says, setting a bag on the table.

He's downright exhausted. There are bags under his eyes and a layer of filth on his skin I'm not sure can be scrubbed off. *That laundry is going to suck.*

"Hi, Daddy," Kennedy says a little too brightly.

Chase looks at her, then at me with a heavy dose of skepticism. "What's going on?"

"Go," Kennedy whispers, shoving her bony elbow into my side.

I give her a look to knock it off. Instead, she tries to hurry me by motioning toward her dad with her head. It's not the subtle encouragement she thinks it is.

"Megan?" Chase asks.

This is going to be a disaster. I can already tell.

"Now," Kennedy whispers.

I suck in a long breath and steady myself. "Chase, we have something to tell you."

hase

"So tell me," I say.

Kennedy moves so she's a couple of feet behind Megan. Megan reaches back and takes her hand, tugging her forward until they're shoulder to shoulder.

My daughter's eyes are shifty. She has a little smirk on her lips that tells me she's done something I'm not going to love. The gesture is more of a shield than anything—her way of bolstering her confidence.

My sights settle on Megan. Holy shit, she's gorgeous. It's hard to believe she's as pretty as I imagined while I was gone. *I didn't make her up. She's real.*

She clears her throat.

"So?" I ask, prompting her to speak. "What do you have to tell me?" *Get it over with so I can get you alone somewhere.*

"I want to preface this conversation by saying everything is fine," Megan says. "There's no need to panic."

My stomach knots. "Maybe if you'd tell me what's happening, I wouldn't."

"Good point."

My high spirits at coming home to my girls dissolve like sand out of an hourglass. I'm draining—all my energy and enthusiasm wane more and more as I wait for an explanation as to why I shouldn't panic.

Megan takes a deep breath. "I got a call today."

"Who from?"

I spin a million thoughts in a few seconds, conjuring up every person who might've called Megan and every reason. *This is not helping.*

"I had the pleasure of meeting Principal Walding and Mrs. Falconberry today," Megan says.

It's the nonchalance for me. I lift a brow and look at my daughter.

My goodwill is gone. The hourglass is empty, and I'm left clutching the back of a chair for support.

I hang my head and will myself to stay calm. *Dammit, Kennedy.* "I know you're being facetious because I've met both people, and it wasn't pleasurable either time."

If it were a different day, I would look at Megan and wink. But it's today, and I don't have it in me to be coy.

"I'm suspended for three days, Dad."

My head whips up. "Excuse me? Please, say that again because I just thought I heard you say you are suspended."

Kennedy doesn't balk. "That's what I said."

I switch my gaze between them. I don't even know where to start.

Every nick, scrape, pulled muscle—they all burn. It's as if the thread holding me together snapped and smacked me in the face.

"What did you do?" I ask my child.

"So it's automatically something I did?"

"Well, yeah, considering *you were suspended*. I'm going out on a limb here and assuming they weren't picking random kids at lunch to go home for three days."

She rolls her eyes.

"Ken, now isn't the time."

She groans into the air as if I just ruined her life. The audacity kills me.

I march across the room, leaving Megan standing with her jaw hanging open, and swing the refrigerator open. It's stocked with food—containers of whatever they've been snacking on while I was away stacked neatly next to the milk, juice, and tea.

It only serves to frustrate me more.

For once, I didn't just feel like I was surviving. There was a reason for me to come home beyond taking care of my daughter, and that was really fucking nice.

And instead of sitting down with the two of them, piecing a meal together, and listening to them tell me about their day, I'm grabbing a beer out of the fridge and figuring out why Kennedy is suspended.

Fucking hell.

The more I think about it, the more the frustration adds to my exhaustion.

I slam the fridge closed and pop a beer open with more force than necessary. "So someone better talk."

"Mrs. Falconberry wrote Kennedy a disciplinary action for stealing a cupcake," Megan says.

My eyes bulge. "A what?"

"One of those individually wrapped things that taste like garbage," Kennedy says. "I wouldn't eat that if I had to—especially when Megan made the best cupcakes the other night."

I rub my forehead. *Make it make sense.*

"She also said that Kennedy engaged in a verbal altercation with her," Megan says warily.

I pace the room and try to figure out what to do. I'm at my

wit's end. Somehow, I had convinced myself that she was doing better—that she could manage two days without blowing something up.

But I was wrong. *And I find out about it when I get home.*

"What did you say to her?" I ask. "What kind of *verbal altercation* did you engage in?"

"Chase, listen, I don't think—"

"I want to hear her take responsibility for whatever she's done to get *thrown out of school for three days.*"

My voice rises as disbelief in what I'm saying takes over.

"You want to know what I did?" Kennedy asks, her voice shaking. "I'll tell you what I did. Mrs. Falconbury said if I had a mother, I'd know how to behave."

What the fuck? I set my beer on the counter.

My blood runs cold as I force myself to remain calm. *A fucking adult said this to my child?*

Heads are going to roll.

"And I told her that …" Her bottom lip trembles. "I told her that not having a mother had nothing to do with my behavior because I have the greatest dad ever."

She turns on her heel and bolts toward the hallway.

"Ken!" I shout.

"Leave me alone!"

Her feet pound against the stairs. The sound is punctuated by her bedroom door slamming.

"Fuck," I say, rubbing a hand down my face.

Megan comes to me. She burrows the side of her face into my chest. She holds me tight despite the mud, dirt, and oil all over me.

"Give her a second," Megan whispers. "Let her have a minute to herself."

I close my eyes and focus on steadying my breath. Megan's embrace helps. It centers me. And I'm sure it helped Kennedy today too.

"She's a good girl, Chase," Megan whispers.

I wrap my arms around Megan and kiss the top of her head.

Thank God she was with Kennedy today. I'm eternally grateful that my daughter didn't have to battle the school alone. But I wonder … *how long has this been going on? Has this happened before? Why has she never said anything to me?*

Have I been wrong this whole time? A stream of memories floods my mind. *No, I haven't. She's snuck out, stolen my truck, gotten detention—gotten suspended.*

Is this a stage? Are there layers to all of this that I haven't seen? Have I been focusing on the wrong thing?

More importantly, when does it end?

"I hate that this is where we are," I say. "That it got to the point that she got into a sparring match with a fucking teacher, of all people. Did I miss something?"

Megan pulls away. "In her defense, her teacher is horrible. And if I can offer some advice—someone needs to contact the superintendent or school board about her. If she's acting this way to Kennedy, she's probably not the only kid she's messing with."

"I'll tell you what I did. Mrs. Falconbury said if I had a mother, I'd know how to behave."

What else has she said to my daughter?

I grit my teeth. "Yeah, well, I'll be seeing Mrs. Falconbury again, and it'll be less pleasurable than the first."

"Want me to go with you?"

I look at Megan. "Actually, why am I just now hearing about this? Why didn't you call me today?"

"Because what would you have done?"

I look at her. *That's not the point.*

"You asked me to handle things, Chase. I handled it. You were however many hours away, and she was safe. There was no need for you to hurry home. You can handle it now."

I raise a brow. "That's not your call to make."

"*What?*"

"This is a big fucking deal—especially if the school isn't doing what's right by Kennedy. I should've been there to advocate for her. Why did no one call me?"

"Probably because I'm on the emergency list because *you* added me."

I scrub a hand roughly down my face. *This is not going well.*

"If you don't trust me with her, you shouldn't have added me to her contacts list," Megan says, her words sharp.

"That's not what this is about."

"Then explain it to me because I'm confused."

I groan, wrapping a hand around the back of my neck and squeezing.

It's not that I don't trust her with Kennedy. It's not that at all. Actually, aside from my mother, I trust Megan with her more than anyone else.

The problem is that I feel removed from what's going on with Kennedy.

But I don't want to fight about it. I have bigger fish to fry.

"So does this have any effect on her schoolwork?" I ask, forcing myself to mentally move on for now. "Does she get to make up whatever they do in the three days she's gone?"

"I don't know."

Breathe.

"Are you mad at me, Chase? Because I get the feeling you are."

I turn around and face her.

A genuine concern glimmers in her eye, and my heart softens as I take her in. She took care of my kid today in a situation that was probably frustrating as hell. *Am I mad at her*? No. I'm just mad at the situation. At myself. At Mrs. Falcon-fucking-bury.

At everything.

"No, I'm not mad at you," I say honestly. "I've just hit the limit on the fucks I can give today."

"What's that supposed to mean?"

"It means I don't have the energy to coddle you right now."

Her jaw drops. "I haven't asked you to do a damn thing for me."

Dammit. Don't take it out on her. "Megan, I'm sorry."

I start to tell her that I'm sorry for being a dick. Then I consider that I should probably apologize for her having to deal with Kennedy getting suspended. That's followed by the horrible laundry in my bag that will need to be washed, the fallout from this suspension, whatever comes next with that—the fact that I want to grab a shower and fall asleep for three days.

"Your mom is coming home tomorrow," she says. "Do you know that?"

I still. *Shit. I forgot.* "Yeah. She told me." I finish my beer and toss the can in the trash.

"So ..." she says.

"So what?"

"So what does this mean? What do you want me to do?" She holds her hands out to her sides. "You said we'd talk about things when you got home."

"Now's not the time."

I stand across the kitchen from Megan and see reality clearly for the first time.

She's waiting on me to answer. For direction. For my attention. And I don't have any answers or directions, and my well of attention has officially run dry.

And that's what does it. That's the kicker—the one thing I can't overcome.

If I ask her to stay with us, I'm relegating her to *this*. It's a life of chaos and turmoil, of teenage drama. Me being gone. When I come home, being too tired and annoyed to be a good partner.

She didn't ask for this shit, and she definitely deserves more. She deserves attention. Friendship. The ability to create the life she wants instead of inheriting mine.

But, dammit, if I don't want to keep her here with me.

"What do you want to do?" I ask her.

"About what?"

"Do you want to stay here, or do you want to go home?"

She stills. "What do you want me to do?"

I shake my head and sigh.

I want to ask her to stay. To beg her not to leave me. Ever. I want to spill my guts and confess that the only time my life has made sense is the last few weeks with her. But saying all of that will affect her decision. I know it will because that's who she is. If she thinks I need her, she won't leave … even if it's the best thing for her.

She nods, licking her lips and blowing out a breath. "I thought … never mind."

I know what she thought, and I thought it too. But the truth is, we might've had a great couple of weeks, but that's not the real world. *Why would she want to be sucked into this with us?*

"Look, Megan, I've slept about five hours since I left here the other day. I have a pile of paperwork to do tomorrow. I have to talk to Kennedy. I have to call the school, deal with my mom coming home, and who knows what else will happen by morning." I frown. "I'm dirty. I'm tired. And … And I don't know why in the hell you'd want to be a part of this. If I were you, I'd go."

"But what about the swing? All of that?"

"Do you want to do this, Megan? Really? Do you want this to be your life?" I spin in a circle, holding my arms out to the side. "Do you want to be stuck here raising my kid? Making me dinner? Waiting for me to come home?"

She blinks at me.

"Where will you work? What will you do for fun? How will you have a life here?"

Slowly, a look of sadness mixed with anger slides across her face. Although it kills me, I find some relief in it. If she's feeling those things, at least she's not upset.

But also—at least she feels enough for me to care.

Dammit.

"And why are you just thinking about this now?" she asks. "You sure weren't coming from this angle the other day."

"Because maybe I see things for the way they really are. Maybe reality just hit, and I'm thinking clearer without you sitting on my lap."

That's not fair, and I know it. But I can't recant it. It might not be reasonable, but it *is* the truth.

Megan sniffles, her eyes narrowed. "You're right. We got ahead of ourselves. It was just lust, after all. Don't you think?"

My heart cracks. I can't answer that. If I try, I'll blurt out what I know is the truth—*that I love her*. And that will really complicate this.

That would be unfair.

She smiles, blinking back what I think are tears. "Okay. Thanks for letting me know."

Megan gives me a wide berth when she walks toward the hallway.

"Can we talk about this tomorrow?" I ask, my chest slicing right down the middle. It takes everything in me not to reach out to her. *Let her go, Chase.*

"Sure."

I should follow her. I should call out her name and pull her in my arms. But it's probably better for both of us to just let her go tonight.

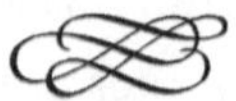

egan

I ROLL OVER AND LOOK AT THE CLOCK—TWO O'CLOCK ON the dot.

My chest is heavy, and my stomach is sour. I managed not to cry until the house got quiet, and I was sure no one was coming by my room. Kennedy texted me good night and thanked me for helping her today. Chase, on the other hand, didn't acknowledge my existence. I did hear him talking to Kennedy for a long time.

If nothing else, he's a great father.

I flip on the bedside table light and sit in bed. I'm afraid to go downstairs to get a snack. The last thing I want is to run into Chase. I have no idea why he grew so cold to me tonight, and I have even less of an idea about what to say to him.

How did he go from practically asking me to move in, to telling me I was just a piece of ass?

"Because maybe I see things for the way they really are. Maybe reality just hit, and I'm thinking better without you sitting on my lap."

"Oh, fuck off," I say, replaying his words for the hundredth time.

I grab my phone and find Calista's name.

> Me: Are you awake?

> Calista: Yup. What are you doing awake?

> Me: Well, me and Mr. Marshall had a falling out tonight.

> Calista: Wanna call me?

> Me: No. I'm afraid he'll hear me talking.

> Calista: Got ya.

I get off the bed and wander over to the window. I remember the first time I was here. The excitement of it, the wariness. How nervous I was, yet not—because Chase was ... Chase.

Calista: What happened?

Me: Kennedy got in trouble at
school. Chase came home from a
work trip, found out, and got all
pissy with me for not telling him
until he got home. Then he
started saying shit like I didn't
sign up for this and there's
nowhere for me to work here—like
I would want to stay here and
mooch off him.

Calista: Okay, I didn't know you
guys were serious.

Me: We weren't. I mean, we talked
about things. Sort of. You know …

Calista: So he was into it, and
you were backpedaling out of a
healthy relationship?

Me: Sometimes I hate you.

Calista:

I sit on the edge of the bed and sigh.

Calista: So what's the status?
Are you going home?

Me: I don't know. We left things
up in the air.

Calista: REMEMBER WHO YOU ARE.

Me: Don't shout. It's late.

Calista: Very funny. But I mean
it. Remember who you are.

Me: 😶 What's that supposed to
mean?

Calista: It means that you are
beautiful and intelligent, and
kind. And if he wants to treat
you like anything other than
that, fuck him.

I chuckle. *I did that. Hence, my predicament.*

Calista: You like him, huh?

I pause, hoping I can honestly tell her that I don't like him as much as I thought I did. Finally, I frown.

Me: Yeah. I thought I was falling
for him. I actually thought that
maybe this whole thing was some
kind of kismet. That the universe
was paying me back for some good
deed I did in another life. But I
was wrong. He turned out to be
another frog and not Prince
Charming.

Calista: That's what men do. They
trick you. And here's another
thing men do—they say shit they
don't mean. Don't be surprised if
he wakes up and regrets it all.

Me: I say shit I don't mean. I
understand how that works. But he
basically said I don't fit here,
and that was … cold.

Calista: Let's give him the
benefit of the doubt. You thought
he was a good guy up until now.
You're a good judge of character.
Maybe he had a bad day and
spouted off some shit. Or maybe
he got scared. He's not as badass
as we are.

Me: 💪

Calista: 🤍 What are your plans?
Are you sticking around there or
going home?

I'm not sure.

My gaze drifts through the window and into the dark sky. I consider my options. None of them feel right.

Me: I'm going to see what
tomorrow brings.

Calista: Remember that you're
Megan Kramer. Don't take any
shit. I don't care how good his
cock is.

Me:

Calista:

Me: I'll keep you posted. Good
night.

Calista: Love you. Night.

I put my phone back on the nightstand, cut the light, and start counting sheep.

CHAPTER 33

egan

I WRAP AN ELASTIC AROUND MY HAIR AT THE CROWN OF MY HEAD. Turning my head side to side, I check out my reflection in the mirror.

Not bad. You almost can't tell I cried off and on all night.

Just to be sure, I add another layer of mascara.

I shove my stuff back in my makeup bag and carry it to my room. I toss it in my open suitcase that holds most of my things. Preemptively, I gathered my belongings at five o'clock. It kept me from pacing the floor.

This morning brought clarity I wasn't expecting. Of course, it might've had something to do with Calista's shouty texts, but I won't admit that to her.

"If Chase wants to be a dick, he can be a dick." I slip on my sneakers. "But I'm here until Maggie gets back. Then I'll go."

I slide my phone into my pocket as I leave my room.

"Morning," Kennedy says, coming out of her room too.

I stop in front of her. "Hey. Good morning. How do you feel today?"

"Okay." She smiles. "Dad apologized last night and let me explain things. We had a long talk that's not so normal for us. But it was good."

How lovely for you. "I'm happy he did that."

"Me too." She jams a thumb toward the bathroom. "I'm gonna wash my face and stuff. Gram is coming by to get me in a little bit. She needs me to help her get their stuff put away."

She's back. I lift my chin, steeling myself to the possibility of going home today.

"I'm gonna grab a coffee," I say.

She nods and moves on down the hall.

I take the steps at a quick pace and round the corner to the kitchen. My feet falter when I spot Chase at the sink, but I keep going. *Remember who I am ... not a woman who just fell in love with you, and you tried to break her heart.*

He glances at me over his shoulder but returns to the dishes. I consider saying good morning, but he didn't bother, so I don't either.

"Do you want to stay here, or do you want to go home?"

That remains to be seen.

"Good morning," Maggie sings as she comes in the door. Her cheeks are rosy. "How are you kids?"

"Hey, Mama," Chase says, kissing her cheek.

"Hi, Chase." She air kisses him back. "How are you, Megan? Did you have a good time with Kennedy?" She walks to the hallway and shouts, "Ken, I'm here!"

"I had a great time," I say, popping a coffee pod into the machine and shoving a mug under it. I press the magic button. "Kennedy was a lot of fun."

Maggie looks at Chase out of the corner of her eye, then switches her attention back to me.

"How was your trip?" I ask as cheerfully as I can. "Do you want a coffee?"

"Oh no, honey. Lonnie got me up at four this morning to make it the rest of the way. I've had more coffee than my bladder can handle in one day."

I smile at her. "Kate is good? Did you have a nice time?"

"We did. Oof," she says, wrapping her arms around Kennedy as she practically dives into her grandmother. "There she is. Hi, sweetheart." She squeezes her tight. "I missed you."

"I missed you too, Gram. Where's Pap?"

"He's at home waiting on you."

Kennedy beams. Seeing her smile like that warms my heart. *She's going to be just fine.*

"What are you doing today?" Maggie asks. The question is a generality, but she's looking at Chase.

He side-eyes me. "I'm heading over to Luke's to help with his fence for a little while."

Maggie looks surprised. "Oh. Okay. What about you, Megan?"

Come up with something. Don't look lame.

I slide my phone out of my pocket. "I'm having brunch this morning."

Me: Hey, Gavin.

Gavin: What's up?

Me: Busy?

Gavin: Why?

Me: Pick me up in 20.

Gavin: Why?

Me: You're taking me for brunch.

"Who are you having lunch with?" Maggie asks.

I smile. "Gavin."

Chase flinches, but he doesn't say a word. *Fucker.*

Maggie laughs. "Tell that boy to come by the house today, all right? Kate sent a few things home with me for him."

"Sure."

Gavin: I am?

                         Me: You are.

Gavin: Does Chase know this?

                         Me: He does now.

Gavin: Are you trying to get me killed?

                         Me: I'll protect you.

Gavin: You're paying.

                         Me: Fine.

Gavin: Give me ten.

                         Me: Hustle.

Gavin: You're bossy for someone desperate for a brunch date.

                    Me: I'm really not in the mood for your mouth.

Gavin: Take it or leave it.

                         Me: Take it. Hurry.

I put my phone in my pocket again.

"Well, we'll see you guys later," Maggie says, tapping Kennedy's back to head to the door. "Have fun today." She practically skips to the door. "I love all of my kids doing things with each other. It just blesses this mama's heart."

I laugh and turn back to my coffee. Chase's gaze stops me.

"Yes?" I ask, taking the creamer out of the fridge.

"I didn't know you were going out with Gavin today."

"Well, you haven't talked to me, so how would you know?"

He glares at me. "Are you fucking with me?"

I sigh dramatically, ignoring how hot he is when he's mad. "No, Chase, I'm not fucking with you. But I'm also not sitting alone in your house on this beautiful day. That would be a little awkward, don't you think?"

He turns away from me, not expecting that reply.

My feelings were more hurt at his about-face before, but now I'm just mad. His behavior makes no sense. I'm willing to cut him some slack because I know he's stressed, but I'm not going to tolerate him being a dick for no reason.

"Besides," I say, adding the creamer to my coffee. "Your mom is back now. There's no reason for me to be here, and I want to tell Gavin goodbye."

I hold my breath and wait, hoping he'll give me a reason to stay.

"Are you glad she's back early?" he asks.

"Yeah, if you're back to this grumpy cat bullshit, I am."

He stills momentarily before going back to searching through the junk drawer.

"I don't know why you aren't talking to me," I say. "But it's not a good look."

"I'm talking to you. That's what this is. Talking."

"You know what? I'm glad you're doing this."

He turns around to face me. His eyes hold the shield between us that I haven't seen in a long time.

"You almost had me convinced you were different," I say, denying the lump in my throat to settle in and make itself at home. "But if you can act like this when I didn't do anything but try to help you, then I can only imagine what you would be capable of in an actual fight."

His chest rises and falls.

"You're pathetic," I say as Gavin pulls into the driveway.

I slide the creamer back in the refrigerator. Then I blow past Chase, leaving him brooding beside the sink.

Jerk.

"Stop looking at your phone," I say. "Give me attention."

Gavin looks up. "You realize we aren't dating, right?"

"Obviously. I'd never date you."

He snorts.

"I wouldn't. You're best friend vibes, not *hot guy I wanna fuck* vibes."

He shakes his head like he can't believe I'm saying this and returns to his phone.

"I'm not paying for your food if you don't give me company," I say.

"You are needy. *Damn.*"

"And you're a terrible best friend. *Damn.*"

He sighs and exits whatever app he's on. Then he sets his phone on the table. He folds his hands on the tabletop and smiles politely. "There. You just cost me a hookup on social, but *there*. Happy now?"

"Thank you."

"What would you like to talk about?"

"First," I say, swirling my straw around my Sprite, "I want to know why you let me fall for your brother."

"*Oh no.* I warned you."

I gasp. "You most certainly did not."

"Well, knowing you, it wouldn't have mattered anyway. You have this propensity of doing what you want regardless of what others think."

I scoff.

"You do," he insists.

"Like what?"

"Like … falling for my brother." He grins. "You really fell for him, huh?"

I roll my eyes.

"So," he says, sinking back in his chair, "what is this brunch thing, anyway? You aren't using me to make him jealous or something, right? He'll kill me, and that'll be on you. Can you live with that?"

"I'm not making him jealous. You are literally the only person I know here, and I wasn't about to sit in Chase's house while he goes and does whatever today. It's … awkward."

Tabitha comes by and places our food in front of us. She makes quick chitchat with Gavin before scampering off to another table.

"Why are you guys fighting?" he asks, chomping on the end of a fry.

"Honestly? I don't know."

He looks at me like I'm joking.

"I don't know," I say again. "He told me last night that he didn't think I was a good fit for his life—"

"*What?*"

"So I should go home or whatever." My chest pulls so tight that I wince. "So screw him."

"I don't think screwing him is fixing your problems."

"Ha."

He takes a drink and watches me over the cup.

My energy begins to wane, and reality begins to settle in. Chase didn't stop me from leaving this morning. He didn't try to apologize. He didn't even try to talk to me.

I frown. "I have a ticket back to Texas this evening."

Gavin slowly places his glass back on the table.

"Could you take me to the rental car place this afternoon so I can get to the airport? I'll pay you," I say.

"*Megs.*"

I shove a fry in my mouth so I can't respond.

He grimaces, moving his head around his neck. "Don't do this."

"I didn't do anything," I say after I swallow.

He picks up his phone again. His fingers fly over the keys.

"Will you take me?" I ask. "If not, I can try to find a taxi, but I don't know that they come all the way out to Chase's."

He doesn't look up from his device.

"Hello? Gavin?"

He looks up and sighs. He's torn, but he gives in. "Yeah. I'll take you."

"Thanks."

"But let's order dessert."

I make a face. "What?"

"Dessert." He eyes his phone for a moment and then sets it down again. "We're ordering dessert. If this is your last meal at The Wet Whistle, then we're getting cake."

"Then you're paying."

He grins. "Fine."

"Fine."

I don't know what I expected or what I thought might happen. *No, that's a lie. I wanted Chase to ... chase me. I wanted him to think I was someone he couldn't just discard.*

Instead, I'm leaving. *Kinda like I always knew I would.*

CHAPTER 34

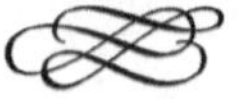

hase

"I thought you were going to Luke's?" Mom asks, taking the last coffee mug from their trip out of her car.

"I am. Or I was. But he just called and said he has to swing by work for a little while, so I'll wait for him to come home. Otherwise, I'll get out there and do all the work."

Mom laughs. "You aren't wrong."

Kennedy comes out the front door and jogs across the lawn. "Hey, Dad! Wait."

"What's wrong with her?" I ask Mom.

"No clue."

"What's up?" I ask as she gets closer.

She comes to a stop next to me. "Hey, can you run me home real quick? I forgot my phone charger, and because your parents refuse to use Apple products like the rest of the world ..."

Mom shakes her head. "I like my phone just fine."

"Get in," I tell my kid as I climb into the driver's side. "I'll bring her back."

Mom nods and goes back to cleaning out her car.

Kennedy gets buckled in, and I hit the gas. We roar down the gravel road toward our house.

"So," she says as soon as the engine dies down. "We need to talk."

I snort. "Oh really?"

"Yes. Really."

I make a face and look at her. "I thought we got on the same page last night."

"We did. About us. But we didn't talk about Megan."

And here we go.

My palms sweat as I regrip the steering wheel and ensure I don't swerve off the road.

I knew this conversation was coming. *I'm not sure how it's going to go. Does Kennedy know she's leaving? Does she want her to? Does she care?*

Where are you going with this, kiddo?

"What are you doing, Dad?" she asks like she's my mother, and she's highly disappointed.

"Um, driving you home."

"Dad ..."

"What, *Ken*? This is none of your business."

"That's cute."

I laugh. "Excuse me?"

She scoots around as much as she can to face me from the waist up. She gives me a look of total seriousness. There's not a crack in this girl's veneer.

I blow out a breath.

"Why did you let Megan stay with us?" she asks.

"Because I didn't want to leave you alone."

She rolls her eyes.

"What?" I ask. "That's why. I was afraid you'd run off and get married while I was gone." I run a hand over my chin. "Instead, you got suspended."

She smacks my arm. "Stop it."

"Fine."

"So why did you ask her to stay with us? Because you said no at first."

God, help me.

"Dad, I hate to tell you, but you're in love with Megan."

I swerve around a pothole a little too sharply. It takes me a second to regain complete control.

"Try not to kill us," she says.

"Ken …" I wipe a hand down my face. "I'm not in love with Megan."

"Uh, yes, you are."

I groan.

"Well, if you're not, you should be," she says as we pull into our driveway. "She's still here after your antics last night. That says something."

"My antics?"

"I listened to your conversation, and you weren't very nice to her."

I put the truck in park. "You shouldn't be eavesdropping."

"Yeah, well, you shouldn't talk so loud. I had to pee. I can't help it that your voices travel through the radiator, and our walls are made of paper."

My eyes close, and I try to remain calm.

"Megan didn't have to fight for me at school, but she did. You should've seen her. She put Mrs. Falconbury and the principal in their place, and *it felt so good*. She sees me and understands me. It's the best thing."

"I'm glad you like her. But that doesn't mean I'm in love with her."

"You are in love with her."

"Stop saying that."

She grins. "Do you know what I think? I think you're afraid to love her, Dad. I think you believe that if you trust her to come into our lives forever, something bad will happen, and you'll feel responsible for it."

Whoa. My head spins as I try to accept that Kennedy just said this.

"Megan taught me to stand up for myself. To not be the victim of someone's moods. My side of the story is just as important as anyone's."

Did she? My heart softens as I think of Megan sitting down with Kennedy and discussing her feelings in depth. And for giving her wise advice … when I wasn't there. *For going to bat for my child.*

"My side of the story is that Megan feels a whole lot like a part of our family," she says. "When she's around, you smile and joke around."

I do?

"You sneak off with her and go down to the lake."

I narrow my eyes. She shrugs, and that's relieving. She doesn't seem to know what we were doing at the lake.

"You don't look so stressed all the time," she says. "You aren't so stiff-looking. I don't worry you'll have a heart attack and die at work."

I sit back in my seat. "You worry about that?"

"*Yeah,*" she says like I'm ridiculous for thinking she doesn't. "And Megan looks at you like you're the most handsome man in the world. And she cares about me. *Me.* I can talk to her about stuff I can't talk to you about."

Like what?

Maybe I don't want to know.

"I like it just being us," she says. "But I think we can add Megan too. We *should* add Megan too. She needs us as much as we need her."

I rest my head against the leather and squeeze my eyes shut.

I can't discuss this with my daughter—even if she does make good points. Even if she says what I'm feeling.

Megan does belong here. The past twelve hours have killed me. I've fought with letting her go and asking her to talk because I don't know what's best for all of us.

Is it right to ask her to give up her freedom for this small-town life? She couldn't do the things that excite her here. The things she's used to. Her whole life would change.

Ours would too.

But it would be worth it.

My phone buzzes in the console. Once my truck's off, I pick it up and see a list of texts from Gavin.

Gavin: ARE YOU LISTENING TO ME?

> Me: Why are you blowing up my phone?

Gavin: Look, I'm sitting at The Wet Whistle with Megan. She's pissy, and it's pushing me over the edge. Plus, she's bought a plane ticket to go home tonight— and I don't mean home as in your house. You better fix this.

> Me: She's going back to Texas?

Gavin: Yup. And she wants me to take her to pick up her rental car.

Holy shit.

I don't know why I felt I had more time to get my shit together, but I was wrong.

My heart pounds.

Me: You're at The Wet Whistle?

Gavin: Yes. Come. Save me.

Gavin: She won't shut up.

Gavin: Also, she's mean, and I'm
scared of her.

Gavin: Also, bring your wallet
because you should have to pay
for this.

Me: Just … stay there.

Gavin:

My chest rises and falls. My hands tremble.

"All men set me up for failure. That's why I'm thirty years old, alone, and childless."

My lips twitch.

"Are you saying you have a crush on me, Mr. Marshall?"

I chuckle. *No. I'm saying I love you.*

"Ken?"

"Yeah?"

"I need your help."

"If I help you, do I get ungrounded?"

This kid.

I open the truck door. "No, but you might get Megan to stay forever."

"Deal!"

egan

"The longer I sit here, the madder I get at your brother," I tell Gavin.

Gavin holds his head in his hands.

"You're not very supportive." I sip my Sprite. "You're a disappointing best friend. Calista is so much better at this than you."

"Call her. I'm happy to turn over the reins."

I gasp. He shrugs.

"I'm ready to get back to Texas," I lie. "I might even return to my old job and give the West Coast another good ole college try. I didn't hate myself there."

The idea of doing those things makes me hate myself. I don't belong there—in Texas or California. I belong *here*. There's just no room for me.

I blink back the tears my strong girl persona has battled all morning. But the less there is to say, and the more there is to think and feel, the harder it gets to stay above it.

It's also harder not to be angry.

I haven't felt this way in a long damn time, and honestly, I hoped I was immune to it. I truly thought I had outgrown feeling lonely and unwanted—like the black sheep.

But I guess not.

"Do you guys need anything else?" Tabitha asks.

"A headache pill, if you have one," Gavin mumbles.

I shake my head at him. "You aren't helping."

"A shot of whiskey?" he asks, looking at Tabitha with pleading eyes.

"Not at this time of day," she says. "Sorry, buddy."

The front door opens, and my attention snaps to the two people walking in.

Kennedy marches straight toward me. She doesn't look around. She doesn't smile at Tabitha or say hello to Gavin. Instead, she stops beside me before wrapping her arms around my neck and hugging me for dear life. *Oh, this girl gives great hugs.*

Behind her is Chase.

He's a beautiful disaster.

His jeans have holes in them. His black T-shirt was in the dryer last night and is wrinkled to beat all hell. The blue-and-black flannel on top makes his eyes look even greener, and I can barely manage to keep my emotions intact.

I want to jump into his arms—have him hold me and make the insecurity I'm fighting disappear.

But I can't. I refuse. I'm not giving him that.

"My father would like to say something," Kennedy says, stepping back.

"He would? That's nice."

Chase dips his chin. "Can we talk?"

"Yeah."

"Where do you want to go?"

Where do I want to go? I shrug. "Right here is fine."

"Not right here."

I look at my wrist like there's a watch on it. *There's not.* "It's getting late. I have a plane to catch."

"The hell you do."

I steel my gaze at Chase's. "Don't worry. It won't inconvenience you. Gavin is taking me to get a rental car so I can drive to the airport."

Chase laughs haughtily. "No, he isn't."

"Gav …" I warn.

Gavin covers his face with his hands. "Don't do this to me, guys."

"You're on our team, Uncle Gavin. You want her to stay."

What? My insides soften as Chase's features smoothen out.

"I have something to ask you," Chase says.

"Yes," I say, much to his surprise. I stand and grab my purse. "You can buy my brunch." I head for the door. "Come on, Gavin."

"Gavin, don't you dare," Chase growls.

"Megan. Wait," Chase says.

I keep walking.

The sun shines high in the sky on this beautiful day. I walk across an empty lot beside The Wet Whistle toward Gavin's truck.

"*Megan!*" Chase shouts behind me.

"Nope. You had your chance to talk. Now that I've accepted that I'm leaving—*oof.*"

I'm spun around by a frantic Chase. Kennedy is on his heels. Gavin follows with his hands shoved in his front pockets like he'd rather be anywhere else besides here.

I pant, trying to catch my breath. "What do you want?"

"Talk to me."

"Why? Because you decide it's convenient for you?"

"Listen to him, Megan," Kennedy pleads.

I take a long, deep breath and summon my strength. "Talk."

Chase twists his hat around backward. "I don't want you to leave."

"Cool. What else?"

"What does that mean?" he asks.

"That means I heard you, so you can continue to your next talking point."

He furrows his brow, annoyed. "Why won't you just talk to me?"

"We're talking, Chase. But you hurt my feelings last night. You embarrassed me this morning in front of your mother. And this …" I look at Kennedy, then Gavin. "This isn't exactly great for my ego either—not that I care about my ego. It's just that you aren't doing me any favors."

"I just need five minutes."

"You get five seconds."

His eyes widen. "What?"

"One. Two. Three."

Chase panics, digging in his pocket.

"Four. Fi—"

"Will you marry me, you giant pain in my ass?" he asks.

"—ve."

My eyes grow as wide as saucers. I swear my heart skips a beat. I stare at a thin gold band he holds and wonder if this is real.

"I mean it," he says, cutting the distance between us.

"Wha … Did you just *propose* to me?"

"He did," Kennedy says. "You should say yes."

I shift my weight from one foot to the other. "What's going on here?"

"What's going on here is that I can't let you leave," Chase says. "Kennedy and I can't let you leave us."

"We love you," Kennedy says.

Tears fill my eyes, and my bottom lip trembles. A flock of geese flies overhead, calling to one another.

My breathing is ragged, but I'm afraid to reach for Chase. Instead, I pull Kennedy toward me, and she buries her head in my chest.

My gaze falls on Chase and his bright green eyes. The way my soul calms when I look at him is remarkable. It's amazing how the situation between us remains, I think, yet just being close to him feels right. It doesn't feel over between us. I don't know if it could ever feel that way with him and me.

"What are you doing?" I whisper to him.

Chase smiles shyly. "I love you, Megan."

My heart jumps so wildly that I take a step back. Startled, Kennedy pushes away from me. My sneaker hits a mud puddle, and the sole doesn't grip the wet surface. It slips, sending me flailing through the air. I land on my back with a huge, noisy splash.

Chase runs to me and takes my hand, pulling me to my feet. Kennedy watches, unsure of what to do. Gavin, the prick, laughs.

I blow dirty hair out of my face and feel the muddy water drip down my forehead.

"Are you okay?" Chase asks.

His voice brings me back to the present, and I can only do one thing—I laugh.

I laugh not because it's funny or because I'm embarrassed. I don't laugh because mud finally got the best of me.

I laugh because my heart slowly melds back together.

"One day, you'll wake up and realize that a piece of your heart resides outside your body. You'll feel a draw to that place no matter where you are in the world. You'll only feel whole and content when you're there—and that will be your home. That's where things make sense. That's where you're meant to be."

I get it now. I understand what my mom was saying.

Peachwood Falls is where my life makes sense. I've only ever felt like myself, with intense peace and contentment, in the walls of Chase Marshall's home. I've never been drawn to a place like I am in Chase's arms.

I suppose that's why nowhere else has ever worked out. I belonged here with this beautiful man, his adorable daughter, and his goofy brothers.

Maybe I had to go through everything in my life to prepare me for this moment—I don't know. But I'm absolutely positive that I'm supposed to be here.

My heart is here.

Chase gets down on one knee.

"You're in the mud puddle," I say, grinning so hard my face hurts.

"I acted like an idiot. I started thinking I knew what was best for you, and that's ridiculous."

I glance at Kennedy and catch her grinning.

"If you'll forgive me for being an asshole, I promise never to do it again."

I reach out and brush a strand of hair off his forehead. "Ever?"

His eyes twinkle. "Ever."

"Ask her already," Gavin says. "I have shit to do today."

Kennedy smacks him, making me laugh.

My heart is full. My soul is at peace. All of the questions I've had about my life—where I belong, what I should do, who I am—I now know why I didn't have the answers.

Because I hadn't met them yet.

"Marry me," he says. "Marry me today. Tomorrow. Next week. Just marry me, Megan."

"I'll stay without marrying you."

Kennedy's face splits with the biggest smile I've ever seen on her.

"Did you ask her to marry you?" a voice says from the road.

We look over to see Tucker's Towing truck crawling down the road. Tucker's head sticks out the window.

"I'm trying to get her to say yes," Chase shouts.

"It's rude to eavesdrop, Tucker," I say.

He chuckles and gives us a wave. Then he continues down the road with a honk of the horn in his wake.

I turn back to Chase. "You don't have to do this." *But please do.*

"You don't get it," he says. "You've already agreed to be mine. So now we're committing. We're trusting each other. You're not going to walk around and feel like it all might end someday because you and I are never ending, Megan."

I bite my lip to keep from crying.

"Let's start a family," he says. "Me, you, Kennedy—maybe a baby or two."

"Yes!" Kennedy squeals. "Have a baby. Please."

"I think I'm gonna puke," Gavin mumbles.

I laugh. "One thing at a time, okay?"

Chase slides the thin band on my finger. "I'll get you another ring. This one is Kennedy's. It's all I could find."

"I don't need a ring, Chase. I just need you."

"Is that a yes?" he asks, his eyes twinkling.

I hold his face in my hands and plant a kiss on his lips. "That's a yes."

egan

"Oof." Chase drops my bag onto the floor of his closet. "Is that everything?"

He stands and holds his shoulder, wincing as it moves.

"Come here," I say, sitting on the bed.

His eyes grow wicked, and it makes me laugh.

"I'm going to rub it," I say.

"Should I take my pants off?"

I snort. "I mean your shoulder. For now."

He sits in front of me and tilts his head to the side. I work the muscle back and forth, kneading him.

The house is quiet. *Finally.*

After the story broke that Chase and I were engaged, the house was a revolving door of people. Maggie and Lonnie. Gavin, even though he complained most of the time. Luke and a beautiful Alyssa. Patti from the hotel swung by to say hello and invited me to lunch soon. Neve and her mother even stopped by and offered their congratulations and to pick up Kennedy—who left with a wink.

Chase was right. Dealing with Kennedy feels slightly different when you're responsible for her.

"Have you told your mom?" Chase asks. "I thought you mentioned telling her earlier."

I smile. "I had to tell her before your mom did."

Chase laughs.

"She was over the moon," I say. "She screamed—legit *screamed* into the phone. And I have a suspicion."

"What's that?"

I press into the skin up his neck. "Your mom and mine might've collaborated on getting me here."

"You think?"

I hum. "I don't know. Maybe." I shake my head. *I'm imagining it.*

"That feels good, Megan."

His compliment makes me tingly.

"We have a lot to do," he says, moaning as I go down his back.

"Like what?"

"Like plan a wedding."

I laugh. "Chase, I don't care about that. Let's invite everyone over and get married by the pond."

"No. You and the mud aren't friends."

"True." I giggle. "Maybe we could get married at The Wet Whistle. Just open the doors, and whoever wants to come can come."

"Not a bad idea."

The more I think about it, the more I like it.

"Right there," he says. "Harder."

"I think you need to go to the doctor. Want me to make you an appointment?"

"Will that make you happy?"

"Yes."

"Okay. Then do it."

I laugh again. "I like this side of you."

"You mean you like to get what you want?"

"Yeah."

"I bet."

He turns around and puckers his lips. I press a kiss against them.

Just like the first time he kissed me, my knees go weak. *I hope it's this way forever.*

"I need to figure out how to get my stuff here from Mom's," I say.

He stands and peels off his shirt. "We can go get it or hire a moving truck. How much stuff do you have?"

"Not much."

"Maybe when Kennedy is out of school for winter break, we can visit your mom and get it."

I watch as he slips off his pants. "I'd like that."

Chase tosses his clothes into the hamper, then moves to the dresser. He busies himself organizing his things.

It's a chore to watch him—*my fiancé*—in his boxer briefs. *He's my fiancé. What the hell?*

It takes everything I have in me not to giggle. I haven't felt pure joy like this ever in my life. There are lists of things to be done in the back of my mind, but none of them matter. They all feel secondary.

Because I'm marrying the sweetest, kindest, hottest man I've ever seen.

Chase Marshall is mine.

Grinning like a loon, I lie on the bed and let my mind wander. For the first time in a long time, I don't feel like I have to manage my thoughts. It's okay to think, wonder, and ask questions—because the most important one has been answered.

I wasn't destined for a life of uncertainty. Despite my

pessimistic thoughts, I wouldn't roam the world looking for meaning for my entire life. I just needed to experience everything I needed to know before finding where I was meant to be.

My experiences have taught me about kindness. I know bullying. I've met despair face-to-face and won. I've lived alone, traveled alone, and relied on myself to make it. I've found success, experienced loss, and had enough relationships to know precisely what I don't want in a significant other.

It felt like individual strands of something that would never come together. Starts and stops of different lives that never amounted to anything.

But I was wrong.

All those things led me here—to the Marshall family. And every one of the lessons I've learned has already come in handy.

Would I fit as well if I didn't bring my unique set of experiences to the table? Would I know how to love Chase? Would I understand Kennedy?

Probably not. And suddenly, I'm grateful for everything that, until now, I've viewed as a failure or dead end. I didn't have the whole picture yet.

"What are you doing?" I ask him.

"Making you room in the dresser."

I hop off the bed and find my bag. I rummage through it until I find what I want.

"Make me room later," I say. "Let's take a bath."

His head snaps up. "You don't have to tell me twice."

I set a bag of bath salts on the tub's edge and turn on the water. As I strip down, Chase checks out the black crystals.

"Make Me Wet?" He looks at me and grins. "What's this?"

"Bath salts. Dump them in the water."

"Okay."

He rips the top open and deposits the eucalyptus-scented salts into the tub. The room immediately fills with the minty, piney scent. I take a deep breath and relish in the perfection of this moment.

Chase loses his underwear and tests the water. It must pass inspection because he slips inside.

Our gazes connect.

"I love you," I say.

He smirks. "Get in here."

I climb in and sit between his legs. He takes a handful of water and trickles it over my chest.

"You are going to be Mrs. Marshall," he says, a hint of pride in his voice. "How do you feel about that?"

"Great. Looking forward to it."

He chuckles.

I rest my head on his chest and tap my fingers against the water. "Chase?"

He hums.

"I was thinking …"

"What about?"

"How do you feel about being called Daddy?"

His body tenses. Immediately, his cock gets hard against my back.

I try not to laugh. *This man is so predictable.*

"What are you telling me?" he asks.

"Nothing," I say.

"You swear?"

I turn around and smile coyly. "I mean, eventually, I want to have your baby, and it can call you Daddy. But not right now."

He grabs my face and brings it to his. "I can accept *you* calling me Daddy for now."

I burst out laughing, but his mouth captures the sound.

Luke Marshall's book is up next in TRULY. It's a feel-good, swoon-filled, spicy romance that will make you smile.

Chapter 1 is next for your reading pleasure.

Chapter One
Laina

"What do you mean you're on the run?"

Stephanie's question is valid, as is her curious but mostly nonchalant way of asking it. After all, it's me we're talking about. But she should've been more prepared.

"Do I really need to break it down for you—*darn it!*" I pry my heel out of a slit in the asphalt. "Besides, when your best friend calls and says she's on the run and needs your help, the only question you should ask is *whose car are we taking?*"

"You're *so* funny."

I glance to my right, then to my left. A trail of sweat trickles between my shoulder blades. Aside from two men in fitted suits and sunglasses from the security team, I'm in the clear.

"There's nothing funny about this," I say, darting across the parking lot as gracefully as possible despite the layers of tulle.

"The last time I saw you—which was approximately fifteen minutes ago, give or take—you were in your wedding dress, looking stunning, I might add, waiting for your father to show up to walk you down the aisle."

Fifteen minutes? Man, I work quick.

The crowd roars from the other side of the safety barrier Landry Security erected three days ago to keep fans and paparazzi—mostly paparazzi—away from the church. Brickfield has been teeming all week with spectators eager to see what the media has deemed the wedding of the century. Former classmates were interviewed. My kindergarten teacher was on the front page of *Exposé* magazine this week. Alleged encounters with the "men in my life" since I became famous have been dissected and analyzed to death. If only half of what was printed were real, my life would be far more entertaining.

I would've felt bad for Sheriff Jones in his plight to organize a response to this level of anarchy in a town of five thousand people if he hadn't used my wedding as the launch of his re-election campaign.

"What's going on, Laina? Are you joking around, or is something really the matter?"

"Considering I'm currently hiding between two sheds and hoping no one is flying drones overhead, I'd say something is the matter."

"Why are you between two sheds?"

I spit a piece of my veil out of my face. "I can't marry him, Steph."

My best friend goes silent. I imagine her face—mouth agape, brows arched higher than the lamination treatment should allow, and a wrinkled forehead defying her Botox. She wore the same expression when I told her I was marrying Hollywood heartthrob Tom Waverly a year ago—complete and utter shock.

"I should've listened to you," I say, taking a steadying breath. "I never should've accepted his proposal at all, let alone plan a wedding and invite one hundred fifty people to the church and another two hundred to a reception that cost more than ..." Dread rolls through the pit of my stomach. "Let's not even go there."

"Okay." Her voice is cool and tempered. "What do you need?"

"Ironically enough, I need you to ask whose car we're taking because the answer is *I don't know*. I didn't think this through. I excused myself from the room, shut the door, and left."

"We're throwing a plot twist at the last second, but that's okay. I think quick on my feet, so don't panic."

"Strangely, I'm not. I don't know whether that's because I'm blocking out the ramifications of this wholly impulsive decision or if this is my gut's way of thanking me for following it." I peer around the side of one of the sheds, nearly getting busted by the best man. "I'll take it either way."

"We're going with the latter. Now, where are you, exactly?"

"Behind the church. There are two sheds with a hedgerow behind them. I'm between the buildings."

The crowd roars once again. But instead of the ordinary screams and whistles, they begin to sing the chorus of the most popular song on country radio.

"Guess Sam's here," I say, sighing.

"Don't worry about who is here. Let's worry about getting you out of here."

"Therein lies my problem." I nibble the lip stain that took me six months to pick out. "People are everywhere. I can't just walk out the gate and onto the street. I get recognized in a wig, hat, and sunglasses, let alone a freaking wedding dress."

My heart pounds as the weight of my actions sinks in.

Tom will be humiliated. The biggest movie star in the world will be left standing at the altar by the pop star the world is quick to label *frivolous*. My parents' fury will be immeasurable. *How dare I be so careless with my image when so much of their success is riding on it?* My PR team will be inundated with calls and emails. My assistant *must* stay out of sight until this cools down, and my fans will jump to conclusions and assume the worst about me. *About Tom.* Critics will claim this was a publicity stunt when it's nothing more than a woman trying to salvage her future amid a few bad choices.

"Maybe I should just go through with it," I say, a chill prickling my skin. "The ramifications of this—"

"It's ten years from now, and you're on a beach."

"Can we talk about vacations later?"

"And you look to your left, and there's Tom," she says. "How do you feel?"

Sick.

Uneasiness stirs in my stomach. Instead of imagining Tom gazing adoringly back at me, I instantly notice the angry lines around his eyes. His voice sweeps through my head.

"There are calories in those drinks, you know."

"We're going to have to talk about you easing up on the music thing when I start filming my next project in the winter."

"Can't you choose more conservative costumes? You're a grown woman, for fuck's sake. I don't want my wife out there looking like a whore."

I grapple with how to phrase that, but Stephanie saves me the trouble.

"Now imagine that you look to the left, and he's gone," she says. "How do you feel now?"

Peaceful.

Relief eases the tension in my shoulders and quells the knot in my stomach. I don't try to answer her this time; it's unnecessary.

"The ramifications of going back in that church and marrying Tom are far worse than the inconvenience it will cause everyone else if you don't," she says. "I'll support you either way. But your father was just in here looking for you, and while I can stall him for a little bit, you need to decide."

A shiver runs the length of my spine. A flush stings my cheeks. My heart somehow lodges in my throat, and each beat reminds me of the seconds ticking by.

I can't do it. I can't return to that church and walk out as Mrs. Tom Waverly. The thought makes me want to hurl.

"The media will have a heyday with this," I say, my back pressed against the shed. "I can see the headlines already."

"Ignore all of that. You're going to wake up married or not. What's it going to be?"

My breath quickens. "I'm not."

"You're sure."

"Yes."

A door closes in the background. "Okay, this is the plan."

A smile tugs at my lips.

"I could borrow a car and pick you up, but someone has to be here to head off your parents and Tom until you've made your exit," she says. "The security team is our best bet, I think. They're under an NDA, and you hired them, right? Not Tom?"

"Yeah, I did."

"Okay. Let me find one of them and get them to pick you up. You stay put. I'm going to bide you some time with your father. Who should I contact on your team?"

"My agent. Anjelica Grace at Mason Music," I say. "Tell her I'll call her as soon as I can."

"I'm on it. Do you need me to do anything else?"

I take a long breath. "Don't be the one to tell Tom. Let someone else do it."

"Got it. Now, hold tight. I'll have a car there as fast as I can."

"I love you, Steph."

"Love you more."

"Oh! And my engagement ring is in your purse."

"Got it."

The call ends. I drop my arm to the side and avoid looking at the phone screen. People are probably already sending texts and looking for me. I can't deal with it. Not yet.

I'm really doing this. I'm really running away from my wedding.

My head begins to spin with all the immediate decisions I must make. I have to get my things from the hotel before it's taken over by the wedding party again. *Can anyone track my phone? How will I get out of here without alerting the media and bystanders?*

Is that even possible?

Before I can go too far down the rabbit hole, a black SUV rolls up perilously close to the shed. The windows are jet black, making it impossible to see inside. Nerves ripple low in my stomach as a man in one of those tailored suits slips alongside the vehicle.

He takes his glasses off so I can see his gray eyes. *Troy Castelli. Thank God.*

"Ms. Kelley, I heard you'd like a ride."

A chuckle escapes me. "I can't believe I'm doing this, Troy."

"I'm happy to take you wherever you want."

"I just want to get out of here without my picture being splashed on social media. Can you pull that off?"

He opens the back door. "Absolutely." He turns to offer me a hand and then sees, for what seems like the first time, the tulle that must also go in the SUV. "How do we get all of ... *that* in there?"

"It's tulle." I bunch as much of the fabric in the front as I can. "I hate it."

"Then why did you choose it?"

The question makes me pause. *Why did I choose tulle over lace? Surf-n-turf over chicken strips and sliders for the reception? The diet drink over the full sugar soda at the rehearsal dinner?*

"Troy, it seems I'm a bit of a pushover."

"No offense, ma'am, but a lot of people inside the church would probably disagree with you."

I grin, standing a little taller. "You're right. Now shove this godforsaken dress in the car, and let's get out of here."

With a little work and a lot of pushing white fabric into every vacant space in the back of the SUV, we make it work. Troy is in the driver's seat in the blink of an eye.

"We'll go out the back service entrance," he says, holding my gaze in the rearview mirror. "You can breathe, Ms. Kelley. It's going to be all right."

I exhale, the sound taking up all the room the tulle isn't. *I hope you're right.*

My heart pounds as we roll to the back of the church. Troy makes a hand signal to a police officer at the makeshift gate, and it's immediately moved.

The crowd has nearly tripled since I arrived two hours ago. The streets have been closed, and people have filled the block surrounding Mt. Calvary Church. Lawns of the nearby houses are littered with bodies. Television crews are set up on sidewalks with vans and microphones.

It's a mess.

And about to get messier.

I glance at the clock on the dash. The ceremony is set to start in two minutes. I squeeze my eyes closed and try to ignore the fire blazing in my stomach.

"Ms. Kelley?"

I open my eyes. "Yes?"

"Where are we headed?"

Oh. Right.

Good freaking question.

Adrenaline flows through my veins, and my palms start to sweat. *Where* are *we headed?*

The hotel is out. The bridal party will inevitably return to their rooms to gather their things. Not to mention, there's no way I could get into the hotel discreetly and make it to my room. My parents' house is a definite no. I'd be emotionally *and* physically burned at the stake. I could ask Troy to drive me to the airport, but that's an hour and a half away, *and* no reservations have been made. My passport is at the hotel. *And what do I do with all this damn tulle?*

Breathe, Laina.

There must be somewhere I can go.

I sort through every person I still know in Brickfield—which isn't many. I've lost contact with nearly all my old friends since I left six years ago. I can't trust anyone to hide me until I figure this disaster out, anyway. I can't even get a room in Peachwood Falls because someone would wind up seeing me, and I'd get trapped with no way out.

"How about ..." Before I can ask him to find a back road to kill some time while I think, the answer pops in my head.

It is safe. *Probably.*

I may not exactly be welcome, but I won't be forced to leave. *I don't think.*

There will definitely be nothing to eat, the bedding will need to be washed, but I'll be able to let myself inside.

My lips curl slowly into a smile. And, for the first time today, I don't feel like the sun is setting on my soul.

"See that sign for Peachwood Falls?" I ask. "Head there."

This book is live now on Amazon and Audible.

ACKNOWLEDGMENTS

First and foremost, thank you to my Creator.

I keep thinking that writing books will get easier. This one, after all, is my thirty-fifth story. (35!) I should be in a groove.

[Narrator: she is not, in fact, in a groove.]

But, there is a silver lining, and that is the community of people around me that help me get all the things done. (Except washing my hair. I have to do that at some point. Ugh.)

I'll be hugging my husband and children today (post-shower) because I haven't seen them in a while. I can hear them on the other side of my office door. I wonder if they've grown? Thank you for your patience, guys. I love you. Now we can watch a movie or play a game. (But, please, no chess.)

My husband's parents will be happy to hear that I've wrapped this book. Now my mother-in-law won't feel compelled to start every text with—*I know you're writing but ...* You two are the best. Thank you for your patience and support.

Kari March slayed this cover. Jane Ashley Converse nailed the image. Dane Peterson and Maddi Hansen's love in the photo is palpable and I'm honored to have it, and them, on my cover.

I sent my assistant an email a while ago. Hopefully, she still works for me and isn't tired of sailing the ship while I write. If you're still here Tiffany—thanks for everything. I'm happy we're still a team.

Ashley Reynolds, the amazing human that I dedicated this book to, slid in like Tom Cruise in Risky Business and pulled me up by my bootstraps. (She was fully clothed though. I think.)

There aren't enough ways to thank you for your time and energy (and patience and kindness), so I won't make it weird. Just thank you. (A lot.)

Michele Ficht never, ever fails me. Not once in all the years I've known her has she been too busy for me. I don't think I'd be that nice to me. But, thank God, she is and I'm honored to call her a friend after over ten years. Love you.

Thank you to Susan Rayner, Jen Costa (kind of—ha!), and Anjelica Grace for beta reading for me and sharing your insight. I adore you all. And to Alexandra Hale for keeping me energized—your messages and enthusiasm were so appreciated. A huge thank you to Lara Petterson for just being … everything. How would I sum up all the ways you support me? I don't know. I'll work on that.

I'm grateful for Marion Archer and Jenny Sims for their editing work on MORE THAN I COULD. Thank you for helping me tighten and clean up these words.

Mandi Beck—we're back! I love you. I love our late-night writing sessions. Please never leave me. (If you tried, I'd find you. Don't bother.)

S.L. Scott is a source of light and love in my life. Thank you for always tricking me into thinking I can do things. I'm really gullible. (But keep it up!)

I'm really surprised Jessica Prince still talks to me after I bailed on her more days than not. But, like the friend she is, she continues to text me. I'm keeping her forever.

Brittni Van can energize me like no other. Her ideas, questions, and excitement about my books and the book world in general feed my soul. You are a true gem in my life, friend.

Big thanks to Candi Kane PR for working with me on the promotion of MORE THAN I COULD. (I remembered the cover this time. Just adding that here for posterity.) I adore you.

Sending lots of love to Kaitie Reister for always checking on me, to Stephanie Gibson for literally always being there (and I mean always), and to my favorite place in the world—Books by Adriana Locke on Facebook. Thank you for cheering me on and reading my work.

Last but most certainly not least, to you, dear reader—thank you for taking a chance on me. I hope you loved this story. I hope it made you smile.

ABOUT THE AUTHOR

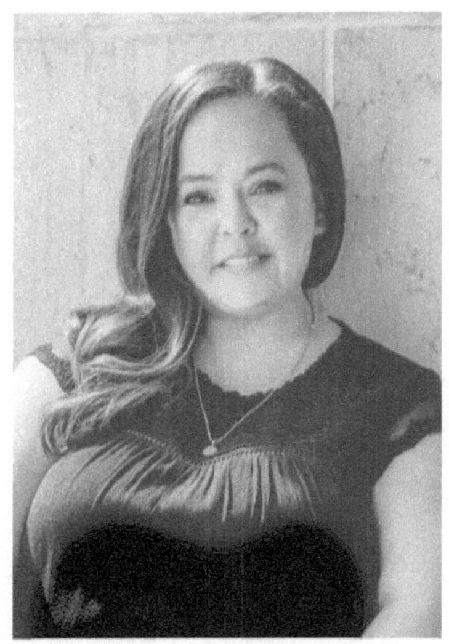

USA Today Bestselling author, Adriana Locke, writes contemporary romances about the two things she knows best—big families and small towns. Her stories are about ordinary people finding extraordinary love with the perfect combination of heart, heat, and humor.

She loves connecting with readers, fall weather, football, reading alpha heroes, everything pumpkin, and pretending to garden.

Hailing from a tiny town in the Midwest, Adriana spends her free time with her high school sweetheart (who she married over twenty years ago) and their four sons (who truly are her best work). Her kitchen may be a perpetual disaster, and if all else fails, there is always pizza.

www.adrianalocke.com

www.ingramcontent.com/pod-product-compliance
Lightning Source LLC
Chambersburg PA
CBHW021215310726
48971CB00006B/1570